I0572631

TILL THE RAPTURE DO US PART

A NOVEL

RUTH HARBOUR

Published by Redemptive Writing

Cover Art: Evelyn Randall
Cover Design: Robin Axtell
Editing/Interior Design: Michele Chynoweth

ISBN: 9798992193008

DEDICATION

This book is dedicated to
THE DYNAMIC DUO
at North Glen Elementary School,
Glen Burnie, MD
1962-1985

Frances P. Pearson, my mother,
And her best friend and co-teacher,
Jane Purkins, my Aunt Jane.

CONTENTS

ACKNOWLEDGMENTS

First, I want to acknowledge that the Holy Spirit put an insatiable thirst in me to understand the end time prophecies. I had to know when the Rapture was going to occur. Some theologians believe it will come before the time of immense suffering (called the Great Tribulation) under the reign of the Antichrist. Others believe the Church—believers in Christ—will be taken up to join Christ in the sky in the middle or end of the Tribulation. I am grateful for my friends who gave me literature to help me understand that Christ will return for his Church before his wrath is poured out on the world during the Great Tribulation.

Thank you to my Professor, Debbie, who made the book of Revelation come alive at the Conservative Baptist Seminary in Shiluo, Taiwan.

Thank you to all who have prayed for me as I labored over this story—Sparrow's House ladies, Beautiful Women's Fellowship, Taiwan Harvest 119 co-workers, Judy and the Women's Intercessory Prayer group at Grace Bible in Allentown, NJ. You are the reason this book is completed.

I am grateful for my dear husband, Mark, for often getting dinner on, and trying to protect my time.

Fellow writers—Marlene, Amy, and my coach, Michele—thank you for your inspiration, encouragement, and guidance.

Thank you to Kevin and Dr. Ray, for being the first to finish reading my book and giving me very encouraging feedback.

To Theo, my grandson—your enthusiasm, curiosity, and suggestions have spurred me on to improving the story. Thank you.

The cover illustration is the creation of Evelyn Randall. Evelyn, you were a joy to work with. I love how you communicate through your art. Thank you for your patience and perseverance.

PROLOGUE

Izzy's heart sank to a deep, dark place. She sat with her mom, who lay in a hospital bed by the front window in her own home, eyes staring blankly ahead. The curtains flung open, sunlight streaming in, could not dig Izzy out of her depression.

Her mother stirred. "Mom, how about a sip of water?" Izzy quickly brought a thick swab of water to her mom's parched lips. She looked down into her mom's face. Brain cancer had taken its toll, and the sixty-year old's flushed cheeks and bulging eyes made Izzy recoil in anger.

God, how could this happen to Mom? Her church has come to pray. I've prayed. You made her an intelligent woman, a wonderful teacher, only to reduce her to this. Where is the love she always talked about?

"Mommy, you'll be alright. I love you. You're my Mommy Dear, the world's best friend, and

top-notch teacher—you and Aunt Anna, the dynamic duo." Her voice cracked with grief, her hand extended gently along her mother's face. Tears flowed unbidden.

Then Mommy lifted her hand up to Izzy's face. Izzy watched her eyes. *So sad...searching for words which flee away, ever since they bombarded her whole brain with radiation.*

Mommy Dear spoke one word—"God."

That is the dangling question, Izzy thought, her face in a scowl, but she turned away so her mom would not see. *God? Do you care?*

God? Do you answer prayer?

God? Are you there?

1. <u>ON YOUR MARK</u>

The mark became a fashion statement long before the Beast made it law. The technology had been in use for twenty years already with the rise of credit and debit cards. People exchanged hard cash much less often as time went by. Then everybody began doing transactions—buying and selling—on their cell phones. Someone asked, "Why fumble for plastic cards anymore? Why not plant the chips where they would always be easy to find—on our bodies? So, lots of people had already rushed out for the chip, which was easily either stamped in the forehead or on the right hand. And to make it even more tempting, the chip could be administered in a tattoo shop, with a free tattoo.

Isabel Defranco did not like throwing away her money. Called Miss Frank by her second graders, Izzy made them use the same cup all day if they forgot their water bottles. When it came to drawing, both sides of the paper had to be used before they could get another sheet.

One day, Izzy struggled to get the zipper shut on her wallet as she came out of a convenience store. A scraggly middle-aged man came up to her and asked, "Do you have any spare change?"

Two perfectly good arms and legs. Of course not. She looked him straight in the eye, pushing her blonde hair out of her face, and said flatly, "No."

A girl sitting in the driver's seat of a rusty white pickup truck behind her piped up and said, "I'll give you something."

Izzy felt miffed. *Why do perfectly healthy people beg? Surely that guy is just saving up his change until he has enough for a beer!* She definitely didn't like throwing money away.

Izzy stewed about it all the way to Aunt Anna's house—an old Victorian-style home with brown shingles and white window frames, a rounded tower covered with ivy, and an inviting swing on the front porch.

The TV blared with an ad as Izzy poked her head in the door of her aunt's cozy haven.

EZ CHIPS ARE HERE TO STAY. NO MORE NEED TO
LUG AROUND YOUR PURSE OR WALLET!
PUT THE PLASTIC WHERE YOU'LL NEVER LOSE IT—
EVEN TATTOO IT—IN YOUR HANDS OR FOREHEAD.
YOU'LL BE GLAD YOU DID.

"I'm not inclined to waste my money or time on tattoos. But planting my credit card in my hand, that's an idea that is long overdue." She stuffed her wallet in her purse as she draped it over the coat rack at the door.

Izzy's Aunt Anna—not her blood aunt, but her mom's best friend—gave her a warm welcome hug. "Oh, Izzy, you don't want that chip on your body. Carry your plastic, that's already so convenient." Anna wiped her face with a towel and motioned towards the table, already laden with a pile of steaming pancakes topped with melting butter, a plate of crisp bacon, scrambled eggs, and coffee.

"But what if I get somewhere without my purse, and I need money? This new tech takes away that worry." Izzy sat down and spread the napkin on her lap.

Anna looked both ways and cupped her mouth with her palm towards her adopted niece's ear and whispered, "It could be the mark of the Beast! It's not worth it."

Izzy's eyes opened wide as she tried to fathom how someone as smart as her Aunt Anna could believe in fairy tales. "Come on, Aunt Anna. You can't be serious. The mark of the Beast? Have you been watching horror movies or something?" She grabbed a couple of pieces of bacon. Saturday mornings with Aunt Anna had been tradition since before her mother passed away.

"Shush! You know better than that. No, Pastor Michaels has been preaching on the end times for a while now. And in the end, a man named Antichrist will arise and head up a one-world government. He will require everyone to take his number on their hand or forehead in order to buy and sell."

"O…kay…but the chips they are offering now seem legitimate, a handy substitute for plastic. No one is embedding anybody else's number. I think I'll go for it." Izzy took a swallow of her orange juice and eyeballed her aunt.

Aunt Anna's face flushed. "Think about what your mom would say, please, Izzy."

After licking the grease from her fingers and wiping them on her napkin, Izzy walked around the table a few steps and planted her hands firmly on Aunt Anna's shoulders and began to massage them. "You know better than I do what a good teacher Mom was." Izzy dug deeper into her aunt's hard shoulder with her elbow. Her mom and Aunt Anna had been a well-loved team at Overbrook Elementary School just around the corner in Wynnefield, Pennsylvania—a hilly community lined with shade trees and brick row homes set back from the road by one or two tiers of cement steps, as well as blocks of old Victorian houses like Aunt Anna's.

Izzy had fond memories of her childhood. *I got to have you both as teachers. Aunt Anna for Language Arts, and Mom for Reading. Neither one of you tolerated slackers, but you both inspired kids to do their best. They were the best years of my life.* Izzy leaned over Anna's shoulder and smiled. "I love the way you and Mom kept your hair bobbed, like twins! Now your hair's a lovely silver gray, and you look so adorable in those teal cat-eyed glasses." She gave a squeeze to Aunt Anna from behind. "I'm so glad one of the dynamic duo is still alive."

Izzy shifted to use her fingers to knead between Aunt Anna's shoulder blade and spine.

"Oh. Oh. A little lower!"

Izzy enjoyed Aunt Anna's appreciation. *Mom used to give the best massages.* Her deep blue eyes filled to the brim, and Izzy used the back of her round soft hands to swipe away the tears. "What would Mom say about this mark of the Beast business?" Her hands found the knotted muscles and began to work them over.

"Ouch!" Aunt Anna leaned away from Izzy's prying hands.

"Oh, sorry. I was thinking Mom would have said that I need to take time to gather all the facts before I decide."

Izzy recalled someone at school had also said some mumbo jumbo about anyone getting the mark of the Beast would have no way of getting into heaven at the end of time. *I'm not sure I want to go to heaven. Where was God when Mom passed away?* Izzy shook her head. Sadness filled her heart like sand in an hourglass. Suddenly tired, she sat down again across from her aunt.

Aunt Anna leaned forward, clasping her thin knotted hands. "Well then, may I suggest you join me at church to hear some of Pastor Michaels' messages on the end times?"

"Maybe someday." Izzy waved her hand like she was shooing a fly away. *How can anyone know God and the Bible are true? He sure did not hear my prayers when Mom got sick with a brain tumor!* "How about we watch the news for a while, to see if there is a beast roaming around the earth who wants to plant his ID on us?"

The next Saturday, on the way to Aunt Anna's, Izzy stopped by the convenience store to pick up some orange juice for breakfast. She got to the counter and realized she had forgotten her credit card. *This is when the chip embedded in my wrist would have come in so handy.*

"Aunt Anna, I am so sorry to come empty-handed." She sighed, holding her empty hands out dramatically. "I stopped by the convenience store for some orange juice, and guess what?"

"No, what?" Aunt Anna looked up from flipping pancakes.

"No money. No credit card. I completely forgot to stick them in my pocket. Just think how handy it would have been if I had already gotten the chip implant in my hand."

"I, for one, am glad you haven't!" Aunt Anna waved her spatula in the air. "Let's keep following the news together. What seems so convenient today may come back to bite you later."

2. **<u>COLLISION COURSE</u>**

On Monday, Izzy's friend, Laura, sat with her during the lunch break in the teacher's room. Izzy noticed her usually cheerful countenance was marred by red, puffy eyes.

"Laura, what's happening? You look like you've been crying." Izzy put her hand on her young friend's shoulder—Laura was the one person at school she could talk to. In the beginning, Laura, the school librarian, shared new books with Izzy for her second graders. Izzy especially enjoyed the picture books Laura shared, like newly found treasures. Izzy always looked forward to their chats.

"Izzy, I might be asked to leave my position." Laura shoved a book into Izzy's hands, and took off her round dark-rimmed glasses to wipe away her tears, causing her long brown curls to cascade down and hide her face.

Izzy inspected the book. The pictures inside shocked her, and she closed it to study the cover.

"What in the world? I had heard the school system had adopted this new curriculum, but this is too suggestive for our little ones. This does nothing but arouse sexual curiosity in kids who would normally be blissfully unaware."

"Exactly. But, as the librarian, I'm responsible for what goes on the shelves. I don't want to put this out, but Ms.

Hitchcock insists it go on the new books table…or else!"

Izzy hid the book under her bookbag on the table and patted her friend's back. "Let me talk with Ms. Hitchcock. Maybe there's something that can be done. I certainly don't want our children exposed to this either."

Laura gave Izzy a big hug. "You're a sweet friend, Izzy. But there's more where that came from."

"Leave it to me. There should be room for appeal." Izzy pulled out her tuna sandwich. "Other than this, how are things going?" *Lunch break never seems long enough!* She began to scarf down her sandwich.

Laura smiled, and a twinkle returned to her eyes. "I have some news. Just found out."

That's more like it. Izzy sat forward to hear.

"I'm pregnant!" Laura whispered, her soft brown eyes radiating joy.

"Oh, congratulations! That's wonderful. Amazing, you and Brad haven't been married that long! Are you two ready?"

"I guess we are now! Though it is a little bit of a surprise." Laura blushed. "The Lord will provide."

"Oh? Are you a believer?" *Maybe God will hear her prayers, at least.*

"Yes, we are. God's a big part of our lives." Laura reached out to cover Izzy's hand with hers.

"Yeah. I can see your faith means a lot to you." Izzy squeezed her friend's hand. "You're going to need it. I don't know how things will go with Ms. Hitchcock but maybe your prayers will help."

Izzy stood up, trash in one hand, hugging the book and her bookbag with the other. "We're going to do some finger painting this afternoon. Pray they don't paint the walls!"

After school, Izzy donned her running clothes to go for her customary jog around Overbrook Elementary School. It had been a disturbing day. She wanted to think things through as she exercised. The wind blew gently, causing the fall leaves to flutter down upon her. *Ahh. I love the fall colors and the crunch of leaves underfoot.*

It's a shame all of life is not this beautiful. Izzy sighed. She felt like she had run into a cement truck today when she appealed to Ms. Hitchcock for Laura. She cut around a young mom helping her little one put her coat on in the middle of the sidewalk. Izzy began to replay the conversation with her principal in her head.

"Good afternoon, Ms. Hitchcock. Do you have a minute?" Izzy felt comfortable talking with her principal of three years.

"Hello, Izzy. How was your day? Please, sit down." Ms. Hitchcock motioned to the sofa for Izzy and sat down in an easy chair across from her. Her clothes were fashionable, with layers for the top, and leggings to match her modest but above-the-knee skirt. Her strawberry red hair fanned out to one side while the other side had been shaved close to the scalp.

"Laura showed me another treasure today from the library." Izzy pulled out the picture book from her bookbag and gave it to her principal. "Pretty suggestive, don't you think?"

Ms. Hitchcock opened the book and flipped through it.

Surely she'll agree. Izzy waited until the principal looked up at her. "I don't want to expose the children to this kind of education. It's totally unnecessary, don't you think?"

"Yes, I agree it is unnecessary." Izzy's principal sighed and closed the book. "But it must be put in the library. The Board of Education has agreed to promote the current discussion concerning gender affirmation, to align with the Pennsylvania Human Relations Act. These books are meant to provide the platform for further discussion. And it must begin in the library and the classroom."

Izzy jumped to her feet. "But surely little ones should not be forced to explore their bodies and gender like this. They are carefree and ready to explore their world of play, and colors, ABCs and numbers! Why force this on our children when they are not even inclined to ask about it?"

Ms. Hitchcock got up and walked to the window, gazing out for a while without speaking. Children played twenty feet away on the blacktop. One little boy with tight blond curls sat on his haunches at the corner of the tarmac, drawing with a stick in the dirt.

Finally, Ms. Hitchcock turned around and said, "Izzy, we live in a changing world and culture. We have to grow with the culture. If we fail to do that, we will be left behind."

"Surely this new culture is not owned by the majority, but by a very small minority."

"Do you see that child drawing at the corner of the playground?" Ms. Hitchcock pointed from where she was standing. "Max. His parents are lesbians. He is asking questions. We need to help him cope."

"It feels so unnecessary, messing with kids' minds like this. I'm not sure I can let my students check out this kind of book." Izzy couldn't help the impatience and frustration creeping into her voice.

"Then you may have to go, Izzy. My job is even on the line because of it."

Izzy's eyes stung as she blinked back some tears.

The breeze and the fall colors beckoned her to toss her cares away as she continued to jog, willing the memory of her conversation with Ms. Hitchcock to vanish.

CRASH! Izzy's head bumped something hard, and her arms tangled with someone else's as she went sprawling onto the cement sidewalk. *What in the world? Ouch!* Izzy sat dazed for a moment.

"Whoa, whoa, whoa! Are you two okay?" Izzy heard a male voice and realized she had bumped heads with another jogger. She was still too dazed to speak when the man talking to her offered his hand. Izzy looked up into the boyish face of her rescuer. She took his hand and stood up shakily. Then she tasted iron and put her hand to her lip.

"You've cut your lip. Here, take this." Babyface handed her a handkerchief from his pocket. "It's never been used," he said with a grin. Then he leaned over to help his fellow jogger up. "You okay, Old Man?"

Old Man? Izzy looked at the older man. *His scraggly salt and pepper beard makes him about fifty,* she estimated. *Maybe the younger man's dad?*

"Sure, just took a hard knock. I'll survive. How about you?" Old Man asked Izzy.

"Still a little dazed, but nothing major." Izzy leaned against the stone wall skirting the property. She surveyed her elbows and knees. *A little scraped, but I'll survive. I hope I didn't break a tooth.*

"My name is Marty," said Babyface. "This is Professor Amos Asher. I suggest we go across the street to the coffee shop and recover over a cup of coffee and a snack. They have bathrooms where you two can clean up."

What a sweet idea. Izzy looked at Old Man to see his response.

"Sounds good to me, Cradle Boy."

Izzy covered her mouth with the handkerchief stifling a

giggle. "Count me in. Very thoughtful suggestion, ah…what did you say your name is?"

"Marty, Marty Goldstein."

One timid smile into the café's bathroom mirror revealed no broken teeth. *Whew! What a relief.* Izzy took out her ponytail and ran her fingers through her sleek blonde hair. She took paper towels to dampen and clean the dirt on her arms and knees. Within minutes she had regained her equilibrium. *I hope Mr. Asher is okay.* One last touch to her hair—which she chose to leave down on her shoulders—and Izzy went to join the men.

Marty rose as Izzy reappeared and offered her a seat at a cozy little table away from the glare of the large front window and the busyness of the counter.

Such a gentleman! Izzy took her seat as Marty helped her scoot in. She could not help noticing his well-formed biceps under his tan polo shirt.

Mr. Asher rose and offered his hand "You okay?"

"Nothing a little betadine won't cure." Izzy smiled.

"Oh, you're brave! I'm a neomycin man myself. But I got away without any scrapes or bruises!" Marty raised his arms skyward revealing well-defined muscles. "How are you, Old Man?" He grinned, showing his even white teeth and a dimple.

"It's mostly only a bruise." Mr. Asher rubbed his head. "I need all the brain cells I can hold on to, so I'll be more careful the next time I round the corner! So sorry I collided with you, Miss…"

"You can call me Izzy, Izzy Defranco."

"Yes, Miss Defranco. So sorry to bump heads. It's been a long time since that happened to me!"

"That's because he's had more time since childhood. Mr. Asher is visiting us at the University on official business for Israel's irrigation and water recycling program. Rather impressive." Marty gave him a thumbs up.

"Oh? Is that so?" Izzy sat up, her hands folded on the table in front of her. She leaned forward. "I did detect a little bit of an accent. But it's not strong. So, Mr. Asher, you are from Israel?"

"Well, I was born in Israel. Then I grew up in Chicago from the time I was three when my folks came here to serve. But by the time I was a young teen, we returned to Israel. There I studied and began to work. I'm afraid it's already been twenty-five years since then."

"He's back actually to teach as an adjunct professor on water preservation. I have learned a lot in his class." Marty's big brown eyes gleamed with pride.

Water preservation meant a lot to Izzy. From the time she was seven, she came home from school admonishing her mother, "Please turn off the water while you brush, Mommy. We have got to preserve our water!" Now, as a teacher, she would not let her students keep the water running when they lathered up to wash their hands. "After getting some soap, turn the water off, sing 'Happy Birthday to You' while you scrub, then rinse your hands off," she would tell them.

"Water is so important for the life of the world. What are you learning, Marty? I'd love to learn, too." Izzy leaned forward.

"I'd love to share. But let's order our coffees before they kick us out." Marty unwound his long legs to stand up and head to the counter to place their order.

Izzy thoroughly enjoyed her surprise class on advanced technology used in Israel to recycle industrial water and salt water. She enjoyed Marty's enthusiasm, and Mr. Asher's expertise.

When their coffee cups were empty and the flurry of discussion slowed down, Marty sat back and looked at Izzy. "What do you do, Miss Conservationist?"

"Fill me in when I get back. We can stand another drink, can't we?" Amos stood to place another order.

"Oh, how about water this time? I'm thirsty." Izzy touched her throat.

"Sounds good." The professor walked off.

Izzy blushed as she observed Marty's dark eyes staring at her, awaiting her answer. She leaned forward. "I'm a second-grade teacher right here at Overbrook Elementary School." She felt proud and happy inside, until she remembered the foreboding she had when she and Professor Asher collided.

3. <u>TALK ABOUT TROUBLE</u>

Happy Saturday! Izzy once more seated herself at Aunt Anna's kitchen table. "How are you, Aunt Anna? You're looking good."

"Oh, no complaints." Aunt Anna leaned onto the table and gingerly lowered herself down to sit with Izzy. "Got to go to the Baltimore Harbor yesterday with my Sisters' Fellowship. Enjoyed some crab cakes!"

"Sounds like fun. But I'm sure the crab was not as good as you make it." Izzy gave her aunt a big hug.

"I enjoyed them. . . labor free!"

"I'm glad you went. I enjoy the Harbor, the smells, the people, even the sea gulls floating on the breeze. The Baltimore Harbor is so quaint."

"How about you, Sweetheart? How's it going? Is that a bruised lip I see?"

"Oh, you noticed. I tried to cover it. Yes, you wouldn't believe who I ran into yesterday, literally! A Professor Amos Asher, teaching this week at the University on Israel's water recycling and irrigation. I even got to sit in on a lesson at the coffee shop…after we bumped heads together. Couldn't believe it! I must have been preoccupied with my thoughts and BOOM! I crashed into him as I rounded the

16

corner on my run around Overbrook Elementary School."

Aunt Anna came closer to inspect. "Smile for me."

"No worries," said Izzy, "Thankfully, no broken teeth."

"So, how old is this Professor Amos?" Aunt Anna said nonchalantly.

"He's at least fifteen years older than I am. But he was running with one of his grad students, named Marty. He's the one who suggested we all clean up at the Café." Izzy could not hide a smile thinking about their happy meeting the day before.

Aunt Anna gave her a quizzical glance. "You know I promised your mom I'd do what I could to make sure you married right. Maybe you could invite this thoughtful young man over for breakfast some Saturday morning."

"Not so fast, Aunt Anna! I don't even know if we'll see each other again."

Looking downcast, the would-be matchmaker said, "You didn't exchange phone numbers?"

"No, but we are connected now on Instagram. Not to worry! I'll keep you posted."

The two dug into their breakfast after a prayer of thanksgiving from Aunt Anna which lasted longer than usual as she enumerated the added blessing of Izzy's new friends. Before long, Izzy remembered the worries of the day before.

"The librarian at Overbrook, Laura, is expecting already."

"Wasn't it her wedding you went to a couple of months ago?"

"Yep. She and her hubby, Brad, are already expecting a baby! She's very happy. But it comes at a time when her job is threatened." Izzy frowned and shook her head.

"How could that happen? She seems to be a sweet and competent person. Why should her job be in danger?" Aunt Anna took off her glasses and cleaned them with her shirt, revealing soft crow's feet at the corners of her eyes.

"The Board of Education has instructed her to put some picture books and other material on the shelves concerning gender education. She showed me one of them yesterday. I thought it was way too graphic and suggestive. Another book presents the idea that the equipment you're born with does not necessarily make you a boy or girl. It's just sowing confusion into the minds of young kids! Let them enjoy their childhood, I say. So, I talked with the principal after school yesterday."

"How'd that go?" Anna took a sip of coffee.

"Well, it turns out there are children at school who have transgender or gay parents. They're asking questions. The new books will help encourage acceptance of all choices moms and dads are making concerning their sexuality. But I think it goes a step further and oversteps the boundaries and beliefs of most families. Principal Hitchcock said we have to grow with the culture. If not, she said, we need to find other jobs. She said even her job is threatened!"

Aunt Anna was clearly agitated as she folded her napkin, pushed it onto the table, and got up to walk to the front window. She stood there, head bowed for a minute. Then she came back to join Izzy. She reached across the table to grab Izzy's hand, her puffy cheeks red. "When we gave up the absolutes of right and wrong, we killed our civilization!" She threw up her hands and said, "Even what constitutes a boy or a girl is in question! And if a child says she's a cat, they give her kitty litter to defecate in! Reason has been thrown out the window. Oh, Izzy, I'm so sorry it's come to this." She fanned her face with her napkin.

"Whoa, Aunt Anna, please don't get too worked up! I would hate for anything to happen to you!" Izzy leaned over, rubbing her aunt's shoulder and back. "Those were real fighting words. Scary, too. So, you think American civilization is dying?" Izzy eyed the bacon but refrained from picking it up.

"In my day, the Word of God was honored in the schools, as was the pledge of allegiance. I used to lead children's Bible club after school. Now they have banned prayer from the schools and even tell students to leave their Bibles at home and threaten them with litigation if they share their faith with their peers! And yet the Bible is God's handbook for us—the manual for happy and fruitful lives given to us by our Creator! It is happening just as the Bible warns, that in the last days people will call good evil, and evil good." Aunt Anna clasped Izzy's hand, and said, "And now you have to deal with it."

"Hey, we can always hope for the best and live by our principles." Izzy tried to soothe her aunt, rubbing the hand that clutched hers. "Thank you for your concern. You're the best auntie anyone could hope for! And your delicious breakfast is getting cold." Izzy picked up a piece of bacon and took a big bite.

Aunt Anna smiled weakly and acquiesced.

The two finished off the meal and cleared the table in silence. Then they retreated to their recliners in front of the FOX29 morning news.

"Wow, look at this. A documentary on ISIS." Izzy sat forward to listen.

A group of twenty Coptic Christians knelt on the beach, all clad in white, facing the surf. One by one their ISIS captors asked them to deny Christ and pledge allegiance to Allah. Each of them died by beheading. There happened to be a non-believer from Chad in the group that knelt on the beach. He watched his peers go down, confessing faith in Christ. When his time came he said, "Their God is my God, too!" And he died like the rest.

"This is unbelievable!" Izzy said. "The oppression! And

to turn to God like that. Could you have done that? I don't think I could have."

"I sure hope so." Aunt Anna spoke slowly. "We need to pray daily for the persecuted believers around the world and pray for ourselves. Yes, if I were in that situation, I could not deny my Jesus. May God give me strength."

"Do you think something like that will ever come to America?" Izzy worried about the conversation that had bedogged breakfast.

"It already is happening to some degree."

"How do you mean? I haven't heard of pastors being killed, or anything like that."

"I'm afraid drive-by shootings have been directed at street preachers. It's a sick world. A couple in our church, who run a bakery in town, are threatened with bankruptcy now because they refused to make a wedding cake for a gay couple, who in turn took them to court. It's been brutal— murder of a different sort. People ought to be able to live by their convictions."

4. <u>RIPPLE EFFECTS</u>

Izzy zeroed in on the picture of Professor Asher featured in *The Hawk*, St. Joseph University's campus newsletter. The headline read:

ENVIRONMENTAL SCIENCE DEPARTMENT DIVES INTO WATER CONSERVATION

The article below it featured "Israel's foremost water conservationist and specialist, Dr. Amos Asher." Izzy took a screenshot and sent it on to Marty, writing, "Enjoyed my lesson, Mr. Conservationist!"

A minute later, Marty shot back, "I was just wondering if Miss Conservationist would be interested in taking in a Hawks game this Friday. It's Hawks vs. Villanova. Ought to be fun!"

Whoa! That was fast. Friday. Monday evening, Izzy lay on her bed enjoying social media after finishing with lesson plans and grading papers. A smile spread on her face as she remembered Marty's soft brown eyes and the dimple when he smiled. *I imagine Marty has played some basketball. He's so tall and muscular.* She wrote him back—Would love to! Meet you? What time?

Marty's classes ran late on Friday, so she met him at the stone gates marking the entrance to St. Joe's University. The breeze, crisp and cool, blew gently through her hair. She wore a Hawk's shirt with jeans and tennis shoes. She laughed when she saw Marty wearing the same thing. "Great minds think alike. We couldn't have planned it better."

"It suits you. After all, second-grade teachers have to be athletic, right?" Marty offered his arm as they turned down the lane onto campus.

Izzy hesitated. *Gentleman? Or bold? I'd say gentleman.* Then she took his arm. "Yes, I stay pretty active with the little ones. Today I had playground duty, and got the kids involved in a game of kickball. I pitched!"

"Sounds like fun." Marty chuckled.

"How about you? Do you exercise? Play basketball by any chance?" Izzy looked up into Marty's face.

His soft hair lay over his right eye in a crescent. He brushed it back with his hand and smiled. "I have two favorite sports—tennis and track. Even though I am tall and seemingly built for basketball, it's not my forte."

"Tennis? I play tennis, too." Izzy forgot herself and hugged her escort's arm in her excitement. Then she let go.

"Well, then, I've been looking for someone to play doubles with. It's in the early hours of the day, before it gets hot, and before the rush of the day. Here at the courts. Would you be interested?"

Wow. Mornings are not good for me. It's all I can do to get to school on time. But maybe... "How about Wednesday mornings. I have a free period first thing that day. Library for the kids." Izzy held her breath, hoping that would be a good day for Marty.

"Wouldn't you know. Wednesday is a perfect day for me, too. I'll sign up and see if it's a go, and will let you know." Triumphant, Marty offered his arm again, and Izzy accepted.

The game between the Hawks and Villanova put the Hawks down, 11 to 20 by the half-time intermission. "The Hawks will come back. You'll see." Marty led Izzy out to get a snack.

"Oh! Snowballs! Surprised they have them this late in the year. But they're my favorite."

"Yeah? What flavor?" Marty followed Izzy over to the stand.

"Spearmint, with marshmallow. And you?"

"Chocolate's my flavor, for everything! Just chocolate. Everything else is too sweet for me." Marty waved his hand back and forth to show his displeasure.

"So, marshmallow is probably overkill for you then." Izzy peered sheepishly up at her new friend.

"Na. Whatever appeals to you, Dear. You will be the one eating it." Marty took out money for two snow cones, a spearmint with marshmallow, and a chocolate.

They ended up standing outside looking in for the beginning of the second half because no food or drink was allowed in the gym.

"They should have told us." Izzy groaned as she peered through the window.

"My oversight. I knew, but just thought a treat would be fun." Marty shoveled down the ice as fast as he could.

"I don't want to waste it. But I can't eat cold food that quickly." Izzy savored the marshmallow and spearmint.

"That's okay. Let's sit this quarter out and enjoy our snack." Marty led them to a bench opposite the gym door.

Izzy tried to enjoy her treat. But there was a lot of excitement going on in the gym. Several times Marty got up and ran over to see what all the raucous was about.

"Hurry up. Our team is about to pass by Villanova." Marty paced back and forth in front of Izzy.

"Hold your horses. You're the one who came out for

snacks." Izzy felt on edge.

"But you're the one who wanted a snow…" Marty stopped midstream and started chuckling. "It's no big deal. Look, Izzy, I'm sorry. We can always watch the recaps. Take your time."

My, this man just gets absorbed in what he's doing. Me, I've got to breathe for a minute. "Give me a moment." Izzy almost didn't want to finish her snowball, but she hated anything to go to waste. So she drank it down. Then she walked slowly to the trashcan, breathing deeply as she went. When she returned to Marty, who was peering through the door of the gym by then, she could smile and mean it again.

The second half saw the Hawks soar past Villanova with a twelve-shot lead, including two triples, bringing them to 32-15. Villanova called for a timeout, then came back strong. They gave the Hawks a real beating, stealing balls off the rim and laying up twelve shots in quick secession. Marty began to groan. Izzy squeezed his arm, giving him a thumbs-up. "They'll turn it around. Don't worry." Then the Hawks fought back with three triples and one free throw. Marty threw his fists into the air, ecstatic.

He looked over and smiled, brushing his hair away from his right eye. "You okay?"

Izzy gave him the thumbs up. "You see. They're winning!"

"It's going to be tight."

The closing moments of the game had everyone on the edge of their seats. The teams fought and rallied to a tie. With the clock running down, the guard threw a free-throw which cinched a Hawks' victory.

Marty ecstatically hugged Izzy.

She hugged him back and gave him a high five. "Congratulations! Your team won!"

"This calls for a celebration. Let's go back to the Café

where we met. What do you say?"

"Let's go for it. Should we drive? Do you have a car?"

"Yes, all prepared. I parked outside the gym this afternoon to be ready for this moment." Marty offered his arm, and Izzy hugged it. He led her to a black Toyota Camry.

"Nice car." Izzy looked at him across the top of the car.

"Hope it's comfortable enough for you." Marty smiled

On the road, Izzy sat quietly thinking about Marty. *He's a real athlete. That game really meant something to him. Me? I need to relax and get into the game more. I never get very worked up about games.*

"You okay? Did you enjoy the game?"

"Oh, it was far more than I anticipated." Izzy laughed.

Ten minutes later they pulled into the restaurant parking lot. "You were pretty intense back there. I mean, that game really mattered to you. It gave me a little bit of an epiphany about myself."

"What's that?" Marty sat across the table from Izzy, his elbows resting on the table, hands folded. His dimple showed and Izzy saw a twinkle in his eye.

"Well, maybe I need to live more in the moment. I mean, that was a fun game to watch, but I couldn't quite enjoy it as much as you. You were a real example to me."

Marty chuckled. "Well, I do tend to get worked up over games. But if they don't win, that's okay, too. I've done my part rooting for the team." Marty looked at the menu and handed a copy to Izzy. "How about a dessert? Or a drink?"

"Um, I don't drink. My father was an alcoholic, and he made Mom a widow when I was just fourteen years old."

"Oh. I'm sorry to hear that. Actually, I don't drink much either. Maybe wine with steak."

Izzy found a custard tart she wanted with some decaf coffee.

"I'll have a house salad, and some pop," Marty added.

The waitress came to take their order. WRTI, Philly's classical radio station, played Massenet's *Thai Meditation.* Izzy and Marty smiled at each other. Izzy felt like she was on an adventure getting to know her new friend.

Marty apologized. "Hey, listen. I'm sorry for getting so caught up in the game. I know I was rude to you, the last person on earth I'd want to hurt."

"The last person on earth?" Izzy grinned. "Don't be melodramatic. I understand. It's easy to get sucked into the excitement of the moment. And I'm glad your team won." She gave Marty a high-five, something she often gave to her students.

"So, it must have been tough living with an alcoholic."

Izzy nodded, looking down. Then she raised her eyes to meet Marty's and said, "It certainly tested my faith in God. How could he allow such suffering? My mother was so intelligent and had so much love and wisdom to impart to her students, but there was always that uncertainty and trepidation about the situation with Dad at home. I just ran to my room as soon as we got in the door." She wiped a tear away and looked down.

How did we get started on this line of communication? "How about you? What do your mom and dad do? Where are they?"

"Dr. Harold and Ruth Goldstein, humble servants of the people of Tanzania."

"Tanzania? That's Africa, right? Do they both do medical work?"

"Yes. My father is a general practitioner, and my mother a nurse. They are what you would call rare birds in Tanzania. Doctors are few and far between. They have been there for over twenty years. Before that, they served in South Africa, and even in Chicago, in a clinic."

"Chicago? I thought you had a little bit of an accent. It's

cute. I noticed you ordered pop instead of soda."

Marty looked down and laughed. "You're very observant. Yeah, but my accent is a mix. On the compound and at the international school, there were people from all over, Holland, Italy, Germany, UK, not to mention the locals. I learned a little Swahili." Marty folded his hands, looking up. "Karibu."

"What? Is that an animal, kind of like an antelope? Right?"

Marty pursed his lips, shaking his head. "Welcome! Karibu means welcome!"

Just then Marty's pop and salad, and Izzy's tart and coffee arrived. Izzy raised her cup to Marty, and said, "Karibu!" They both burst out laughing, and it felt good.

"Hey, are you at all interested in following in your parents' footsteps? Is medicine a field you are interested in?" Izzy sat back comfortably with her coffee in hand, peering at Marty over her cup.

"Yes, I guess that is what has brought me here to St. Joseph's. I started out at Illinois University and got a degree in Environmental Sustainability and Conservation. I guess Uncle Asher had a real influence on me. But I discovered that I love the math and the bio and aspire to tinker and create useful tools which will help people and our world. So I went on to finish the Masters of Biochemistry here. Then the school encouraged me to get my doctorate in Health Education; they might have a job opening for me, plus I would continue to do research in their labs... too good of an opportunity to turn down!"

"Brilliant! Beyond me. Give me some crayons and drawing paper, or a book to read to my kiddies, and I'm happy!"

"Don't put yourself down. We're all made for different work. What you do with your students, I'm sure, will make a good impact on their lives." He reached across the table and took Izzy's hand in his long, slender hand. He noticed Izzy frowned and let go of her hand.

"Oh, no. You're fine." Izzy brushed her hair behind her ears. "It's just that my teaching position and liberty is being tested right now. My friend, Laura, is the librarian. She showed me the books the Board wants us to make available to children for gender education; we don't have any choice. But I don't want to muddy the water for my little ones. I just want them to grow up secure and confident. They don't need to worry about sex and their identity now. That'll come, but much later if you ask me."

"So, what can you do?" Marty put his hand on Izzy's.

"We are working with our principal, Ms. Hitchcock, hoping to put in place some safeguards. It's a big deal to me right now." Izzy squeezed Marty's hand. "But you are definitely a bright spot in my days. I'm looking forward to our first match on the court on Wednesday."

"Yes, me too. I'll be talking to God about your situation, though."

The stone plopped into the lake at Woodland Park, causing concentric waves to ripple out. Closer to shore, where Izzy and Marty sat comfortably on a wooden bench, blackened leaves bobbed up and down and congregated in a mass like children huddling before a fire. Izzy tossed another stone with greater resolve to get the rings to make it to a branch, raised like an arm beckoning for help, a little way from shore. Her forceful throw made its mark as the ring of water broke around the branch.

"Ah-ha! Superwoman!" Marty put his arm around Izzy's shoulder.

"I wish all of life were so easy." Izzy took Marty's hand

draped on her shoulder and interlaced her fingers with his. Sitting there under Marty's arm made her feel more secure. Still, the recent ripples in her school, from the gender affirmation push in the state, had been challenging.

"How's it going in school?" asked Marty, gently pushing a loose strand of Izzy's soft hair behind her ear. He sat back and propped his left leg upon his right knee.

"Somewhat encouraging. Ms. Hitchcock allowed us to survey our teachers. The results were remarkable—seventy-five percent of the staff believe we need to let parents know about the nature of the books and invite them to weigh in on whether or not their children may check them out."

"That's good. But does it change anything?" Marty stood up to stretch and throw another stone in the water.

"Well, at least the books have been put up on one shelf behind the librarian's desk, which is now labeled Gender Education. Ms. Hitchcock included a blurb in her communication home about their availability for parents who are interested. She also asked parents to sign a form giving their children permission to check out the books if that's what they want. If she doesn't have that signature, Laura does not allow the children to take the books home."

"Sounds wise. But what's to keep the kids from sharing with others on the bus ride home, or on the playground?" Marty heaved a stone out into the deep and it skipped way past the beckoning branch.

"Oh, that's another thing. Ms. Hitchcock told Laura to prepare envelopes for the books to go home in. The children are not allowed to bring out those books while at school."

Izzy shivered as the wind rustled more wildly in the trees and pushed a cloud over the sun. She received a sideways hug from Marty who rubbed her shoulder briskly to warm her up.

"It's getting chilly. I guess it's time to head home,

considering I'm not finished my lessons for tomorrow. It was a great match yesterday morning. But the weather's turning. What do you think?"

"Let's take it a week at a time. If it's too cold to hold the racket, I'd say take a break. But you're good. I enjoyed playing tennis with you." Marty offered his fist to bump Izzy's fist. "A teacher's work is never done, so you'd best get home. I've got a test to prepare for, too—Professor Asher's class. I guess we both need to hit the books."

"Good luck. Then for your reward, why don't you join me at Aunt Anna's house for breakfast Saturday morning?" After a pause she added, "And invite your teacher, Mr. Asher." Izzy teetered from foot to foot, her hands sunk deep into her jacket pockets, a whisp of long blonde hair whipping across her face in the chill wind.

"Well, thank you! My Lady is inviting me home to meet the family?" Marty said with a smile.

"Be on your guard, My Lord," laughed Izzy, "Or we'll grill you for breakfast! I'll text you the address." Izzy jumped up and down to get warm. "Karibu!" She waved briefly, then turned to jog home as quickly as she could through the stiff breeze.

Marty Goldstein, I do believe I'm falling for you!

5. <u>MEETING THE FAMILY</u>

Aunt Anna made the perfect picture of Mrs. Claus—her plump figure wore a red Christmas apron, and her short silver curls protruded from under a red felt Santa hat. Her kitchen smelled of coffee. The dining table sported a green tablecloth, red napkins, and crystalline plates with flatware, butter in a crystal dish, and coffee mugs. A big round red candle etched with Mary holding baby Jesus sat burning in the middle of the table.

Izzy wore a red scarf around her neck, over a white long-sleeved shell and red pleated skirt which came just above her knee. White leggings with shiny black boots made her a perfect elf, especially with her blonde curls bouncing on her shoulders. She paused in the doorway, her arm looped over Marty's. They never meant to but had an uncanny way of dressing to match one another, except that Marty's Christmas color was hunter green, which highlighted his soft brown hair. Dressed in a hunter green scarf and bowtie with a white long-sleeved knit polo shirt and long green pants with glossy black shoes, he and Izzy again looked like they belonged together.

Aunt Anna gasped as she saw the happy couple coming

in. "Oh, you look so wonderful together. Let me get your picture, please." She quickly took a shot, then placed her phone in her apron. "Welcome to my humble abode!"

Izzy was at her aunt's side, giving her a peck on the cheek. "Aunt Anna, the house is so warm and inviting. All dressed up for Christmas!" She motioned toward Marty. "I want you to meet my friend, Mr. Martin Goldstein. He's doing grad studies over at the university."

Aunt Anna took a step toward Marty and offered her hand, craning her neck to look him in the eye. Marty took her hand and squeezed it. "Please, call me Marty."

"I've heard lots about you," they both blurted out at the same time, which made the three of them burst out laughing.

"It's all good," grinned Izzy. "I only have good things to say about each of you."

"She's been bragging about her Saturday morning breakfasts here with her Aunt Anna. Your warm kitchen is so welcoming this morning coming in from the cold." Marty rubbed his hands together.

"And the coffee is to die for." Izzy grabbed a mug from the table. She turned to Marty. "Please have a seat, and I'll pour you a cup to warm your hands. Aunt Anna, are you ready for some coffee?"

"No, I'm fine for a little bit. Let me get the pancakes on the grill. We've got scrambled cheese eggs and bacon in the oven." Aunt Anna shifted her gaze to Marty. "It's turkey bacon, Marty. With a name like Goldstein, I thought maybe I should avoid serving you pork."

"Aunt Anna, you are so much more thoughtful than I am! I knew the professor was Jewish, but it didn't even dawn on me," Izzy blurted out. She turned to Marty and asked, "So, you are also, Jewish? Do you practice?"

Marty cleared his throat and shifted his weight in his seat. "Actually, I am Jewish. Both of my great-great-grandfathers were rabbis in Israel. But the holocaust obliterated my paternal great-great-grandfather's side of the family, with the exception of my grandfather, who was rescued and spirited away to America. My great-great-aunt raised him, until he decided he wanted to return to a kibbutz outside of Jerusalem." He stopped to take a sip of his coffee.

Izzy rose to give him a warmup for his coffee. She put her hand on his shoulder as she returned to her seat. "What a horrible thing your grandfather experienced. I would hate to think of any of my children being ripped away from their parents, their home." A tear escaped down her cheek.

"Yes, I'm afraid that after the holocaust, and all that grandfather went through, he turned from his faith. At the kibbutz, he met Grandmother, who grew up worshiping the earth there on the farm. Many Jews were angry with God after the holocaust."

"I don't blame them," Izzy said, a cloud darkening her brow.

"Hey, it's the past! Bad things happen." Marty jostled Izzy. "Don't let it spoil the present. I can't resist Aunt Anna's turkey bacon, eggs, and pancakes."

"Well, let's get it on the table." Aunt Anna pulled piping hot plates out of the oven and put them on hot pads in the center of the table. "Give me a few moments, and I'll make some more pancakes while you get started. I'd like to say grace, if you don't mind."

Izzy was accustomed to Aunt Anna's habits. "She wants to pray, to give thanks."

"Oh, that's fine." He quickly bowed his head and closed his eyes.

"Dear heavenly Father, thank you for this happy morning that we can be together. And thank you for providing for all our needs. Thank you for this food. In Jesus' name, Amen." Anna looked up to see Marty still had his head bowed.

Izzy smiled and said, "Hmmm-mmm. Dig in!"

The dimple on Marty's face and the twinkle in his eye nearly melted Izzy's heart. Feeling her face flush, she jumped up to wash her hands at the kitchen sink. After drying her hands, she used the damp paper towel to pat her eyes and cheeks. *Why can't I hide my emotions?* She chided herself.

"So, where is your professor this morning?" Aunt Anna sat down at the head of the table and placed a plate full of soft fluffy pancakes in the middle. She hid many dabs of butter in the steamy pile.

"Uncle Amos?" Marty stopped midway with a sopping scoop of pancakes, resting his hand next to his plate. "He has Saturday morning conference calls with his wife and three children back in Israel. Wishes he could have been here."

"Uncle Amos? Is he your blood relative?" Izzy asked, sitting up in interest.

"Yes…I thought I'd told you, sorry. My mother, Ruth, was fifteen years old when her little brother Amos came along. Then she married her high school sweetheart, Harold Goldstein, a jeweler's son, when she was only twenty and Dad, twenty-one. Before they knew it, I came along. Her little brother, Amos, was only six at the time."

"Only six years between you?" Izzy marveled. "He seems so much more…"

"Mature." Marty helped Izzy finish, adding, "That's because he already has a wife and three kids, I believe they're six, eight, and eleven years old. Two boys and a girl." Marty finished off his pancakes and took a bite of bacon.

"Did you grow up together?" Aunt Anna asked, taking a sip of coffee.

"For a little while. My grandfather and grandmother came

to Chicago for about sixteen years. Mom was already fifteen, and Amos, only one. I came along when Uncle Amos was six years old—just in kindergarten. But it wasn't long before my folks whisked me off to Africa where they ran a clinic for about seven years, that time in South Africa. Finally, when I was in third grade, my folks relocated to help a neighborhood clinic in Chicago. Then Amos had fun introducing me on campus as his nephew. And I was proud to own him as my uncle. We had five good years together. Then one day my grandparents took Uncle Amos back to Israel. They said, 'We have rediscovered God and want to get closer to our roots.'" Marty paused, looking blankly ahead, remembering. But he very quickly shook himself back to the moment, took up his napkin to wipe his mouth and smiled. "We see each other when we can. It's a treat to be able to take his class."

"Now I understand why you call him 'Old Man.'" Izzy reached out to hold his hand. "Did you always call him that, growing up?"

"No, I didn't think of that until we were older. He broke his leg running college cross-country, and I was just a teen. He doesn't enjoy that title as much as Uncle, but I like to razz him once in a while."

"Yeah, youth. They can be cruel sometimes. I should know." Izzy dropped his hand and crossed her arms with a smirk. "But I can see your uncle did not let the broken leg or the name-calling get him down. He's still running."

Izzy held up her elbow with some scarring leftover from her head-on collision with Professor Asher. "See? Living proof. Is he doing okay?"

"He's fine." Marty pushed his chair back from the table. "I, on the other hand, am stuffed!"

"Are you two slowing down? There are still pancakes and coffee." Aunt Anna had the coffee pot in hand, ready to pour.

"Very satisfied," said Marty, "but, yes, I'll take a warm-up. Thank you." Then, looking at his watch, he said, "I hate to be rude, but I wonder if you had heard about the volcanic activity happening around the Pacific Rim? I believe the haze this morning is undoubtedly behind it."

"I'm glad you mentioned it." Aunt Anna stood with her hands on her hips, looking at the clock on the wall in the kitchen. "We like catching up on the news. I did notice those troubling developments along the Pacific Rim yesterday."

Izzy collected sticky plates and flatware from the table. "I heard something briefly in passing yesterday. Some kind of volcanic activity?"

"Yes, it's very volatile and widespread." Marty helped Izzy clear the table, then Aunt Anna led him to the living room.

You're a keeper, Marty Goldstein, Izzy thought. *Not afraid of house chores!*

6. <u>THE NEWS</u>

"You two find it on the TV and settle down. I'll finish up in the kitchen. I can listen while I work." Izzy got busy rinsing and washing the dishes.

Aunt Anna's living room spread beyond the dining area and kitchen. Izzy watched the news from behind the bar where she rinsed the dishes. Four soft leather recliners and two end tables circled a warmly colored loop rug and heavy pine coffee table, facing the seventy-five-inch screen. Marty lowered himself into the first recliner on the right, and Aunt Anna plopped down into the fourth recliner with a sigh. The news anchors, Rod Rogers and Julie Quespie looked starkly clear like they were in the living room.

ROGERS: News from the Atlantic. A string of volcanoes have come to life along the Mid-Atlantic Ridge. What began with the tremendous blast of Mt. Lakagigar just east of Iceland, seems to have awakened some sleeping giants in the Mid-Atlantic, spewing tons of lava and ash into the ocean, even damaging two cargo ships caught by surprise. In the last twenty-four hours another volcano—this one inland—has begun to cause concern.

QUESPIE: That's right, Rod. Mt. Vesuvius has people the most nervous, as it has begun spewing smoke and ash. The Italian government is encouraging people to prepare for evacuation. Over two hundred people—especially those with respiratory illnesses and the elderly—have been treated at local hospitals.

ROGERS: A big worry posted by fishermen on social media is the devastation—even annihilation—of thousands and thousands of fish and marine life.

Pictures of dead fish on the water's surface and dumped onto fishing trolley decks flashed upon the screen. Mesmerized, Izzy joined the two in the living room, sitting next to Marty. She noticed the water looked like blood. "Look at the color of the water," she said in awe.

"That is a chemical reaction due to the demise of the oxygen in the water. It ends up with more iron." Marty leaned forward, face riveted toward the screen.

"Wow! Pastor Michaels read to us from Revelation, how in the end times the globe's water will once again turn to blood." Aunt Anna patted the Bible on the table next to her chair.

"Are you serious?" Izzy sat up to look at her aunt.

Aunt Anna nodded. "It comes right out of Revelation 16:4." She picked up her Bible and put on her red reading glasses—she had red, teal, steel-blue, and black to match whatever she was wearing, as sometimes she served as the lectionary in church on Sunday mornings. She read—

"The third angel poured out his bowl on the rivers and springs of water, and they became blood."

Izzy got up, hand outstretched, asking for the Bible. She

sat back down, silently reading. Marty looked over her shoulder.

"Shades of Moses," he said.

"How do you mean?" Izzy leaned over to see.

Marty sat up taller, his right hand pointing skyward. "God sent Moses to Pharaoh, to tell him, 'Let my people go.' When he didn't, God told Moses to threaten Pharaoh with plagues. The first plague was all the water in the land turning to blood."

Izzy sat up and shook her head. "You mean to tell me you believe that?"

"That's how the story goes from the second book of our Torah, which is Exodus in the Bible. It just seems rather strange that the same plague should appear again in the last book of the Bible. Either coincidence, or I'd say that God hasn't changed."

"Yeah, He's still cursing mankind," Izzy said, scrunching up her face and picking at her nails.

"Well, wait a minute." Aunt Anna frowned looking at Izzy, finger raised. "In Moses' day it was a threat meant to bring Pharaoh to his senses, so the children of Israel could go to worship God in the wilderness. Remember what your mom always said, 'God is…'"

Izzy glanced down at the book in her lap, then looked up wearily at Aunt Anna. "Love, God is love. Mom always said that, and it always rubbed me the wrong way. She said it after my dog died when he was hit by a car the first day I went with her to church. You'd think that if God wanted me to know His love, he would not have taken my pet dog!" She angrily wiped away some tears with her hand.

"Oh, Sweetheart, I remember that day. God used little Rexie to save you from being hit by that car! Rex pushed you out of the way. So your dear mother, of course she wanted you to know that was God's loving way. He spared your life that day."

"Thank God for Rex is all I can say." Marty winked at Izzy.

A smile ever so faintly crept up on Izzy's lips. "Yeah, thank God for Rex." She looked up into Marty's eyes, and knew she was blushing again.

Aunt Anna, as if on cue, leaned forward and raised herself up out of the recliner. She walked off into the kitchen to put away the dishes. Marty leaned over and gave Izzy her first kiss—it was a simple but firm peck which Izzy received with her eyes closed. But when she opened her eyes, there were Marty's tender eyes, and the dimple on his cheek. He gently brushed her hair off her forehead. She sat up, dazed, but totally at peace for a moment.

Then Izzy glanced to see if Aunt Anna had seen. She seemed busy putting the dishes away in cupboards along the far wall. Her eyes met Marty's and she could not suppress a smile. "You're such a sweet guy, Marty Goldstein."

Wow, God, Marty is grateful I'm alive. I guess I owe you an apology for holding Rex's death against you all these years. Thank you for Rex's sacrifice. It's good to be alive.

"It's rather amazing how God works things out." She curled up in her chair leaning against the armrest, facing Marty. "Shall we join Aunt Anna for Sunday School tomorrow, to see what more the Bible has to say about the end times?"

Marty took both of Izzy's hands in his, head down as if in thought, until a grin grew on his face. "I think it'll be good for us to get to know God better. And I would love to do it with you."

Sunday morning, nine o'clock sharp, Aunt Anna introduced the young couple to her pastor and Sunday School class.

Everybody seemed genuinely happy to see them.

"Please, help yourself to some coffee and donuts if you like. We will begin class in another five minutes." Pastor Michaels stepped forward to shake Marty's hand, towering over Marty. Izzy took a step back, feeling dwarfed next to the pastor's huge frame.

While helping herself to her coffee, Izzy could not help feeling attracted to the gentle giant who moved around the room talking with his people. She gave Marty's arm a squeeze. "I kind of look forward to what Pastor Michaels has to say." He squeezed her hand in response.

Within a few minutes, coffee in hand, Marty led Izzy to join the class. He steered them to a couple of seats next to the window.

"Today," began the pastor, "We will be looking at the rise of the Beast and his partner, The Prophet. But first, what end-times prophecy is being fulfilled in the news lately?" He took off his glasses to look over the crowd expectantly.

Aunt Anna's hand shot up, and Pastor Michaels nodded for her to speak. She stood and said, "Jesus told us to expect earthquakes in the last days. Do you think the volcanoes figure into that?" Leaning on the table, she slowly lowered herself back to her chair.

"Yes, indeed. It all has to do with the birth pangs Jesus spoke of foreshadowing the Last Days. Thank you. Now, let's take a look at Revelation 13. As we read this portion of Scripture, I want you to count how many players there are in this end-time drama. Now we're reading from Revelation 13, beginning with verse one—'*And I saw a beast coming out of the sea. He had ten horns and seven heads, with ten crowns on his horns, and on each head a blasphemous name. The beast I saw resembled a leopard but had feet like those of a bear and a mouth like that of a lion. The dragon gave the beast his power and his throne and great authority.*

One of the heads of the beast seemed to have had a fatal wound, but the fatal wound had been healed. The whole world was astonished and followed the beast'..."

Izzy listened until her head pounded. All the talk of a man given authority by the devil, apparently representing a council of ten nations, apparently experiencing a fatal stab but coming back to life, gave her a headache. Pastor Michaels plowed on to share how he would be validated by another beast who would do miracles, even calling down fire from heaven. And that beast, also referred to as the false prophet, would make an image of the first beast which everyone would be forced to worship.

After church, Marty and Izzy went to Aunt Anna's house for a roast meal. "Whew! I felt like my head was going to explode. TMI…I just could not handle it. It all seemed so surreal."

Aunt Anna, who was putting the mouth-watering roast, rice, and veggies on the table, stopped long enough behind Izzy to cup her chin in her hand while massaging her scalp with the other. Marty got busy putting the silver around the table.

"Ahhh! Feels so good. Thank you." Izzy stretched her arms back to pat Aunt Anna's sides. "I needed that!"

"Give it time, Dear." She stood with her hands resting on her belly. "There is lots to take in. But try to remember the author of Revelation. Go back to the opening of the whole book, and it says, 'A revelation of our Lord Jesus Christ…' Christ gave us this information so that we can be ready."

When everyone finally settled down to eat, Anna said a prayer. "Heavenly Father, Lord of the universe, yet lover of each soul, bless us by this food. And help us to process what we are learning from your Word. For it is in Jesus' name we pray."

All three voices chimed in, "Amen."

"It all seems like a cosmic war," said Marty cutting his meat. "I can't wait to read to the end to see who wins."

Aunt Anna clasped her hands. "Well, good for you! You do just that and let me know what you conclude." Her cheeks shone a bright pink, and there was a twinkle in her eye.

Marty continued, "I actually found it a little scary, I mean if it's really going to unfold as Revelation says. Especially the part about the second beast, or The Prophet, deceiving the world into worshiping the image of the first beast. I can't imagine the whole civilized world reverting to Baal worship! But that this image is going to come alive and cause all who refuse to worship it to be killed! Feels like a sci-fi horror movie!"

"If it comes down to that, I will rather bow down to worship the idol. Better than being killed!" blurted out Izzy with her hand over her mouth full of food.

"Oh, no, no, no!" Aunt Anna grabbed Izzy's hand. "Please give yourself time to think about it more carefully. Life is more than just the here and now. The real you inside is going to live somewhere forever. Yes, it is a cosmic battle for your soul. Our enemy is the deceiver and would love to have your allegiance and worship. But God has revealed all this so we can cling to Jesus through thick and thin and enjoy with him victory over evil and eternal life."

After dinner, everyone contentedly retreated to the living room to watch the news. "Watching the news these days feels like it is marching right out of the Bible." Marty sat down with anticipation.

FOX 29 News anchor Rod Rogers reported with urgency in his voice.

> ROGERS: Now with some breaking news. The Campi Felegrei, or Fire Fields, in Italy has lost its north-western face with a surprise eruption. The

devastating blast caught everybody off guard, and has spread havoc as far away as Spain to the west and Rome to the north—flattening trees and many structures in its path, and spawning a tsunami which has obliterated many Mediterranean ports. The landscape and sky are filled with soot, glass, and ash. Now bringing you a firsthand look from the sky, here is Nora, flying with Brett in Sky One.

Izzy gasped and put her hand to her mouth. Marty sat up and gaped at the carnage. Something had happened to the audio coverage, but what the eye could see caused them to cringe. Tears streamed down Izzy's face. Aunt Anna moved over to grip Izzy's arm. They watched in horror as families on the streets of Rome lay like refuse on the ground in the aftermath of the blast.

Izzy jumped up, her head spinning. "How could people be caught unaware? Surely, they've been tracking the changes in that volcano!"

As if an echo, Julie asked Rod the same question.

QUESPIE: How could this happen, Rod? Have scientists monitoring the situation failed to prepare the populace?

ROGERS: No. This one caught everyone by surprise, Julie. It's what scientists attribute to the volcano having a large caldera—a spread out depression which does not give the early warnings of seismic activity or ground swell.

QUESPIE: There are five hundred thousand people living in the Neapolitan area of southern Italy, all sandwiched between two fiery mountains—this one that exploded today, and Mt. Vesuvius. Rod, both for the locals, and for people

who are drawn to that locale for its beauty
and culture, this is such a tragic turn of events.

ROGERS: Certainly, Julie. I'm sure the residents
love their mountains. It's easy to forget that
they are volcanoes. I'm afraid there is no more
time for complacency. These sleeping
giants—volcanoes around the world— seem to be
awakening with a vengeance.

Aunt Anna took the control and turned the TV off. The three sat in silence.

"Why, God, does there have to be such suffering?" Izzy felt heavy, like a weight sat on her shoulders.

"Well, Kids, there are people who need prayer right now. Why don't I lead us in a word of prayer?" Aunt Anna bowed her head, Izzy and Marty followed suit. "Oh, Father in Heaven, the world is shocked. People, families, are hurting. Many have lost their lives. Have mercy on their souls. Give grace and comfort and help to the living. Cause your people around the world to reach out with your love to help them. And help us not to be complacent about your coming. As the world experiences these birth pangs, enable us to prepare our hearts—to be on guard against the evil one, and to be useful in your service. For it is in Jesus' name we pray. Amen."

Izzy said the amen, but a question lingered in her mind. *How can I help?*

7. <u>WATER CONSERVATION</u>

The next day, Izzy asked her students, "When you get thirsty, what do you want to drink?"

Teddy, in his raspy deep voice, said, "Coke. No, Coke Zero."

Valerie, arm outstretched, sitting up excitedly, waved her hand, and said, "Orange juice. Nice, cold orange juice."

Chloe, whose shoulder-length wavy brown hair covered her shoulders, nonchalantly raised her hand and let it hang limp.

Izzy pointed to her and said, "Chloe, what do you drink when you are thirsty?"

"Water. I drink water. My mommy won't let me drink anything else." She tilted her head and raised her hands and shoulders as if to ask, "Why?"

"Chloe, your mommy wants you to grow healthy and strong. With all the running and thinking you all do, your bodies need water to keep healthy."

"You all are so fortunate. Your parents can afford to buy whatever you want to drink. This past weekend, the world was rocked by at least four volcanoes. Besides all the destruction of lives, homes, and crops, volcano eruptions pollute the air with ash. The ash pollutes water supplies, making them poisonous to drink. People there get very, very thirsty. Is there anything we can do to help them?"

Izzy smiled later in the retelling of her lesson to Marty as they took a walk at the park. A family of sparrows splashing in the fountain at the pond added to her mirth. "Some of the kids had some great ideas. One said, "Can we send them some water bottles?" Another sweet little guy said, "Pray for them." Another said, "Talk to Mommy and Daddy about helping them somehow." But the one I liked the most came from Chloe. She said, "Whenever I don't eat my food, Mommy says, 'Think of the kids in Africa' because they are starving. So, I guess we should not dump our water but drink it all up."

Marty chuckled. "I'm glad you are teaching your children about what is going on in the world. You're a fine conservationist. And teacher."

"It doesn't save those who died in the eruptions over the weekend. But it's the little I could do to help. The world water situation has really deteriorated over recent months."

"Yes, it has. Too many distressing things have taxed the world's water supply. This recent spate of volcanoes is only exacerbating the water crisis brought on by the meteors which struck last year. But I have been watching the head of the World Water Restoration Committee, Mr. Bandar. He seems to be doing a lot of good. He's charismatic, and quite the genius. His WWRC has become brokers of funds, water, and resources including personnel. Nations with surplus water and healthy groundwater and springs have begun to share more generously, while other nations are rallying together to give what they have—youthful workers eager for world peace, funding, steel, produce, equipment, and technology for digging new wells and such. It seems to be the making of a new world order."

Their walk had brought them to Belmont Plateau overlooking the glen. A light breeze swirled through the leaves on the trees, making them dance and sway gently. Marty led Izzy to the shade underneath a tree. They ran their hands over the moss to clear away pebbles and debris, then sat down, their backs against the tree trunk.

Izzy brushed her hair back behind her ears and looked up to Marty. "You seem pretty impressed with this Mr. Bandar."

Marty's brows knit, thinking. "Yes, he's a good diplomat and resourceful leader. But Israel has set the example. Did you know that they were the first to respond to the crisis, and pledged eight percent of their water reserves to help their neighbors, even though they live amongst hostile neighbors?"

"My hat's off to them. Very impressive. And Uncle Amos has had a part in all that, right?"

"I do believe so. Makes me proud to be related."

"Me, too. I mean, I'm so proud to know him." Izzy grinned.

Marty ran his fingers through his hair and pulled out his handkerchief to wipe away the sweat on his brow. He frowned at the grime that showed up with his sweat. "Look at this. The air pollution from the volcanic ash is horrible. We had best retreat indoors."

Izzy followed Marty to the Sports Bar in town for a bite to eat. As they ate, the sunset haze shown a rusty red. "I guess this is the fallout from that volcano blast in Italy. What a huge impact it is having on the air around the world. I wonder what the long-term effects are going to be." Izzy wrinkled her nose and looked up at Marty.

"It's definitely a day to stay indoors for the elderly and people with respiratory illnesses, and for those who want to stay healthy."

"Let's call Aunt Anna, to make sure she's okay." Izzy put the phone to her ear while she rested her head on her hand; her blonde hair brushed the tabletop. Marty reached out and crunched a handful of hair in his hand, smiling. Izzy smiled back as the phone rang seven times. She hung up. "She'll call back when she can. Hopefully she's been smart enough to stay indoors with the air on."

"Yes, I'm sure." Marty put his hand on Izzy's arm. "Listen, tomorrow I'll be saying good-bye to Uncle Amos."

"What? So soon?" Izzy put her fork full of food down on her plate.

"Yes, sad, but true. His intensive course has come to an end. It was good while it lasted. But he has a family to get back to. So I was hoping you could join us for a meal tomorrow night, to help me send him off."

"Of course. I'd love to." Izzy squeezed Marty's hand. "Rain or shine, I'll be there."

Uncle Amos wore a brown plaid dress shirt with a tan vest. He browsed the menu, waiting for the couple to arrive. When they came, he glanced at his watch and proclaimed, "Six-fifteen already!"

"Oh, so sorry, Amos, to keep you waiting." Marty slid into the seat opposite his uncle.

Izzy, brushing a little wisp of hair out of her eyes, said, "I had a little emergency at school today."

Setting the menu aside, Amos stood for Izzy, motioning for her to sit down. "Sit down and tell me about it."

"A parent came into my room after I dismissed the children, with her little Eric in tow. She informed me that Eric had told her one of the fifth graders, a boy, had touched Eric inappropriately on the playground. Just what I had feared would happen once the Board of Education insisted we make gender identity books available in the library. It's so tragic."

Amos shifted in his seat, wincing. "I'd hate for that to happen to my second grader, Benjie. I've been following your struggles with the Board through Marty. So, what did you do?"

"I apologized profusely and tried to get Eric to talk about it…but the poor kid just shook his head. I wanted so much to hug him, to comfort him. I told him it's not his fault. Then I told his mom I would talk with the school, and I was sure we would increase our surveillance on the playground." Izzy blew out a deep breath.

Marty put his arm over her shoulder. "So, you talked with the principal?"

"Yes, she's going to adjust the playground duty schedule, and we'll have a teachers' meeting tomorrow after school. Plus, she is arranging to talk with the fifth grader and his parents, tonight."

"Well, you can't blame it only on the books in the library." Amos sat up and straightened his coat jacket. "There's so much exposure to sex on TV these days. I've been appalled by the ads, even, on American TV these days. Worse than I remember it."

A waitress placed water on the table for her three customers. "My name is Patty, and I'll be your server today. Ready to order?"

"No, please give us a minute." Marty picked up the wine menu. "Today I'm treating as we are saying 'Until we meet again' to my uncle here. Shall we get some wine?"

"Sure, go ahead." Izzy raised her glass of water as if to toast the professor.

Amos agreed as he raised his imaginary glass.

After dinners were served, and the bubbly wine sparkled

in his glass, Amos raised a toast to his nephew. "To a promising conservationist; may you succeed in saving our world for the next generation."

"Yes, go for it!" Izzy toasted with water, clinking everyone's glass. Her heart fluttered when Marty's smiling eyes met hers as they sipped down their drinks.

Marty quickly raised his toast, "To Uncle Amos, professor par excellence. May your zeal for water preservation and your expertise and innovation have a far-reaching effect on all nations."

"I'll receive that." Amos raised his glass to Marty. "Thank you."

"Well said." Izzy gave Marty a sheepish grin. Then turning to Amos, she said, "I understand your little Benjie is old enough to be in my class. And today is his birthday. Seven years old, isn't he?"

"Yes, indeed. A very precocious seven-year-old!"

Izzy looked to the ceiling and raised her glass high. "To Benjie, Happy Birthday! May you follow in your papa's footsteps and help this world with your wisdom."

"How sweet of you to remember." Amos lifted his glass toward Izzy.

"Yes," agreed Marty, giving Izzy's shoulder a squeeze.

"I'm kind of wired that way. I feel very happy that his papa will soon be home to help him celebrate. I'm sure he must be missing you." Izzy raised her glass again and clinked Amos's glass.

"It will be good to be home." Amos held his glass with a far-off look in his eyes and frowned. Then he looked up with a slight smile and raised his glass to Marty and Izzy. "I come from a long line of matchmakers, and so I've done my part bringing you two together. May God bless your relationship. It has been a pleasure running into you, Izzy."

That Wednesday morning Izzy woke up with a start and looked at her phone. "Ahh. Six o'clock, I'll barely make it. No coffee for me this morning." She texted Marty—running late, get started without me if you can find someone to play. Then she did her morning routine and ran out the door fifteen minutes later. Her car, a blue Nissan, was covered with frost, so it took her extra time to scrape off and defrost. When she finally made it to St. Joe's tennis courts, she looked at her watch—six-thirty-five. They usually started playing doubles at six-thirty.

Izzy ran to the courts with her racket to find Marty. *I guess I'll be sitting out this match.*

When she arrived at the court where they usually played, a stocky female student walked over and handed Izzy a cup of coffee. "Oh, my goodness, what's this?"

"Marty got it for you. Sweet guy." She shook with the cold and took down her hair from the bun it was in and slipped the band on her wrist.

"Yes, he is. Thanks, uh…"

"Vanessa. He's on that court over there, playing with my partner, Jessica. I stubbed my toe so I decided not to play this morning. I'm heading inside where it's warm. Take care."

"Thanks, Vanessa."

Izzy stood on tiptoe to look for Marty. When she saw him, he'd just hit a hard play off the corner of the court. His partner, a tall brunette wearing neon green, returned the next ball. She was good.

This hot coffee means so much to me this cold morning. Marty, you're a Sweetheart.

Before long Marty waved in Izzy's direction. She held up her coffee and gave him a thumbs up.

She enjoyed sitting out and watching Marty play. He and Jessica seemed well matched. She had a strong backhand. Marty lobbed a few balls and gained a lot of points playing the net. Izzy cheered from the stands. "Woo-hoo! Go team!" When the set ended, Marty's team had won. Marty and Jessica exchanged hand bumps. Jessica waved at Izzy and ran off toward the locker room. Izzy walked onto the court to see Marty.

"Congratulations! Great game. I enjoyed watching you work up a sweat."

"Oh, is that so?" With that, Marty took off his headband and tried to hand it to Izzy.

"Eww. No thank you." Izzy backed away. When Marty threatened to shoot the headband at her, she held up her hand. "Peace. I don't have much time. I've got to run to school. Any news from Uncle Amos? Did he make it home alright?"

"Yes. I've got some great news. But it will be more fun sharing it with you at the Café tonight. How about six-thirty? See you then?"

"Great. I can't wait. Bye." Izzy scurried away, bypassing a sweaty hug.

After school, Izzy went home to freshen up before her date with Marty. She had also worked up a sweat pitching ball for the kids at recess. I feel pink tonight. So she wore a blousy white shirt with roses and a pink jean skirt.

Marty was waiting for Izzy at the door of the Café. He had his hand behind his back, but it was hard to hide the dozen red roses.

"What?" Izzy gasped. "They're beautiful! And look, we match!"

Sure enough, Marty's light pink dress shirt and tan jeans

made them look like a handsome couple. Marty gently placed the roses into Izzy's arms, then asked for help from the hostess to take a few shots before they retreated indoors.

"You shouldn't have gotten me flowers." Izzy stood them up on an empty chair at their table. "I love roses, though. Thank you. What are we celebrating?"

"Well, I am celebrating us. It's been a month already." Marty tried to be serious, but he could not suppress a smile.

The waitress, Patty, came along. "Pretty flowers! What's the occasion?"

"Our one-month anniversary." Izzy covered her smile.

"Yeah, it's been about a month. I remember when you all first came in here. Looked like you'd had an accident. Ha! Turned out to be a good thing. Congratulations. Do you need a minute?"

"No, we can order." Marty seemed to be in a rush. "I'll have your beef stroganoff with broccoli. And you, Dear?"

Dear. He is a sweetheart! "Ah, give me the lasagna and salad. Thanks."

"Wine for the lovely lady?" asked Patty.

"No." Marty leaned over to whisper. "She doesn't drink."

"Oh, fine. So what can I get for you?"

"Water will be fine," Izzy and Marty chimed in together, and laughed.

When Patty was gone, Izzy looked at Marty and started tearing up.

"What?" Marty leaned forward with his handkerchief and said, "It's clean."

Izzy burst out laughing. "It's nothing. It's just that I have thoroughly enjoyed getting to know you, Marty." *You're a keeper!* She thought. "You put a smile on my face when the going gets rough."

"Oh, I'm happy to hear that, because the feeling is mutual." He took Izzy's hand in his. "How are things at school?"

"Going okay. The kids keep me hopping. So far our system for checking out those books in the library is going smoothly. But I want to hear your news from Uncle Amos."

"Alright. Are you sitting down?"

Izzy nodded excitedly.

"Uncle Amos writes—'Hello Marty. I've got some unbelievable news for you. I have been invited by the Prime Minister to head up the Ministry of the Interior in Israel. I will assume that position at the beginning of next month and may even be invited onto the Security Cabinet. It is a position I feel rather prepared for and hope and pray to God to have a healthy influence. With the volatility of this old world—both geologically and geopolitically—I am glad for this platform of service. Nevertheless, it is a rather daunting task.'" Marty glanced up. "Still with me? Okay, he continues, 'On the home front it was a very happy homecoming. Attached is a pic of my happy family upon my return. Please give my regards to Aunt Anna and Izzy. Very fond memories. Izzy's a fine girl, Young Man! –Amos'"

Izzy squeezed Marty's arm as she reread the email on Marty's phone. "He's a sweet Old Man, isn't he?" She could not suppress her smile.

Marty unraveled Izzy's arm and reached over to rub her shoulder. "He's a good judge of character, I'd say. And look at this unbelievable opportunity before him—Minister of the Interior, no less!"

"I am proud of him. Our very own matchmaker…and Minister of the Interior!"

The food came. Then Izzy asked, "Did you notice your uncle frowning just before he blessed us as our matchmaker? I wonder what was worrying him?"

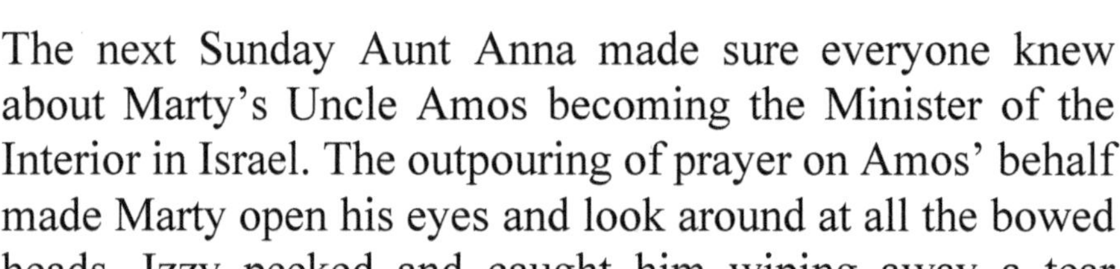

The next Sunday Aunt Anna made sure everyone knew about Marty's Uncle Amos becoming the Minister of the Interior in Israel. The outpouring of prayer on Amos' behalf made Marty open his eyes and look around at all the bowed heads. Izzy peeked and caught him wiping away a tear before he bowed his head again.

Then, Izzy listened hard to what Pastor Michaels shared about Revelation 12 and grappled with it. The pastor shared how the devil and his minions were thrown out of heaven down to the earth. She learned how this fallen angel was also called the dragon that wanted to destroy Mary's son, the Son of God, Jesus. So that when he was born, Herod ordered the killing of all the babies two years old and under around Bethlehem...all because the wise men came to Jerusalem inquiring where the king of the Jews was to be born.

"This is a fulfillment of verses four through six, which says—'*And the dragon stood before the woman who was about to give birth, so that when she bore her child he might devour it.*'

"*She gave birth to a male child, one who is to rule all the nations with a rod of iron, but her child was caught up to God and to his throne, and the woman fled into the wilderness, where she has a place prepared by God, in which she is to be nourished for 1,260 days.*"

Izzy sat with her Aunt Anna and Marty, looking over the room of folks bent over their Bibles listening to the pastor, taking notes, asking questions. *Why would God allow the devils to be thrown down to the earth? So much pain and suffering and confusion. It doesn't seem fair.*

Pastor Michaels continued, "Keep your eyes open. In the last days, the woman described here, which I believe is the nation of Israel, *is going for a flight for her life into the wilderness where she will be nourished for 1,260 days. But we see the dragon, again, trying to destroy her with a flood, but her God, our God, is going to deliver her to a safe place he has prepared for her for 'a time, and times, and a half a time'--that's three and a half years! The 1,260 days from verse six, and the three and a half years we see in verse fifteen, are the same amount of time. In the Bible you will often find God repeating himself to let us know it's a sure thing. We don't know how he's going to do it, but God, I believe, is going to hide Israel in the wilderness during the last three and a half years of the Beast's covenant with the world."*

Over dinner that day, Izzy confessed her confusion. "Why did God send the dragon and his minions to earth to wreak havoc? Why not just send them to Hell? Why here?"

"Honey, that is a very good question. It is much akin to the question we all ask from time to time, 'Where does suffering come from?'" Aunt Anna patted Izzy's hand. "Be patient. It is all a part of the bigger story of God's plan of salvation. And we know who the victor is," she finished, holding up the Bible.

Somehow that did not disburse the discomfort Izzy felt. She was still not very happy with God.

Marty sensed her somber mood and put his hand on Izzy's shoulder. "Hey, this is a cosmic war we are in, Izzy. Today when Pastor was sharing, I realized for the first time that Christ really came for us Jews, but we rejected him at that time. It's something I would like to run by Uncle Amos. Because it appears God has a plan for Israel in the last days."

Wow. Marty really believes God has a plan. I don't really understand, but I hope it's a good plan. "Marty, your trust in God is remarkable. Let me know what Uncle Amos says."

Marty smiled and put his hand on Izzy's. "I will, Dear. If we are patient, I believe that we will see that God has a good plan after all."

"I hope so. I guess I need time, and patience." Izzy breathed a little easier, dispersing the storm that had been brewing in her heart.

Then Izzy shifted in her seat and looked Marty in the eye. "Did you wonder how Uncle Amos and family are going to be affected? Will they be hidden in the wilderness for three and a half years?"

"I'm hoping they'll come to know Jesus as their Messiah, and the Messiah of Israel, before that happens." Marty's eyes smiled.

8. <u>NO TIME FOR IZZY</u>

That evening, Marty took Izzy for a walk in the park. The full moon shone brightly overhead, like a floodlamp showcasing the meadows that ran to meet the forest. They walked in silence, taking in the soft breeze and broad brilliance around them.

"It's at times like this that I can see believing in God." Marty smiled down at Izzy.

Izzy smiled back. *I feel so loved by this man.* She stopped in her tracks and faced Marty, looking up into his soft brown eyes. *Where will the path ahead take us?*

Marty swiped her cheek with his thumb, and said, "You've captured my heart, Izzy, and I want to spend my life with you." Then he dropped down on his right knee and presented Izzy with a diamond ring—its flame danced before her eyes. Her hand covered her mouth, and she stood in shock. The blue hues of the moonlight emanating from the gem were mesmerizing.

"Oh, Marty," Izzy whispered. "You took me by surprise! I am in shock." Izzy sank to the ground. "How can this be happening to me? Marty, it's so fast. But I do love you. You're so gentle, thoughtful, and kind. You're my best friend." Marty embraced her, then lifted her chin to look into her eyes. He wiped away the tears he found there with his handkerchief and kissed her firmly on the lips.

God, how can the man of my dreams be asking me to marry him so soon? Izzy's head spun as she looked from Marty's moist eyes to the moon shining above and back again. Marty grasped her arms firmly in his. How long they stood there suspended between heaven and earth, Izzy did not know. Finally, she nodded her head, and a smile spread upon her lips and pushed all doubt away.

"Yes, I'll marry you, Marty Goldstein!"

Izzy didn't know how she made it through the next day at school. Of course she had to share her news with Laura over lunch. "Laura, you will never believe what happened yesterday." Izzy put on an air of pride, her nose up, head thrown back, and arms crossed comfortably, flashing her ring cooly.

Laura put her finger to her lips. "Mm. Looks like something pretty important. Ah. You got tenure."

"No, I wish. But it's coming soon. I've been teaching for seven years." Izzy rested on the other hip, her hands on her sides this time. "Guess again."

"You and Marty getting along okay?"

Izzy's smile grew bigger, and she nodded. Izzy scratched her nose with her left ring finger.

"Oh!" Laura let out an excited scream. "You didn't get engaged! Izzy? So soon!"

"I did. We did. And I've never been happier. Laura, when you meet Mr. Right, you just know." Izzy sat down to open her lunch and eat it. "It was so romantic. He took me totally by surprise. In the moonlight, at Fairmount Park, at the glen, one of my favorite places. He drew me close and whispered, 'Izzy, you've captured my heart and I want to spend my life with you.' Then he got down on one knee and held the ring up to me. It was unbelievable. I almost fainted."

Later, Izzy and Marty met together for some dinner at a cozy spot on St. Joe's campus called The Perch. Izzy laughed. "I shared our news at lunch today in the teacher's room. I was just talking to Laura, but it was kind of hard to keep it between us. As soon as Laura saw my ring, the whole teacher's lounge heard we were engaged. Everybody came filing by to wish me well."

Marty and Izzy sat in two tall upholstered chairs around a mahogany round table. He smiled and glanced up from his cell phone. "I've shared our news too, with Uncle Amos. Here. See what he says."

Izzy sat back in the chair and read Amos and Marty's chat.

Marty: Uncle Amos, I thoroughly agree with you—Izzy is a fine young woman. As a matter of fact, she is so fine that she has agreed to marry me! We have set the date for three months from now, August 28th. Is it possible you could come? We would love to host you and the whole family.

Amos: Congratulations! You certainly did not waste any time.

Marty: This fish is just too big and beautiful. I could not risk her swimming away.

Amos: Fine. Fine. Will it be a Christian or Jewish wedding?

Marty: A combination, I think. We are still talking through it. But, Amos, there is something I have wanted to tell you. After spending these months studying the Bible with Izzy at church, I believe now that Jesus is the Messiah.

Amos: In Jerusalem, we still look for the Messiah's coming to deliver us in the last days. What convinces you that Jesus is the Messiah?

Marty: Revelation. Fulfilled prophecy, also, from the Torah. I would love to share with you sometime.

Amos: Let's find the time sometime. Today will be a busy day for me. I will meet with His Highness, Mr. Bandar, the head of the newly formed World Council for Emergency Preparedness. This water crisis has crippled much of the world. Say a prayer to God!

Marty: Will do. I'll pray with Izzy. Soon, I will be baptized. Uncle Amos, since believing, I feel more Jewish than ever. Someday we will talk.

Amos: Yes, let's talk. I would love to come to your wedding. Let me look at my schedule. Shalom!

Izzy stretched and grinned. "Big and beautiful fish, huh?" She threw her napkin at Marty.

"You are a beautiful woman, Izzy. And I knew I didn't want you to get away." Marty leaned forward and clasped both her hands in his and kissed them. "You're not a catch, Izzy. To me, you're a blessing from the Father. I am very grateful that God brought us together."

Izzy brushed Marty's fluffy hair back with her hand. "Uncle Amos seemed to take your conversion to Christianity well. He even seems a little interested. Amazing! I think I have more problems with your being baptized than he does."

"You worry too much, Izzy. Is it hard for you to truly trust God? Too many hurts and losses?" Marty sat forward and again took a hand, looking intently at her fingers between his.

The table bedecked with a lace doily and soft candle, and Debussy's "Afternoon of a Faun" softly playing over WRTI made Izzy wish their wedding day had already come. *Mrs. Martin Goldstein. Isabel Defranco Goldstein. Izzy D. Goldstein.*

"Earth to Izzy. Earth to Izzy. Did you hear me?"

Izzy shook herself out of her reverie. She looked at Marty, at the plate of steak set before her, the soft lights, heard the quiet music, and recalled Marty's comment. "A-hem," Izzy cleared her throat and took a sip of sparkly water. "I think the Goldsteins suffered more than I could imagine. And yet you are convinced that God is good and that Jesus is your Messiah. If you can do it, then I can do it."

"Are you saying what I think you're saying?" A bright smile fell from Marty's face.

"Yes, I've decided I will be baptized with you. Let's get baptized together this Sunday!" Izzy watched Marty's brow furrow even more. "What's wrong, you don't like that idea?"

"Well, it's just that I don't want you to do it for me. I want you to be sure you want this, that you're ready."

Izzy felt a little miffed and challenged him. "Who's to say I'm ready or not ready?" *This feels like a spat. Oh no!* She wondered if she resembled a hissing cat, because she sure felt like one.

Marty hung his head, then looked up. "Well…only you."

"Exactly." She tried to soften her tone, as she already felt deflated.

"Okay, sorry, I love the idea then." Marty's tone turned humble, and his face, crimson.

Izzy looked around to see if they had drawn any attention. She rubbed Marty's arm and caught his gaze with an apologetic look. "It's okay. We're okay." *Maybe I'm not ready, but I can't very well not get baptized with Marty. Hopefully, God will make me ready.* "Of course I'm ready to be baptized with you. And in another three months we will become Mr. and Mrs. Goldstein. I can't wait!" She held up her water goblet and clinked Marty's. Then their talk turned to the wedding plans.

Sunday morning, Aunt Anna, sporting a new blue chiffon dress, got to church early with two big white towels and a couple of gold-wrapped presents for Izzy and Marty. She caught Marty's arm as he came through the door, Izzy right behind him. "There you are, here in good time for your big day. Did you remember a change of clothes?"

"Of course, we did! At least, I did. This whole idea of dying with Christ as we go down into the water, and then coming up a brand-new person with a brand-new life has me so excited, I hardly slept last night. I couldn't not be ready!" Marty smiled widely and reached out to put his arm around Izzy's shoulder. "How about you, Sweetheart?"

It's a little inconvenient having to get dunked and then changed afterwards. But Izzy did not want to dampen Marty's enthusiasm. "Oh, it's a happy day, Marty. You and me! Let's do this together. Wish we could go ahead with it, but we have to attend Sunday School first." Izzy put her hand to her mouth when she saw Aunt Anna's raised eyebrow and grabbed Marty's arm to find a seat in class.

In Sunday School, Pastor Michaels introduced the Two Witnesses of Revelation 11. "This brave pair will be sent from God and stand as witnesses against the Beast and all who are in his camp. They will have the power to call for no rain—or any sign or judgment they choose—for the duration of the Great Tribulation. This is the period after the Beast breaks his covenant with Israel and the world by putting an idol of himself in the temple. What the Bible says in Daniel 9:27 is: *'He will make a strong covenant with many for one week and for half of the week (the last half) he shall put an end to sacrifices and offerings. Then on the wing of abominations will come one who makes desolate, until the decreed end comes to the desolator.'*

"The abomination mentioned here is the image of the Beast which he will place in the temple, thereby desecrating the temple. Jesus told his disciples, in Matthew 24:15-21—*'So when you see the abomination of desolation spoken of by the prophet Daniel, standing in the holy place (let the reader understand), then let those who are in Judea flee to the mountains. Let the one who is on the housetop not go down to take what is in his house, and let the one who is in the field not turn back to take his cloak. And alas for women who are pregnant and for those who are nursing infants in those days! Pray that your flight may not be in winter or on a Sabbath. For then there will be great tribulation, such as has not been from the beginning of the world until now, no, and never will be.'*

"For this to happen, the Jewish Temple on the holy mount, Mt. Moriah, must be rebuilt. So, keep your eyes open for the Beast. When you see the temple being rebuilt, prepare yourselves for Christ's return soon! Back to the two witnesses," Pastor Michaels turned and wrote on the whiteboard, THE TRUTH & THEIR TESTIMONY. "Some scholars argue that the two witnesses are not two literal prophets of old coming back to fight against the Beast and to call down God's judgment on his regime. Some biblical scholars make the case that these two witnesses of the Truth of God and of a personal encounter with the The Lamb of God will be the ones to empower every soul that comes to Christ after the Church is taken up with the Rapture. The tall man took off his glasses and looked over the crowd. "I personally like to take the Bible literally, so I would expect two men of God breathing fire out on those who would accost them. But it is comforting to know that, even after the Rapture, souls are going to be saved, people are going to come to know the Lamb of God, and he will strengthen them to be his witnesses in some very tough days!"

Sounds like scary days. But I shouldn't have to worry about it, because I'm getting baptized today! The thought of baptism made Izzy a little self-conscious. *God knows my heart. I'll do my best to live a good life, God. I want to make Marty proud. You, too.* But then the thought of having to please God made Izzy's shoulders droop a little. *How does one live up to God's expectations and standards? Impossible! Oh, God! Please make me fit for heaven, because I'm getting baptized today.*

Izzy stewed about getting baptized until the moment arrived. She and Marty were taken down the hallway behind the front of the church to change into shorts and T-shirts topped off with a white choir robe before the service began. She couldn't enjoy the songs that began the service, because she felt trapped in a whirlpool of worries. *Lord, just as I am, I'm coming. When I have doubts and am disgruntled with you, help me stand strong. Oh, God, I'm going to get dunked. I'll look like a wet cat. Oh, dear, I forgot my hair dryer. My hair's going to frizz.*

"And now, it gives me great pleasure to receive two of our friends into the communion of the Saints as they follow the Lord in baptism. Marty Goldstein, and Izzy Defranco, please find your place behind the stage and prepare for baptism."

Pastor Michaels' voice brought Izzy back to reality. She looked up at Marty, who took her hand with a gentle grip and gave her a warm smile. She mustered a smile and followed him behind the curtain at the back of the stage where the baptismal pool was filled and waiting. *I hope it's warm water.* She shuddered to think it would be otherwise.

Marty was the first to take the plunge.

"In the name of the Father, and of the Son, and of the Holy Spirit, I baptize you, Marty." Pastor's strong arms brought Marty back with a swoop, and then he raised him up again.

Everyone in the church sang out, "Happy day, happy day, when Jesus washed my sins away!"

Yep, Marty looks like a drowned rat. And I'm next. Help me Lord! Izzy wanted to take a towel to Marty's dripping face, but someone else helped him, and Pastor, who was standing down in the water, held his arms out toward Izzy.

Izzy noticed Aunt Anna, white towel in hand, waiting on the other side of the pool. So she took courage and stepped down into the water with her bare feet. *Oh! So cold! What happened to the warm water they promised?* Her face must have registered shock, because she saw Aunt Anna mouth, "It's okay."

So, Izzy plastered on a frozen smile and went down to where the poor pastor had been standing for what must have felt like an eternity.

"So sorry," she whispered.

With his left arm, Pastor led her to the crook of his strong right arm, and taking a washcloth in his left hand, he said, "Izzy, in the name of the Father, and of the Son, and of the Holy Spirit, I baptize you." Pastor covered her nose firmly with the cloth as she went under.

Izzy forgot how cold the water was as she went down beneath the surface and rose up again, water running off her hair and face like a sheet. *We did it! Happy day!*

Everyone sang along while Izzy made her way to the ladder and pulled herself out of the water to where Aunt Anna waited with the towel. Izzy let Anna drape her shoulders with the towel and wrapped it tight around herself. Together, they exited behind the curtains.

Aunt Anna led her to the girls' room to help her change. "Congratulations, Sweetheart. You did it! How do you feel?"

"A wee bit cold." Izzy shivered. "But I'll survive."

"Here, this will make you feel better." Aunt Anna led her to the mirror over the sink and plugged in a hair dryer.

"Oh, you are so thoughtful. Thank you." Izzy took the dryer and brushed out her hair. Then she quickly got out of her wet clothes and redressed in her Sunday clothes—a violet dress with puff sleeves and a matching rope belt over a free-flowing skirt. Then she tackled her hair with the dryer until she felt ready to return to Marty and the church. *It won't be long before we are here again for our wedding ceremony!*

9. <u>PHOTOGRAPHIC NIGHTMARE</u>

Izzy tossed and turned in bed. An endless dream had her in its grasp. She and Marty had been married. Aunt Anna had lavishly prepared an assortment of finger food and a beautiful triple-tier black forest cake with fluffy white icing. The church fellowship hall began to fill with beloved guests and relatives who had come to see the happy couple get married. But Izzy and Marty could not join them immediately. Their photographer had to get some photos for their album. He led them all over the grounds around the church after getting shots at the altar. Izzy thought with each pose, Surely this is the last picture! But the picture taking dragged on for forty minutes. When Izzy finally entered the fellowship hall, it was empty! She turned around to cry on Marty's shoulder, but he was gone! A knot wrenched Izzy's stomach, and she sat up suddenly in bed shouting, "No! No! No!"

Izzy looked around her quiet bedroom. The clock said three-thirty. It had all been a very bad dream, but so vivid. Her stomach still hurt. Izzy plopped back down onto her pillow in relief. It was only a dream!

That day Izzy met Marty for a picnic lunch on the lawn of

his school. Crocuses and daffodils heralded the coming of spring. The breeze felt warm as they spread out a light blanket Izzy's mom had always used for picnics. The red and white plaid blanket, laid out on a patch of grass, made Izzy miss her mom.

Marty saw her wipe away a tear. "You okay?"

Izzy nodded her head. "Sure. Just a little longing for my mom. This was the blanket she reserved for family picnics."

Marty put his arm around her shoulders and rubbed her arm. They stood in silence.

Izzy looked up at Marty, a frown on her face. "What do you think? Is Mom looking down on us enjoying our picnic?"

"Well, Pastor did say something about being surrounded by a great cloud of witnesses, of the saints that have already beat us to Heaven." Marty lifted the food basket and placed it in the middle of the blanket. Then he took Izzy's hand and motioned to sit down.

"Mom, I miss you." Izzy's voice squeaked. She waited to get control of her emotions. "Wish she was here to meet you." She looked up into Marty's face and placed her hand on his cheek. "She would have adored you."

"I'm sure I would have adored her. I'm sorry she's gone. But, yes, I do believe she is watching down on us. Here." Marty leaned over and picked a daffodil and gave it to Izzy, despite Izzy's objections. "Shh, shh. It'll be fine. Let's take a selfie together with this flower representing the mom we are sure is with us in spirit. How about it?"

Izzy held the flower to her chest, her blonde wavy hair hanging down around her shoulders. She and Marty leaned back on their elbows and looked up into the camera. This would be a memory to cherish.

"You wouldn't believe the dream I had last night. It was a nightmare! We missed our own wedding reception because the photographer took us away from our guests. Horrible, just horrible. And then you disappeared on me!"

"What? Me? Disappear on my lovely bride? That was a bad dream. Don't give it a second thought." Marty handed her a sandwich from the basket. "Peace."

Izzy feigned anger and pushed it away. "How can I receive your peace offering when you deserted me?" But upon seeing Marty's moist brown eyes, she quickly repented and grabbed his hand and kissed it. "I know you would not leave me. It was only a dream. But we had better make other arrangements for our wedding album. I don't want any picture taking that day, except for the group shots with family and friends."

"Agreed." Marty offered his fist for a bump from Izzy.

"I know. We should do what Laura, the librarian, and her husband did. Her hubby is from Taiwan. There they always get dressed up in wedding garments rented out by the photographer before the wedding. Then they get to take wedding shots in their favorite places. The album is done and on display the day they marry."

"Well, that's a great idea. We may have to find a different photography shop. I'm not at all sure our guy does that kind of thing."

"I'll ask Laura who did their album. Phew! What a relief. I guess that a bad dream has helped us to make some better plans. Our wedding is coming up fast, though. Just sixty-three days…"

Izzy paused and looked at her watch. "—and eighteen and a half hours."

It took a month to get an appointment at the photo shop. But the day finally came and, coffees in hand, Izzy and Marty met Laura and her husband, Brad, at the Wedding Memories

Photography shop. A dangly bell tinkled gently, announcing their arrival. A Chinese woman appeared from an inner room, her round cheeks shaded with blush, her bright eyes and brows made up and picture perfect, and her red lips curled up in a welcoming smile. "Ah, Laura, so nice to see you again. You look lovely. And you are expecting already!"

Laura blushed. "Yes, the baby is due in three months."

"Congratulations. And thank you for introducing your friends to us. Today is the big day."

"Thank you, Carol, for taking good care of them. Let me introduce you. Carol Hemmingway, this is Izzy Defranco and Marty Goldstein. They will be married next month. Thank you for squeezing them into your busy schedule."

"I am thrilled to make your acquaintance." Izzy shook Carol's hand with a smile. "Laura has done nothing but brag about your service. We love the idea of getting our wedding album made beforehand. Thank you so much."

"You are more than welcome. Now let's sit down to discuss your choices of clothes, and the places you will be going." Carol led them to a cozy little alcove lined with a variety of clothes. There they sat at a small round glass table with a white rim and ornate brass chairs with white cushions.

Izzy felt very cozy. She eyed the clothes hanging nearby, and couldn't wait to try them on.

Carol continued. "Now today your plan is to take pictures at Woodland Lake and Fairmount Park, and, also, at the church where you will marry, Belmont Bible Church, right? You will spend at least forty-five minutes in each place. May I suggest you add the arboretum at St. Joseph's University? We have taken some lovely shots there."

"That will be quite meaningful, as I'm finishing a degree there." Marty looked at Izzy, and she gave a confirming nod, and took his hand in hers.

"How much time do we have for the price that was quoted?" Izzy inquired, flipping through brochures on the table.

"We charge a thousand for every three hours, then fifty dollars for every half hour after that. But that includes your rentals and the basic album. I have pulled out the two dresses and suit you have chosen, Izzy." Carol pushed away from the table and directed Izzy's attention back to the clothes clustered in the center of the back wall of the alcove. They walked over together.

Ahh! Such a lush chiffon! Izzy gingerly patted the white gown featuring a curved neckline lined with baby pearls, a sequined bodice, a skirt which swirled up in the front and fanned down with a frilly train in the back. Smiling, she looked up to Marty for his reaction.

He gave a thumbs up. "You will look ravishing in this. Ahh, it's not bad luck to see the bride in her gown before the day of the wedding?"

"Not if you want your album ready the day of! And we will print your choice of two business-card sized pictures you can make available for your guests, for a nominal fee, of course."

"I remember the cards you had at your wedding, Laura. What a lovely gesture. I use it as a bookmark. So, I think of you often." Izzy reached out to hold her friend's hands in hers.

Laura blushed, obviously pleased at Izzy's remark. Suddenly a ripple ran across her baby bump like a gentle unbroken wave on the ocean. "Oh, Baby Boy seems to be happy!"

Izzy gasped. "I saw that. Your baby is moving! It must be so much fun. A boy, you say?"

"A baby may or may not be born with the extra equipment. But that is not what makes it a boy. You must wait to see how the child develops," a tenor voice came from the front as Carol's co-worker rounded the corner. Tall and thin, with short cropped brown hair which jutted out like the bill of a cap, the woman wore an orange and brown plaid flannel shirt over baggy jeans and black tennis shoes.

"Oh, hello." *She is quite boyish*, Izzy thought. She cast a questioning look at Laura. Laura's expression and slight shake of her head indicated that she did not know this person.

Carol quickly introduced the newcomer. "This is my husband, Jamie. He will be your photographer today."

Laura turned to Carol. "Uhm, I didn't know you were married."

"Oh yes. We have been married for five years. We were among the first to marry after the state recognized LGBT marriages. When you decided to go with us for your photo session, Jamie had gone to Italy to pick up our son, Max. So I hired another photographer for your photo shoot."

"Kitty, I remember. She was very good." Laura nodded approval.

"Your friends won't be disappointed with Jamie's photo shoot, I'm sure." Carol stood with her fingertips together, looking expectantly at Marty and Izzy for affirmation.

Max. Max? Something tugged at Izzy's mind. Then she remembered the lonely little blond boy at the edge of the blacktop the day she talked with Ms. Hitchcock.

Marty, noticing the surprise on Izzy's face, stepped forward and extended his hand to the newcomer. "Jamie, thank you for your help today. We are excited about this adventure."

Jamie clapped her hands and rubbed them together. "Great. We are happy to please. Shall we sign the contract and get out for our pictures? The weather forecast is not altogether promising this morning."

Izzy cast a questioning look at Marty and took his hand.

Marty smiled, then looked at Carol and Jamie, bowing slightly. "If you could give us a moment, we had better make sure we're in agreement." He moved toward the door, but Carol spoke.

"Oh, please take a seat. We will step out and let you two discuss matters."

Brad and Laura started out as well, but Izzy called them back.

Returning to the table, Izzy expelled a long breath and looked longingly at the chiffon dress, then back to Marty, Laura, and Brad. "Our struggles at school seem to have followed us here."

Laura put her hand on her friend's shoulder. "I'm sorry, I didn't know."

"That's okay, Laura, really. Our problem isn't with them, right, Honey?" Izzy turned to see Marty's expression go from a worried look to a small smile. "If you're sure, Sweetheart. Can you be comfortable with your decision?"

"Our purpose at school is to protect our children and give parents a say-so in their children's education, right? Now, time is ticking by. I'm afraid we don't have the luxury of finding someone else. We waited a month for this opening. In just four weeks I'll be married to the man of my dreams. The price is right, don't you think so, Marty?"

"I think it's quite reasonable. I'm just not sure…" Marty looked out the window at the gathering clouds.

"Oh my goodness, the clouds!" Izzy gasped. "Let's go with Jamie. She'll be fine."

Laura motioned to Jamie and Carol to return. "They're ready."

Jamie had on a brown windbreaker when she came in. "If we're going to do this, then we better get going," she said gruffly, then directed them to change into their wedding garments before beginning. She also carried another change of clothes they had pre-selected for the photo shoot.

This is so much fun! Izzy dressed with Laura's help.

"Oh, you make a beautiful bride!" Laura reached for her pocket. "I like your hair today. I found this sequin studded tiara and got it for this occasion." She produced a petite silver tiara from her pocket and handed it to Izzy. "Do you like it?"

Before her friend could finish her question, Izzy had already put her arms around Laura's neck. "Oh, you shouldn't have. It's beautiful."

Izzy emerged with Laura and stopped in her tracks when she saw Marty. He wore a black tuxedo with satin trim, a long-sleeved white shirt with cuffs turned back and fastened with a black button, and a silver vest. "Whoa! There's my man! You are one handsome dude, Marty."

Marty blushed. When he saw Izzy looking like the queen of the ball, he took three big strides toward her and knelt, reaching for her hand. "May I kiss my queen?" He gently kissed her hand and as their eyes met, Izzy felt a breathless longing. He stood, and said, "Maybe we'd better elope today!"

Everybody laughed.

With Jamie's prodding, Izzy and Marty said good-bye to their friends, and followed Jamie to their favorite hang-out, the lake. How often had they come there to chat after work and between classes? It was a comfortable distance for both of them to travel from their schools, being half way between Wynnefield and St. Joe's University.

Jamie did her work well. Beautiful white boulders along the walkway lent themselves nicely for many poses. There were also benches surrounded by roses, and fields where grassy slopes invited a scamper to the glen at Fairmount Park. Izzy wished she had brought her tennis shoes.

Suddenly a huge raindrop splashed on Izzy's nose. She looked into the sky and shouted. "Oh, God. Please don't let it rain! We've just been having so much fun. Please, God, keep the rain away for just a little while. We haven't gotten to the spot where Marty popped the question!"

The rain came down in earnest then, and the three moved as quickly as they could to a shelter fifteen yards away. Izzy had to stop and take off her delicate shoes and make a run for it. Jamie carried her train. "Oh, God! Why couldn't you keep the rain away? I'm so disappointed." Izzy raised her fists to the sky to show her displeasure. Wet curls hung down around her ears. Her mascara smudged at the corner of her eye.

Marty moved to embrace his disheveled bride, but she pushed him away. "If God is so good, why doesn't he hear my prayers? Errr!"

"She just needs to express her disappointment," Marty said to Jamie. "Sometimes the weather lets us down on these missions."

Izzy grew more furious because her husband-to-be was making excuses for her outburst. *Who does he think he is? I'm the bride and I'm allowed to have moments like these. Given the circumstances, I'm entitled to.* "That's it, I'm done." Izzy couldn't imagine how bad she looked, crossing her arms and pouting.

"Not to worry, your next stop is indoors," Jamie said.

Marty hung his head like a scolded sheepdog, and a wet one at that. Water dripped from his hair, his nose and eyelashes and suddenly Izzy saw through her anger and realized how adorable he was.

She took a step into Marty's embrace and buried her face in his chest. He hugged her as she cried. *I guess it's not the end of the world,* she thought. *I've still got my man.*

"Okay, let's go," Izzy managed a smile. "I'm sorry, I kind

of blew it there."

"I thought Mt. Vesuvius had exploded again." Marty grinned, brushing Izzy's hair out of her face.

"Not to worry. We should be able to keep within our three hours if we head over to the church now." Jamie produced a huge golf umbrella to hold over their heads as she guided them back to the car.

Pastor Michaels greeted them as they got to the church. He guided them to the Fellowship Hall, where he had set up the wedding decorations in one corner. Something large and lacy set up on poles drew Izzy's attention.

"What's this?" She held up a tassel at the corner of the structure.

"We have used it before in our Bible teaching. Marty had mentioned you two might be interested in adding some Jewish flavor to your wedding." The pastor winked.

Marty gave Izzy a sideways hug. "That's where we would say our vows, and exchange sips of wine—or sparkling cider. What do you think?"

"I love it!" Izzy said.

Jamie produced a hair dryer from her bag, and beckoned Izzy to come stand near the outlet. She also gave Marty a hair dryer and sent him and the pastor off to another corner. It took only five minutes to spruce up the bridal gown, and another ten minutes to fix Izzy's hair. Then everybody gathered around the canopy feeling more comfortable.

Pastor Michaels, dressed in khaki pants and a polo shirt, put his hand on the structure to explain its meaning. "When the Jewish couple is married, this canopy—or Chuppah—represents the groom's home and protection—a safe haven—and a private place where the couple will consummate their marriage. It is the place where two become one, and so it is the place where you will exchange your vows and your rings, pledging to one another unity and faithfulness toward one another for all your days."

I have always felt safe and secure under your arms, Marty Goldstein! I just can't wait!

"Yes, yes, very lovely," said Jamie. "Now, let's not waste too much time here. Let's get some pictures taken for your album."

10. <u>WINDS OF CHANGE</u>

"Marty, Aunt Anna, quick, look here!" Izzy called from her seat in the living room, pointing to the TV screen. "I believe that's Uncle Amos!"

Marty looked closely from behind Izzy and exclaimed, "You're exactly right! That's our man! He's accompanying the Prime Minister. And look who they are with—Mr. Bandar of the World Council for Emergency Preparedness. Shhh! Let's listen."

The three of them got settled and focused on the news broadcast.

> ROGERS: As we all know, the worldwide water shortage has reached critical conditions. Yet more meteors projected to impact the earth will only exacerbate the situation, resulting in a rise in violence and looting around the world. Israeli Prime Minister Cohen has signed a covenant with His Highness of the newly formed World Council for Emergency Preparedness, or WCEP, Abdul Mutakabbir Asahd Bandar. Let's go to our correspondent on the ground there in Israel. Julie?

QUESPIE: I am here outside of the courthouse in Ramle in central Israel just east of Tel Aviv on the road to Jerusalem. Today a Water Distribution Pact was signed by representatives of the ten nations which have come together for the World Council of Emergency Preparedness. His Highness Abdul Mutakabbir Asahd Bandar has agreed to say a few words. Your Highness.

BANDAR: "Please call me Mr. B. The world is in a crisis, and the Council and I are here to do what we can, together with the great peoples of the earth, to restore peace and hope to the world in the face of recent threats to our water supply. Therefore, we have put into place a Water Sharing Plan. Countries with a healthy water supply and water table have stepped forward pledging a good percentage of water for their neighbors who lack water."

QUESPIE: Your Highness, I understand Israel increased the percentage of their pledge, from eight to fifteen percent. How were you able to get them to approve such a hefty commitment?

BANDAR: "I am not free at present to comment on this matter. But all ten nations have come together with a remarkable display of unity, convening for a period of preparedness for cataclysms for the next seven years. There is the threat of meteors which scientists are monitoring closely. The world has been battling plagues of epidemic proportion. Together, we are keeping ahead of the need through consistent monitoring, research, and sharing of medical equipment and treatment strategies. The volatile situation with volcanic activity around the world requires everyone to be on the alert and ready for evacuation. It has nearly eradicated the saltwater fishing industry. Therefore, maritime countries have agreed to participate in restoration of the waters—the flora and the fauna of the sea—through recycling and simulated saltwater fish biomes. This is a commitment of billions of dollars."

Mr. B seemed so knowledgeable and in control of the ocean water situation that Marty said, "Bravo! That's the man I've been following, Izzy, Mr. Bandar. It seems he has been promoted. He's quite the genius."

But Aunt Anna shook her head, looking troubled. She got up from the recliner and lowered herself into her place around the dining table. "Come." She sighed and reached for her Bible while Marty and Izzy joined her.

Aunt Anna looked up with a drawn face. "Did you notice how many years and how many nations are involved in this pact with the World Council for Emergency Preparedness?"

Izzy responded immediately, "Ten nations, and for seven years. Oh! What did Pastor Michaels say? What does Revelation say?"

Aunt Anna opened her Bible and read from Revelation Chapter 13—"*'And I saw a beast rising out of the sea, with ten horns and seven heads, with ten diadems on its horns and blasphemous names on its heads… One of its heads seemed to have a mortal wound, but its mortal wound was healed, and the whole earth marveled as they followed the beast…And the beast…was allowed to exercise authority for forty-two months.'*"

Izzy shook her head. "I know the ten horns represent the ten nations, but forty-two months, that's only three and a half years."

Aunt Anna, her teal glasses down on her nose, peered up at her beloved children with sympathy. She dabbed at a tear. "Another great book for prophecies concerning the last days is Daniel. Let's see what he has to say." She opened to the middle of the book. "Here it is, in Daniel 9:27. Pastor Michaels touched on this in Sunday School. It says—*'And he shall make a strong covenant with many for one week, and for half of the week he shall put an end to sacrifice and offering. And on the wing of abominations shall come one who makes desolate, until the decreed end is poured out on the desolator.'*"

Aunt Anna suddenly looked very tired. "Remember," she said, "The Antichrist will make a 'strong covenant with many for one week.' That's seven days…which can be translated to seven years. Our Mr. B and his WCEP have signed a pact of some kind with Israel, and with all ten member nations, for seven years."

"I'll try to get the details from Uncle Amos," Marty said, looking confused. "After all, he saw the Prime Minister sign it today." Marty brightened up again. "Absolutely amazing, though, that my uncle should have a part in this significant moment in history." He looked up and reached out for Izzy and Aunt Anna's hands.

This can't be happening! Surely it is just a coincidence. Izzy suddenly felt shaky and leaned into Marty's arms. "This can't be happening. We're just getting started!"

The next morning Marty met Izzy out for breakfast. Lately, summer gardens ablaze with color had heightened Izzy's anticipation of her walk to the coffee shop where she and Marty had first visited. But that day all she could see were the cracks in the sidewalk.

Oh God, is our marriage going to be so short-lived? And what about children? Will we even want to start a family? Her legs felt like rubber as she plodded to her intended destination. She looked up in time to see Marty standing at the entrance holding the door open for her to come in. He wore a light-yellow polo shirt with a brown collar which accentuated his soft brown eyes, and she immediately started wiping away tears. *O God, please let it be good news from Uncle Amos!*

"Hey, none of that allowed." Marty used his handkerchief to wipe Izzy's moist cheek. "Come, a cup of coffee will do you a world of good."

The sweet smell of coffee and pancakes, the clanging of plates, Marty's hand clasping hers across the table, helped Izzy to be at peace. *It's always been a crazy world. Nothing has changed. But now we have each other. I had better not ruin the moments with worry.*

"Looks like our Minister of the Interior Uncle Amos Asher has some amazing news to share. Let's take a look together," Marty said after they had ordered their food. Izzy scooted out of her seat and slid into the booth next to Marty to get a good view of his chat with Uncle Amos.

AMOS: You saw the news? Yes! Today was a pivotal day in history, though it does not come cheaply to the nation of Israel. The situation in the Middle East has been quite volatile because of the scarcity of water. Water table levels have dropped drastically in neighboring countries.

Iraq and Iran have been plagued with sinkholes that have eaten up whole communities.

With our advanced water recycling capabilities and our access to the Great Sea, Israel has been truly blessed by God. So today we took a leap of faith to commit fifteen percent of our water resources to our neighbors.

MARTY: Are you confident about this decision? That doubles your original pledge. What will Israel receive for her generosity? Granted, I applaud the security cabinet stepping up efforts to be a good neighbor in this crisis. Will the water left in Israel still meet the demand?

AMOS: It will be a bit of a stretch, but in return we have an opportunity for which we have long prayed. I can't share the details through this text, but please feel free to call me. Now let's talk about you and Izzy.

Your special days are coming up fast. Your Aunt Abigail and the children were looking forward to attending your eclectic wedding. But with the developments here in Israel, I just do not feel it is a good time to leave. But I want to encourage you both.

We have been married for fifteen years already. Our children are strong olive branches around our table—Daniel is twelve, Hannah is ten, and little Benjie is already a big seven. Can you believe it? May God fill your home with love, joy, and children. Please call me when you can.

Warm greetings to Izzy and Aunt Anna.

"Ahh, so sad they won't be able to attend our wedding." Izzy grabbed a tissue and wiped away a tear.

"Oh, Sweetheart. It is a disappointment. We will just have to plan a trip to Israel sometime soon."

"Now I would be down for that." Izzy nodded her head with a forced smile. "I have an uneasy feeling, though, that there's something very secretive going on. Neither Mr. B nor Uncle Amos felt free to talk about it, at least not publicly." Izzy snuggled under Marty's arm, feeling quite cozy. But then the food came so she returned to her seat on the other side of the table.

"Let's call after we eat. I believe they are just seven hours ahead of us." Marty salted his eggs.

"Of course. Let's. Tell me about your work at the University. How is that shaping up?" Izzy grabbed her cup of coffee.

"Oh, praise God! I have been invited to have a seat on the faculty. This is an exceptionally difficult position to secure. I'd say God is good." Marty pointed his fork skyward.

"Yes. I'm so grateful, too, for your good fortune. Our good fortune. Here we are getting married in just another month. God, you're just in time!" Izzy looked upward after she popped pancakes into her mouth. *Thank you, but must it always be so last minute?*

Izzy put her fork down and leaned forward. "So, when do you get started? And will you be teaching Health Education?"

Marty shook his head as he took a swig of orange juice. "No, they actually needed me to teach biochemistry, but they will give me some doctoral students in the Health Education department to work with. The folks at church will be thrilled that God has answered their prayers. It's quite remarkable."

"For sure Aunt Anna will proudly announce our news this week in Sunday School."

Just then a modern rendition of Amazing Grace began playing over the speakers in the cafe. Upon recognizing it, Izzy laughed and covered her mouth and nose with her hands. "So timely."

"What did you think of Aunt Anna's offer last night?" Marty took one last bite and wiped his mouth with his napkin.

Izzy knew he was referring to her aunt's recommendation that they all start putting up food in her cupboard in the basement, just in case the end times were in the near future.

"Is it really a possibility that this Mr. B and his council are hatching some sort of devious plan?"

Marty shook his head, reaching across to take both of Izzy's hands in his. "It remains to be seen. I doubt it though. My uncle wouldn't be involved on the council if the new plans were evil. Still, maybe it's a good idea to begin preparing for the possibility of not being able to buy and sell. Look at it as laying aside food for any emergency. We can at least humor her."

Izzy broke into a smile. "After you left, do you know what else Aunt Anna suggested?"

Marty smiled, looking up and guessed, "She wants us to move in with her after we are married, right?"

"How did you know?" Izzy pointed at Marty.

"I found a note she had written inside her Bible yesterday. It said, 'Invite the newlyweds to move in.' You have a very generous Aunt Anna. I don't know. Wouldn't you like to have your own home?"

"Of course it would be nice to have our own space." Izzy closed her eyes a moment. "But Aunt Anna knows you are just getting your feet on the ground at the University. Maybe we could start out at her house and then go from there if the circumstances are not just right. Would you like to give it a try?" Izzy tilted her head to see Marty's reaction. *There's that dimple and those dancing eyes.*

"Well, it's different from what I ever imagined. But, sure, let's go for it! We should tell her we will stay with her for our first six months together, and then we can talk about it again. I feel quite blessed to have her as family. And we don't know what will unfold in the days ahead. Which reminds me. Uncle Amos just might shed some light on the future. Let's go for a walk and give him a call." Marty stood up and offered his arm to Izzy. Together they stopped to pay the bill then went out into the sunshine.

Izzy held onto Marty's arm while he took out his phone to reach Uncle Amos. A cloud covered the sun, and Izzy shook with a chill.

"You okay?" Marty put his arm over Izzy's shoulder and raised the phone to his ear.

"Uncle Amos? Hello. I'm sorry to be calling so late. It must be close to nine over there."

Izzy motioned that she wanted to hear, so Marty punched the speaker.

"That's quite alright, Marty. I'm glad you called. Have you heard the news today?"

"No, we haven't. Are you okay?" Marty asked, head down.

"All of Jerusalem is rioting. The word got out about the deal Mr. B brokered with Israel—in exchange for our fifteen percent of water reserves, he got us permission to rebuild the temple. But some of our neighbors are furious."

"The temple is to be rebuilt?" Izzy asked, recalling the words of Pastor Michaels. "Isn't that a sign of impending doom?"

"On the contrary, it's what we've been waiting for all our lives," Uncle Amos said, his voice crackling with the bad reception.

Marty covered his phone and whispered to Izzy, "Let's go to your aunt's house to watch the news on the big screen." Then he spoke into the receiver. "Uncle Amos, are you and the family safe?"

"Our district is pretty secure. I certainly hope so. Let's keep in touch and talk soon."

Izzy called Aunt Anna. "Aunt Anna, Marty and I just talked with Uncle Amos. Some unrest in Jerusalem. Turn on the news, and we will be right over."

Aunt Anna greeted them at the door wearing a green turtleneck top with comfortable gray-green sweatpants. They all filed into the living room to find their customary seats. The TV already showed coverage of stone throwers in the streets, and placards reading "No Capitulation to the Jews" and "No to the Temple" outside the Israeli Knesset.

"Did you hear, Aunt Anna? They're going to rebuild the temple in Jerusalem!" Izzy reached over and grabbed her aunt's hand.

"No wonder there are riots. I hope Uncle Amos and his family are all right." Anna clasped Izzy's hand.

"Yes, we do too." Marty nodded as he sat forward in his chair.

They listened to Breaking News with Rogers and Quespie—

ROGERS: There are more developments in Ramle this afternoon after His Highness Abdul Mutakabbir Asahd Bandar called an emergency meeting with the press to help quell the riots. Julie, you were on the ground there. Tell us what happened.

QUESPIE: I'll narrate the video footage. Watch what happened when His Highness addressed the press. I understand that, for security purposes, this was a closed meeting, open only for the press. Mr. B is dressed in a white dress shirt and gray suit, donning a silver turban trimmed with pink and blue. He is sitting behind a long table, Khalil Yasin Hamza by his side. This is a man they call The Prophet, who seems to be Mr. B's counsellor. His Highness opens his mouth to speak to the press after the guards stop their jostling for position. Folks, the unbelievable happens. One of the reporters stands up and shouts, 'Glory to Allah! Let Allah be avenged of his honor!' Then a scream goes up as the reporter deftly throws a dagger into His Highness's heart.

Anna, Marty, and Izzy all jumped from their seats at once to get a closer look. They saw the world's icon slumped in his chair, blood darkening his chest, while chaos broke out in the room.

"He looks dead!" Izzy could not believe her eyes. Julie Quespie continued narrating the events—

QUESPIE: The Prophet reaches over, removes the knife and presses his handkerchief into the wound. He is heard to say, "Surely, it's just a scratch.' Immediately His Highness sits up and yells, "Seize that traitor!" And the man is wrestled to the ground and is led out in handcuffs. The video ends here. People's mouths gaped open, as was mine. That looked like much more than a scratch to me. Where did this man get his strength?

ROGERS: Now people are talking about His Highness as if he were a god, saying no one can overcome him.

QUESPIE: Listen now to what The Prophet, whose name Khalil Yasin means 'companion prophet,' says in this next clip—

THE PROPHET: This is a sign. Can't you see? His Highness's path is the only path to success and life for the world. Let Ishmael put away his sword. Look with gratitude upon your brother's pledge to give fifteen percent of his water supply to bring relief to his neighbors. Don't you need water? I'm sure I speak for my countrymen in Iraq: With thankful hearts we pledge to provide money, personnel and equipment to expedite groundwater sharing. Let all the great countries of the world join hands and contribute so that everyone has sufficient water.

QUESPIE: With that he tears away the bloodied shirt from His Highness, Mr. B, revealing a cross-shaped scratch with no gaping wound. His Highness B raises his glass of water to The Prophet, and then to all in the room, an action returned by all in the room.

ROGERS: Here! Here! I'll drink to that.

QUESPIE: Ditto, Rod. Remarkable, isn't it? I could have sworn the man was dead, but he walked away with just a scratch.

Aunt Anna reached for the remote control and turned off the TV. She opened her Bible, spreading it out on the counter in the kitchen. Marty and Izzy stood on either side. Pointing with her forefinger Aunt Anna read from Revelation 13, saying, "I'm reading from the Revelation of our Lord Jesus Christ, chapter thirteen, beginning with verse one—*"And I saw a beast rising out of the sea with ten horns and seven heads, with ten diadems on its horns and blasphemous names on its heads. And the beast that I saw was like a leopard; its feet were like a bear's, and its mouth was like a lion's mouth. And to it the dragon gave his power and his Throne and great authority. One of its heads seemed to have a mortal wound, but its mortal wound was healed, and the whole earth marveled as they followed the beast. And they worshiped the dragon, for he had given his authority to the beast, and they worshiped the beast, saying, 'Who is like the beast, and who can fight against it?'"*

"Just like watching the news." Marty sighed and hugged Izzy.

"God, this can't be happening!" Izzy held tightly to Marty, hiding her tears on his shoulder.

"Now, now." Aunt Anna patted Izzy's arm. "We're going to be all right. Do you remember the journals I gave you following your baptism? The Bible gives us a lot of promises, and some in particular are about how God will rescue us from the terrible tribulation of the last days. I want to share it with you, from I Thessalonians 4:15 through 18— *"For this we declare to you by a word from the Lord, that we who are alive, who are left until the coming of the Lord, will not precede those who have fallen asleep. For the Lord himself will descend from heaven with a cry of command, with the voice of an archangel, and with the sound of the trumpet of God. And the dead in Christ will rise first. Then we who are alive, who are left, will be caught up together with them in the clouds to meet the Lord in the air, and so we will always be with the Lord. Therefore encourage one another with these words."*

Aunt Anna looked up from her reading and gazed from Izzy to Marty, tears in her eyes. "May I suggest that before you go to sleep tonight, you spend some time talking to God about all these developments. One way you can do that is to journal your conversation with God. He will talk with you as you write. You will realize you are not alone, and that he is there to help you."

"Thank you, Aunt Anna. It's all very sobering." Marty wiped away a tear and looked at his watch. "Here we are, just ten days away from being married. I would like to say a prayer. Can we kneel?"

For the first time in her life, Izzy knelt down to pray as

her fiancé led them to the living room and fell to his knees on the floor in front of the recliner. Even though her knees were stiff, Aunt Anna followed suit.

Marty began, "Dear heavenly Father, this is terrible news, to realize that the Beast is here. And Izzy and I are just beginning our life together as husband and wife. Father, how long will we have? Help us to cherish each day together, and to trust you. We want to lean on you for wisdom and guidance…and comfort, Lord. Thank you. For we pray in the name of our Messiah, your son, Jesus. Amen."

Everyone chimed in, "Amen." Then Marty helped Aunt Anna up, and the three turned to sit in their recliners. They sat quietly, thinking.

Izzy gripped the armrests of her chair, screaming at God in her heart, her face drained of color, her eyes shut tight. *Oh, God! How could this be happening? It feels like our marriage is over before it even begins. God! I'm so disappointed!*

11. LIFE'S GOOD AND BAD

Time rushed on. Two days before the wedding, Izzy got to meet her in-laws for the first time. Dr. Harold and Ruth Goldstein flew into Philadelphia. Marty put them up in a hotel close to Belmont Bible Church. After school, Izzy joined them for dinner, but not until she had freshened up and changed her clothes. She decided to wear a white puffy-sleeved blouse with yellow polka-dots together with a pale yellow skirt. To her delight, Marty wore his yellow polo shirt.

"Karibu! Welcome!" Izzy tested her limited Swahili on the senior Goldsteins.

"Asante sana." Dr. Goldstein chuckled. "Thank you!"

"You two make a beautiful couple!" Marty's mother said warmly after greeting Izzy with a double kiss—a kiss to each cheek as was their habit in Tanzania.

"Thank you." Izzy blushed, looking up to Marty. "It is such a pleasure to meet you, at last! Did you have a good flight?"

"Yes, but a long one, coming from Africa." Dr. Goldstein spoke honestly folding his hands together. He wore a tan cargo shirt with a pocket where he kept his reading glasses.

Izzy and Marty could not have asked for nicer weather the day they made their vows. That morning—crisp and cool—displayed cirrus clouds, like cotton candy, dangling in the baby-blue sky. The wind blew gently yet occasionally seemed to rush with a puff which sent leaves scurrying across the walk. It brought back memories of the day they met.

That day just eleven months before seemed so distant to Izzy. She smiled as she thought of how the brazen young grad student had suggested everyone go to the coffee shop to recover from their bumps and bruises. *Marty, you were the sly one. Did you have any idea that we were meant for one another? I loved you early on—your smile and bright eyes, your thoughtful ways. God! This should be the happiest day of my life. Why do I need to feel so sad? So what that the Beast is on the world scene. I'm not going to let him ruin our day.* Izzy threw back her shoulders and breathed deeply of the cool air as she stood briefly on Aunt Anna's porch to greet the morning.

Feeling a little sore this morning. But I'm so glad we could get the last of my boxes from my apartment yesterday—such a cozy, inviting place to retreat to after busy days at school. It had almost become a ritual for her to run and get a tall glass of iced water and slip out onto the balcony for some breathing space as soon as she got home. That world of tall swaying trees towering above her perch—the mysterious sound of leaves in mass moving with the wind—worked wonders for her frazzled nerves and renewed her energy for the coming tide of lesson plans and papers to grade. She would miss her shaded balcony.

Aunt Anna came out to the porch with a cup of coffee. "Good morning. Are you recovered from your move, ready for this big day?" She handed Izzy the coffee.

"Good morning. Yes, yes, yes!" The bride-to-be gingerly

took the cup of coffee, put it on the table, and gave Aunt Anna a bear hug. Then she stretched her arms wide and toward the sky. "It's a lovely day for a wedding, our wedding." But her face fell into a frown. "Aunt Anna, I can't help but feel I'm playing a game of charades. It's supposed to be an altogether happy day, but there's this underlying current…"

"I know, Sweetheart." Aunt Anna began to give Izzy a brisk back scratch. "We cannot change the facts, as much as we want to. But let's trust the Father who is planning to send his Son back to us soon. Let's look beyond the trouble to those happy days. The happiness of today is but a foretaste of the joy God has prepared for us then."

Joy…seems…so…elusive. "I will try." Izzy bent over and kissed her aunt on the forehead. "Love you."

The ten o'clock wedding fast approached. Izzy and Anna got busy—a quick bite of cereal with their coffee, Aunt Anna's prayer of blessing on the day, then the rush of doing Izzy's hair and make-up before finally putting on her bridal gown.

Marty had liked her so much in the dress she wore for picture-taking that he wanted to buy it. "No," she told him. "Not like I'm ever going to need it again. One day's use is sufficient." So she donned the chiffon gown that they rented with mixed feelings. *Under different circumstances, I would have enjoyed passing my wedding gown down to my daughter.*

Aunt Anna hired a friend and his car for the couple that day. Marvin—skinny and tall, and smiling like a happy Bassett hound—came to the door wearing a gray suit and maroon tie, his shoes somewhat worn, but polished. Although already nine-fifteen, he had to sit and wait another fifteen minutes.

Izzy put the final touches on her mascara. Aunt Anna

cooed over her hair as she put it up in a French braid and wrapped it around in a bun. Izzy smiled as she put on her veil and fastened it in place with Laura's delicate tiara. A few wisps of golden curls hung down around her face.

"Dear, you look so lovely." Aunt Anna wiped away a tear. "I so wish your mother could have been here for this! But I am positive that she is smiling down on you from Heaven."

Oh, Mom. If only you could have been here. Izzy dabbed her eyes with a tissue, and she almost thought she heard her mom's voice say, "Don't forget—God is love!"

Marty got to the church early. He stopped briefly to take in the view of the place which had become like home to him. The black drive snaked down between trees, then emptied out into a large parking lot. From the lot a white cement sidewalk took people between two beautifully manicured lawns with wildflower gardens. Azaleas skirted both wings of the one-story brick building beyond. A cement circle of about fifty feet in diameter lined with benches—a favorite place for tea time after church—lay before the front glass entrance of Belmont Bible Church.

Marty parked his car at the rear of the building outside of the kitchen entrance. He had the black forest wedding cake Aunt Anna made for the reception after the wedding. Three steps tested Marty's balance. Thankfully the Ladies' Fellowship women opened the door for him and took the cake off his hands. Marty whooped when he saw the wedding decorations, and setting of the twenty tables clothed in white around the Fellowship Hall. "You ladies know how to work wonders. Thank you for your love and hard work for Izzy and me."

Then he searched for Pastor Michaels. The pastor and a

few of the church folk greeted him with warm hugs and handshakes when he walked out into the foyer. "Thank you for all you have done for us. I just want to ask a favor of you."

Pastor Michaels put his hand on Marty's shoulder. "Sure, Marty. What can we do for you?"

Marty took a deep breath. "I know Izzy just wants to be with the family and friends that gather today. Could you please ring a bell or let everyone know when it is time for everyone to go to the Fellowship Hall for our reception? I just want to make sure her worst nightmare of missing the reception because of picture taking doesn't happen."

Pastor Michaels chuckled. "Izzy won't miss it, any more than she would miss the Rapture! I'll see to it that the reception bell is rung. Now, let me commend you for the lovely display you have in the foyer. What a wonderful idea—preparing the album before the wedding! And the give-away photo keepsakes are so lovely." Pastor escorted Marty out to their display table in the entrance. There he picked up one of the business-card-sized photos.

"That one is Izzy's favorite." Marty and Izzy stood facing one another, holding hands, her smiling face turned up toward his. The glen—which lay down the hill beyond them—was hazy. "Of course, that's where I proposed." Marty admired the shot. "We had to pay extra to go back and get that shot because we got rained out the first time."

Pastor picked up another photo between his meaty fingers. The lovely couple sat on a white boulder, holding hands, and looking longingly at one another; they wore matching T-shirts which read, "The Lord is my Rock and my salvation!"

"Whose idea was this?" asked the pastor. "It's quite meaningful, and so true as you marry and become a family."

Marty looked down at the card as he rubbed his thumb

over Izzy's face. "It was my idea, but Izzy loved it, I think." Then looking up, he wiped a tear from the corner of his eye and patted the pastor's elbow. "Hey, thanks. It's about time."

People came into the foyer, first in ones and twos, then in a steady stream to make their way to the sanctuary. But everyone stopped to "Ooh and Ahh" over the keepsake pictures sitting in baskets for the taking.

When Izzy got to the church, her four bridesmaids—all dressed in pastel pink—were sitting on some shaded benches out front fanning themselves. As soon as Marvin pulled up to the curb, he jumped out and ran to the curb side to open the bride's door. He took her by the hand and escorted her to join her bridesmaids. Aunt Anna helped herself out of the car and joined the happy group of women excitedly talking with Izzy.

"Now, now, Ladies. There's not much time to compose yourselves for the wedding march. It's best you get inside to freshen up in the powder room. In ten minutes, you process down the aisle."

As soon as the giddy group made their entrance into the foyer, Marvin's wife, Barbara, presented each bridesmaid with her bouquet of flowers. Small yellow mums with baby's breath sprinkled each spray of pink and white roses.

Izzy admired her bouquet—red and white roses offset by a couple of huge pink tubular mums. *Is this really happening? Marty and I are getting married! This has to be the happiest day of my life.* She peeked into the church through the glass window of one of the wooden doors in the foyer. There stood Marty and his men lined up at the front, all wearing boutonnieres made of small red roses with tiny baby's breath. The pianist played the prelude from Elijah, "If With All Your Heart You Truly Seek Me."

Izzy turned to her ladies and said with a nervous wave of her hand, "Get ready! This is it!"

Laura, her maid of honor, gave Izzy's arms a light squeeze. "You are gorgeous. God bless you. Your future in-laws are here. They are sitting up front on the left. She's wearing violet, with a hat."

As soon as Laura told her the news, the organist began to play the wedding march, and the color drained from the bride's face. *My in-laws! I meant to greet them again this morning. My stars.*

Aunt Anna gave the cue, and Laura began walking down the aisle, bouquet in hand, trying to increase her natural stride to make up for her shortness. Each bridesmaid fell into line every few measures of the march.

Then Izzy began down the aisle, looking straight at her man, smiling, until everyone stood up. Then she lost her equilibrium and stumbled. *Am I falling?*

An arm reached out to steady her. Izzy looked up into Carol's face and saw Max standing beside her.

"Thank you." Izzy mouthed the words tensely, feeling lightheaded.

Oh God, help me get through this. She sent up a quick prayer. But then the heel of her right shoe got stuck in the carpeting and came off her foot. Izzy felt her face getting hot. No more could she make a pretense of smiling.

Aunt Anna came to her aid and let her lean on her while she got her shoe back on.

Izzy became painfully aware of a problem with the heel picking at the carpet as she walked. So she tried walking on tip-toe so as not to snag the rug. Finally, sweat beading on her forehead, and the curls limp around her face, Izzy pulled off her shoes and handed them to Aunt Anna who had anxiously followed her down the aisle. A few more steps, and Izzy stood within reach of Marty, but she did not dare look at him. *I'm a mess!*

Laura, who was to receive the bride's bouquet, took her handkerchief to dab Izzy's face. She wiped her cheeks, whispering, "Let me handle this." Then stepping up to the microphone set there for the ceremony, Laura said, "We know the old maxim, 'Something old, something new, something borrowed, something blue!' Well it was my borrowed slippers which were the culprit this morning, but I think the bride has proved herself quite resourceful! Marty, congratulations." With that, everyone laughed, and Laura took Izzy's flowers and turned her around to face her husband-to-be. The chuckles in the crowd restored Izzy's smile as she looked longingly into Marty's face, concern etched in his eyes.

Marty whispered, "I love you."

The mic picked it up, and a few "ahhs" rippled through the crowd of well-wishers.

But Marty's words made Izzy's pent-up tears start falling. Marty took his handkerchief and gingerly rolled back Izzy's veil and wiped away her tears.

Pastor Michaels, who stood at the microphone wearing a gray suit, tie, and boutonniere, cleared his throat. "You may now kiss the bride."

Izzy, Marty, Aunt Anna and the whole congregation looked shocked at the pastor.

"Just wanted to lighten the moment," the pastor said, and everyone gave a small laugh.

Someone brought a glass of water for Izzy. *Wow. I really blew it this time. But there's a lot of love in this place. And Pastor Michaels is a gem.* Izzy turned around to hug the gentle giant waiting to lead their ceremony. "Thank you." Izzy laughed quietly.

When she turned her gaze to Marty, his smiling brown eyes and dimple put all her confusion to flight.

Pastor Michaels' voice boomed, "Today we are all gathered to celebrate the love between this man—Martin Goldstein—and this woman—Isabel Defranco—as they exchange their vows in holy matrimony. Who gives this woman to this man?"

Aunt Anna, dressed in her blue chiffon dress with long white gloves, stood beside Izzy and said, "I do." Then she kissed Izzy on the cheek and put her niece's hand into Marty's and sat down in the front.

Izzy enjoyed the rest of the service. Pastor Michaels encouraged Marty to love her like Christ loved his church and gave his life for her. His admonition to her, "to honor and obey Marty," seemed an easy command to keep in the light of his willingness to die for her. *Would he really be willing to die for me?*

The time came for the two of them to exchange their vows. They wanted to say their own vows from their hearts. So each had written them out and stood ready to recite them.

Marty's turn came first. He took the mic in one hand and Izzy's left hand in his other. "Izzy, I have never met a more vivacious and caring individual. I vow to love you all my days—all our days together upon this earth. I will love you in good times and bad, in health and in sickness, through wealth and in want, even through misunderstandings and failure, I pledge to cling to you in love forever, and to protect you with my life, God helping me."

Izzy noticed a tear at the corner of Marty's eye. She reached up and wiped it with her hand. Then she leaned into the mic on its stand and took both of Marty's hands in hers. She proclaimed her vows to Marty freely with a crisp, clear voice. "Martin Goldstein, I vow my unending love, honor and respect for you. You are the light of my life. I will stay with you, my husband, even in the dark times, in sickness and in health, in the good times and the bad, even when confusion strikes like it did today…"

Soft laughter slipped from the guests gathered, many reaching for the hands of their spouses.

"…and I thank you for your patience and kindness to me. But if someday you should falter and fail me, I promise to always, always be here for you, and pick you up when you fall. I will love and honor you until our life on earth is done…"

Izzy paused. *Can I trust God to help me?*

"God helping me."

The pastor smiled at the two joined as one. "Now, you may kiss the bride!"

"Ahh, such a whirlwind of fun and memories." Izzy brought a glass of champagne to sit next to her hubby later in the comfort of their honeymoon suite at the Sheraton Inn near Hershey Park.

"Cheers to my beloved bride. Isabel Defranco Goldstein, my love for you is as deep as the ocean, and as high as the sky! I am so looking forward to doing life with you."

My dear Hubby, yes, let's try to do life together, and cherish the moments. Izzy tried to raise her glass to Marty, but she blinked back some tears and had to put it down.

"Hey, don't cry Sweetheart. Please." Marty gently took Izzy's chin in his hand and gave her a kiss.

"I just felt so embarrassed…" Then Izzy nearly burst out laughing.

"What?" Marty looked taken aback.

"No, no, I'm not laughing at you. I'm remembering how Pastor Michaels saved the day." Izzy tried to mimic the good pastor—"You may now kiss the bride."

"Oh! I've never been more shocked and unprepared." Marty laughed, rubbing his knees, looking with interest at his wife. "I'm so glad you can laugh at yourself."

"Yeah. That was such a sad situation turned around by some friends. Laura, I couldn't believe how brave she was, making excuses for my clumsiness. What a sweetheart." Izzy shook her head. "Didn't you love the Chuppa! It even made *me* feel Jewish."

Marty smiled. "Yeah, me, too. It was lovely. Our family *especially* enjoyed it. It kind of took the sting away from it being a Christian wedding."

Scooting over and wrapping Marty's arm over her shoulders, Izzy snuggled down, blinking away sleep. "It was special saying our vows there under the canopy. I felt so warm and secure. I caught a glimpse of your dear mother wiping away a tear. So special that they could be with you— with us—as we begin life together."

"Yes, I felt their presence as we made our vows in the Chuppah. I think they were pleased." Marty rubbed his eye.

"It's a shame they couldn't stay longer." Izzy sighed and stroked her hubby's prickly chin.

"Yes, I agree. Although they are retired, the work keeps them quite occupied there at the compound. Father and Mother make quite the pair—doctor and nurse—serving their community in Tanzania. You know, in that part of Africa medical help is very hard to find. Especially quality health care. I…think…that's why it's next to impossible to keep them here."

Does my guy look lonely? Izzy tousled Marty's soft brown hair. "Wasn't the bridal party table done up nicely? Oh, I wish I had had more time to visit more fully with everyone who came. Such memories we made today." Izzy rested her head on Marty's shoulder. He stroked her hair, and they sat in silence for a moment.

"Your Aunt Anna took the prize for best hostess of the year, I think. She made sure everyone had plenty to eat, surprising us with extra trays of tasty treats from the kitchen until it was time to cut the cake."

Izzy nodded. "Her Sisters' Fellowship really made sure we had plenty prepared for our guests. So very, very precious."

"Yes, praise God! That church has become like family to me. Marvin was a hoot. Did you see him smash his cake into Barbara's face after we shared our cake with one another?" Marty stretched out his legs, laughing.

"Hilarious! I didn't know he had it in him. He and Barbara are always so prim and proper in Sunday School. He even helps Pastor teach parts of the lessons sometimes. Who would have known?" Izzy shook her head, but her smile faded fast as she stretched to stay awake.

"Somebody's tired." Marty reached over and started massaging Izzy's shoulders. "I tell you what, let's say a prayer of thanks to our Rock before we have some more fun, if you know what I mean." He took his stand in front of Izzy and bent over to rub noses and give her a kiss. Then he gently pulled her out of the couch and took his place on his knees before it. She followed suit.

Wow. What a lover of God I have married. I've never knelt so much in my entire life. And on our wedding night!

12. <u>THE HONEYMOON'S OVER</u>

"While you were away, Mr. B rose to the top of the charts." Aunt Anna huffed a little as she stacked water bottles on the pantry shelf in the basement, the newlyweds by her side.

"We avoided the news this trip. This was our honeymoon. No time to let the cares of this world get us down." Marty gestured as he talked with one hand but rested the other hand squarely on his bride's shoulder.

"Well, good for you. That was smart." Aunt Anna continued to share the news. "But you won't believe this. One day the world watched as Mr. B pointed to the stormy sky, snapped his fingers, and watched the storm clouds roll away leaving blue sky and sunshine for the dedication of the World Council for Emergency Preparedness administration building. Another day, as he observed a crying infant in the crowd that thronged to see him, he reached out his arms to ask to hold the child. The mother hesitated and the baby howled even louder. As soon as she released the child to his embrace, to everyone's delight, the baby began to laugh, squeal, and clap his hands."

"No wonder people are calling him Prince of Peace. We heard it on the news coming over here today." Izzy raised her shoulders in disbelief.

"I know of only one Prince of Peace." Anna muttered. "But this Mr. B seems to be winning the hearts of many. Seeing as he has just embarked on a seven-year journey with the nations of the world, I think perhaps he will be Mr. Nice Guy for a while."

"Yeah, here we are stacking the pantry shelves for the day we won't be allowed to buy and sell anymore, but nothing has yet been said about taking the mark with Mr. B's ID." Marty scratched his head.

"I'm happy we don't have that threat yet. It never hurts to put up some extra food for a rainy day or emergency." Izzy nudged a box over to Marty, trying to feel hopeful. *Wouldn't it be lovely if these weren't the last days and the time of the Beast?*

Marty opened the box of canned soup and shoved it closer to Izzy. Izzy smiled back at him and kissed his nose. Together, they loaded a shelf.

Aunt Anna sat on a stool and wiped the sweat off her brow with a handkerchief. "Tell me more about your honeymoon, you two lovebirds."

Izzy grinned at Marty, and he winked back.

"We had a blast." Izzy looked up at Marty with a twinkle in her eye. "Didn't we, Sweetheart?"

"Uh, quite! Especially at the amusement park. We rode every ride…sometimes three times. Unbelievable!" Marty drummed on the seat of his chair between his legs.

"Wait a minute, you two enjoy those roller coasters? One of them goes upside down and backwards. What do you call that one?" Anna heaved some more canned goods onto a shelf.

"Corkscrew, yes. That was the best. I've never had so much fun in my life! Except we did learn there is a limit to how much a body can take, didn't we Marty?" Izzy recalled her new husband bending over a trash can and losing his lunch.

Marty seemed to turn a little piqued at the thought. "Yes, Dearest, you would remember. A little merciless, I think. That third trip ruined a perfectly good memory."

Izzy giggled and put both hands on Marty's cheeks. "Oh, Marty, I didn't mean to be unkind. Let's just remember the good times."

"Hmmm, yes." Aunt Anna agreed. "So, what else did you two enjoy about your trip?"

"The food, definitely." Izzy pointed up in the air. *I'm picking up on Aunt Anna's habits.* "Hershey isn't too far from Pennsylvania Dutch country. There were cute little breakfast places with horse-drawn carriages parked on the street. The silver dollar pancakes piled high with butter, powdered sugar and pecans were to die for!"

"Not to mention the smorgasbord in the heart of Lancaster. It's so easy to eat too much there." Marty, wide-eyed, winked at Izzy and patted his belly contentedly.

"That's right. I always start by taking small portions—mashed potatoes and gravy, fluffy and melt-in-your mouth, freshly cut moist roast beef or ham, good old fried chicken, fluffy tall biscuits with butter or gravy, and—" Izzy looked up trying to recall the broad selection of sumptuous food.

"Don't forget the beans—green beans, baked beans, peas and mushrooms, black-eyed peas! Salad, of course, with your pick of dressings. Cottage cheese and apple butter. Pickled beets—"

"Hold on, you two. You're making me hungry!" Aunt Anna chuckled, holding her belly.

"But we haven't gotten to the desserts yet. Black forest cake, but not nearly as good as you make, Aunt Anna." Izzy paused to give Anna a hug. "Apple pie with a scoop of vanilla ice cream, raspberry crumb cake, cheesecake—"

"You ate all that?" Anna wiped away some drool.

"Just a little of each." Izzy grinned with pleasure.

"Dark chocolate cake with chocolate frosting, tall and moist. Mm-mm!" Marty looked up from his reverie. "I'm done."

Izzy chimed in. "But then we walked off the heavy meal down in the gift shop, wandering through row upon row of gifts and souvenirs. Which reminds me, Aunt Anna. Hold on a second." Izzy scampered off to their bedroom. A few moments later she reappeared with a beautifully wrapped lavender gift box, about twenty-four inches square. She put it down on top of the stepstool in front of her aunt, a grin tugging at the corner of her mouth.

Aunt Anna gasped and clasped her hands together in surprise. "What is this?" Her eyes opened wide, her eyebrows raised, and her face flushed with pleasure.

"Open it." Marty put his hand on Anna's shoulder. "You deserve a Pennsylvania Dutch house-warming gift seeing as we have taken you up on your hospitality. Please." Marty nudged the gift toward their generous hostess.

"Oh, you shouldn't have." Anna clasped her hands together like a child at a birthday party. Then she gingerly untied the wide silk lavender bow and lifted the lid off the box. When she pulled back the crisp white paper to peek inside, Anna could not contain her joy. "It's gorgeous!" Out of the box she gently lifted a colorful quilt.

This is killing me. I can't wait to see it laying out on her bed. Izzy put her arm around her aunt and gave her a big sideways hug as she stroked the red oak leaf pattern.

Soon the square quilt lay on display on Aunt Anna's bed; nine oak leaves dressed in shades of red, yellow, orange, green, blue, and lavender were hemmed with a border of pastels and prints. Everyone stood silently enjoying the moment and the colors.

"You know, we met in the autumn. So, I could not pass this one up." Izzy lightly pinched Marty's elbow and looked up into his smiling face.

"Thank you, Darlings. It is a wonderful keepsake. Every time I see it, I will pray for you. God bless your marriage and your home." Aunt Anna wiped away a tear.

One morning after breakfast, Marty opened the Bible to the story of the prodigal son. "I'm reading from Luke 15." Izzy and Aunt Anna sat with their coffees and Bibles open— Anna read from her big family Bible, and Izzy read from her on-line Bible.

They never had time for more than ten or fifteen minutes together, but Izzy knew that Bible time meant a lot to Marty. *I know this is a good habit for us. Thank you, God, for Marty.*

Marty concluded that morning with this thought—"I don't care who you may be, or what your background is, but, like this prodigal son, you can find a Father in Heaven who is looking for you and waiting for you to come home!"

"Amen. Amen." Izzy and Anna both clapped.

Then came the usual buzz in the kitchen to get out and get to work. Aunt Anna had assumed the job of packing both Marty and Izzy's lunches and leaving them on the counter for them to pick up as they went out the door. There were hugs all around, and a kiss for the newlyweds as they headed off to work.

When Izzy came up the walk at school, Jamie was dropping off Max. Blond curls bouncing, Max slammed the door to the car and ran inside. *I wonder what that was about.*

That morning, the new "Mrs. Goldstein" had black-top duty, watching the children as they sat, grouped by classes, waiting for the morning bell to signal the start of school. Lots of kids sat in clusters, talking and laughing. But Max sat with his back to his classmates. When she walked toward him to say a special "Good morning," one of the boys poked him in the back and said, "Who brought you to school this morning, Maxine? Was it your Mommy or your Daddy?" Max put his head down between his knees.

"That sounded a lot like bullying to me." Izzy stooped down and peered at the ruddy face of the guilty boy. "Stand up, please. Now what's your name?"

The child shuffled his feet. "Andrew."

"What's his name? And look at me, please."

"Max."

"Andrew, how would you like it if someone poked and teased you? Does that ever happen?"

Andrew nodded his head.

"Andrew, sometimes we forget to be kind. You need to remember the Golden Rule—'Do unto others as you would like them to do to you.' Do you understand?" Izzy bent over to get eye contact with her pupil.

"Yes."

"Do you have anything to say to Max?"

Andrew looked at the ground, and said, "Sorry."

"No, are you talking to the ground, or Max?" Mrs. Goldstein prodded.

Then Andrew raised his eyes and looked at Max's shirt. "Sorry."

"Are you sorry you teased him?"

Andrew said, "Yes, I'm sorry I teased you, Max."

Both boys avoided looking the other in the face. Izzy rubbed Max's back and put her hand on Andrew's shoulder.

"Now both of you shake hands. Let's be friends."

Andrew extended his hand, but Max did not. He held his hands to his waist hard and fast and would not look up.

This one is not ready. He's hurting. "Andrew, that's okay. Please be kind next time, alright?"

"Okay." Andrew answered, looking up at Mrs. Goldstein. She shook his hand, saying, "Good."

Then Izzy, realizing the bell would be ringing shortly, put her arm around Max's shoulder and led him aside to a quiet spot. She got down at face level and looked him in the eye. "If that ever happens again, please let me know, Max. Do you have anyone in your class you like to play with?"

"Um, not really." Max looked up at Izzy with a frown.

Forlorn little puppy. "Hey, you've got friends here, you just haven't discovered them yet."

"Really?"

"Really. Now keep your eyes open for people you can play with or help. You'll find them." Izzy patted Max's curls.

He turned to go, saying, "Thanks."

At lunchtime, Laura and Izzy sat together eating their lunches. Izzy found a note left by Marty, and she shared it with Laura. "Look at this. Marty is quite the artist. And he wrote, 'Don't forget, the Father is looking after you." The picture he drew showed a father figure, arms outstretched from the top of a hill, with a little curly-headed child running up the hill.

"Ahh, so sweet! I wish Brad were an artist and left little notes for me." Laura laughed.

Izzy smiled, but she could not shake a thought. *Max ran the wrong direction this morning from his father figure. He seems to be struggling.*

"Do you remember little Max that we saw at the Photo Memories shop? Carol and Jamie's adopted child?"

Laura nodded. "Yes. He has been checking out some of those Gender Education books. I wonder, sometimes, what it's like for him, and for his parents. I'll tell you a secret."

Izzy curiously cocked her head. "What?"

"I invited Carol out for teatime next Saturday. She and I met at the grocery store and got to talking about this and that. You know, she's really quite funny. Just felt like chatting more, maybe catch the chance to encourage her in her journey toward God. Would you like to come?"

Hmmm. It was nice of Carol to attend our wedding with Max. She saved me from falling! But journey toward God? Sounds frustrating.

Just then, the bell rang. Izzy stood to go. "Time for class. Thanks for the invite. I'll think about it. But I'm glad you're doing it. I think this family could use some TLC right now."

That afternoon Izzy helped the students into their cars at pick-up time. Jamie pulled up to the curb and rolled the passenger window down as Izzy opened the back door for Max to get in.

Jamie craned her thin neck back toward Max, revealing her lithe profile with freckled cheeks, pointy nose, and thin lips to Izzy. *Except for her boyish haircut she's actually quite feminine.*

As Max slid in, Jamie asked, "Did you get a new book from the library?"

"Yes, I got your book." He pulled the envelope out of his bookbag and frowned.

Jamie grabbed the envelope and shoved the book toward Izzy peering in at the door. "Why are these books covered like this, in an envelope?" Her eyes flashed.

"Is this from the Gender Education shelf in the library?"

Izzy asked.

"Yes, but what's the big deal? Should we be ashamed of these books?"

Izzy noticed a grimace on Jamie's face. *What am I going to say?* "Jamie, the school has left that judgment up to each parent. You know that you had to sign your permission for Max to check out those books. But not all parents have signed."

"There should never have been such a distinction made." Jamie sat up and rolled down her front passenger window all the way and continued. "There should never be a distinction made. It makes Max feel ashamed, checking out a book which has to be covered and hidden from all his peers. This is not right! And I will report it to the Board of Education!" Then she pushed the button to roll up the passenger window and drove off.

Nice way to end the day. Why can't she be satisfied with having the books anyway? Why must she force them on the whole school? Izzy suddenly felt very tired. After her duties were over, rather than grade the kids' papers at her desk—as was her custom—she gathered them to take home, together with her lesson-plan book.

Izzy smelled something baking when she walked in the house. She took a deep breath and sank into one of the recliners in the living room, her eyes closed before she settled in her seat.

An hour later, Marty walked in, put away his briefcase, and tiptoed over to his sleeping bride. He slipped into the recliner next to her and reached over to gently hold her hand. Her eyes fluttered open, and she smiled. Marty brought Izzy's hand to his lips and planted a kiss. "Hey, how was your day? You don't usually nap when you get home."

Izzy remembered her encounter with Jamie and sat up with a frown. "Talked with a disgruntled parent. Jamie is going to take the matter of hiding the gender education books in envelopes to the school board; she says it makes Max feel uncomfortable in front of his classmates."

"I suppose that is understandable. It sets him apart from his peers." Marty reached over and massaged Izzy's shoulder. "Maybe you can work it out for students to put those books into their bookbags and not bring them out until they are home. Dispense with the envelopes."

Izzy sat with her head in her hands. *Now what? If the Board gets involved, we may have trouble.* "I'll call Jamie right away and let her know I'll talk with the principal about her concern. It would be nice not to involve the Board."

Aunt Anna joined them in the living room. "Couldn't you just let her know when you see her?"

Izzy ran her hands through her hair. "That's okay. I have her number from doing business with them."

She retrieved her phone from her bag and dialed. "Hello, Jamie? Listen, I understand how Max must be feeling. Believe me, we do not want him to be set apart from his peers. We are making efforts to encourage him to make some friends at school. I will talk with the principal tomorrow to see what we can do to help."

"You're a little late. I've already registered my complaint with the Board via email. You'll have to take up the matter with them." Click. Jamie hung up.

"Argh! She hung up on me, and it has already gone to the Board!"

"Shhh, shhh." Marty rubbed Izzy's hand. "It'll be alright. Let's pray about it."

"I don't feel like praying about it!" Izzy got up and walked to her bedroom and slammed the door. *Oh Marty. Shhh! You don't have to pray about everything. Just listen, okay?*

13. COPING WITH PRESSURE

The next day, Izzy felt like a stranger in her own school. *Why am I tiptoeing about my classroom? This is ridiculous. Let's begin with something light for the kids this morning. Izzy drew a tall, slender book off the shelf of favorite books next to her desk. Why can't all books be so delightful?*

"Good morning, children. As soon as you put your things away, please put your chairs under your desk and find your place on the reading rug." A couple of girls said, "Ooh! Reading rug!" and a little boy put his thumbs up with a big smile, saying, "Thank you, Ms. Frank." After a brief scurry, all of Izzy's students sat cross-legged on the floor, attentively listening.

Izzy also sat cross-legged on the floor, book in hand, her heart melting as she looked over the beaming faces of her eager students. *Hello, Sweethearts. You do a teacher's heart good.* Izzy showed the children the cover of the book and asked who could read it.

Chloe—pigtails swinging—wriggled as her arm shot up.

"Chloe, go ahead." Izzy nodded.

Chloe read *The Night Before Christmas*, by C. C. Moore.

"Very good. Now let's listen to find out what happens one Christmas Eve." Izzy cleared her throat, and began—

"'twas the night before Christmas and all through the house, not a creature was stirring, not even a mouse.
The stockings were hung by the chimney with care,
In hopes that St. Nicholas soon would be there.
The children were nestled all snug in their beds,
While visions of sugarplums danced in their heads..."
KNOCK, KNOCK, KNOCK!

Izzy turned the page, annoyed to hear someone at the door of her room. She looked over to see who was intruding on her sacred time with her kids. *Ahh! I've got to stand up.* Izzy stood up, pushing the hair out of her face, blowing out with a puff. It was Ms. Paige, one of the substitute teachers who often served at Overbrook. The children's heads all turned toward the intruder. "Ms. Paige, good morning. Could you please wait while we finish our story?" Izzy pulled a strand of blonde hair back over her ear.

"I'm afraid not, Mrs. Goldstein. You are wanted in the office. I've come to take your class." Ms. Paige stepped over to the rug and offered her hand to retrieve the book.

Oh, no. Wanted in the office? Someone at the Board did not want to waste any time. Izzy relinquished the book and looked upon her children.

"Children, I must go to the office." The children's faces fell, and suddenly everyone began talking with their neighbor.

Izzy clapped her hands. "It's okay. I have some business to tend to in the office. But Ms. Paige is a great storyteller, and she will start over from the beginning. One Christmas Eve some mysterious things happened. Now listen closely and, when you are finished, I want you to draw what happened. When I return, I'd love to hear your stories as you share your pictures. Now sit up straight and give Ms. Paige your undivided attention. Make me proud." She tried to smile despite her misgivings as she left the room.

Ms. Hitchcock, dressed in a black suit and a bright blue blouse with a flouncy bow, sat at the head of the long table to the far side of her desk. She gave Izzy a cursory nod as she entered and motioned for her to join the small crowd of representatives from the Board's Policy Committee, all wearing business suits.

Izzy looked over toward her seat, and realized that Laura, looking quite pregnant, seemed to plead with her through swollen eyes. *Oh dear, Laura, I should have warned you.*

"Now that we are all here, let's get started." Ms. Hitchcock, looking at Laura and Izzy, continued, "It seems we had a complaint sent to the Board yesterday from one of our parents. They accused our school of discriminating against the students who wish to check out the gender affirmation books."

Izzy sat up and raised her hand slightly. "Yes, I talked with that parent yesterday at pick-up time. Her child…"

"The proper pronoun for the parent, Izzy, is he/his. You are talking about Jamie, Max's father, am I correct?" Ms. Hitchcock interrupted.

Izzy faltered. "Yes, yes, I am. The parent complained that Max felt embarrassed by having to keep the books hidden in an envelope. This was the first I had heard of his feeling that way, and I called her afterwards to assure her we could talk about a solution."

"Him, you called him afterwards?" The principal spoke sharply, standing up to make her point. Then, looking around at the committee members, she decided to lead the conversation.

Ms. Hitchcock cleared her throat. "When the books provided by the Board for gender affirmation came into our library, some of our faculty took issue with the content. The fear was expressed that the books gave our younger students more sex education than they were ready for."

"Why, of course, not! We had our team of experts vetting the books…" a board member interjected.

"If there was a problem, why would you not first bring your objections to our committee?" Grumbling and discussion ensued. Izzy and Laura looked at each other sadly. They knew they were caught in a no-win situation.

Finally, the discussion died down, and Izzy saw her chance. "I realize now that, of course, I needed to go to the source with my concerns. I am sorry I missed that chance to build trust with our Board. I know we are all concerned for the welfare of our children. Please forgive me for not going through the proper channels. If I may, I would like to share my primary objection to the gender education material for our children."

Ms. Hitchcock looked around at the representatives from the committee, particularly their leader—a woman in black who sat with her arms folded. Seeing no dissenters, she waved Izzy on to speak. "You may proceed, Mrs. Goldstein."

"My mother was extremely protective of me, and of what I was exposed to growing up. She succeeded in shielding me from sex so that when I was thirteen—until it happened to me—I thought a period was only the punctuation at the end of a sentence."

Some chuckles told Izzy she had her audience.

"But, unfortunately, try as moms may to protect their children from danger, unwanted influences can still touch their children's lives. I was one of those casualties of porn on the web. My phone and the computers at home all had been programmed so that pornographic material would be blocked. All I had to do was go to my friend's house without telling my mom, and I was exposed.

"I was in junior high when that happened. That stage of my life I had interests in dance, reading, and music. It was the time for building friendships and exploring the world of social need in my community and world. But I must confess that, instead, I got sucked into porn. It was a long, hard, uphill battle to break free of it.

"Frankly, I believe what the Bible says about God making people, male and female, and that anything more than that is only confusing our children. I believe our children need to stretch their wings and grow as they pursue age-appropriate interests in their world. They do not need to be derailed by too much sex education too soon.

"So our attempt here at Overbrook Elementary School was to include our parents in the decision about what kind of literature their children would be exposed to, how much sex education they would be exposed to. The envelopes were not meant to ostracize the children who had their parents' permission to check out the books. We regret, I regret, that it had this effect on Max. Someone suggested that instead we could just have the books put into bookbags until they got home."

"You presuppose that parents have the right to make that judgment for their children, but we disagree." The woman in black speaking—the head of the committee—wore heavy eyeliner and dark lipstick to match her black suit, and had half-inch plugs in her ears. Her tone put Izzy on edge. "Both child psychology experts and early childhood educators vetted the books which should be on your shelf in the library and freely distributed to all the children."

I would not want you making decisions for my children. Izzy opened her hands to appeal to Ms. Hitchcock for support. But Ms. Hitchcock could not come to her rescue because her head was down. Izzy decided to speak her heart. "Let children be children. Let them explore their world, and pursue nature, things that go, the miracles of light and color. Young children, I believe, would not even think about gender and sex unless it is presented to them. I wanted to protect my students, and we discovered by a survey of our teachers that seventy-five percent felt that parents should be involved in deciding this issue of gender education."

Someone groaned. *Did Ms. Hitchcock groan? Oh, Dear.* Izzy had never experienced Ms. Hitchcock's censure before, but today she did not look very happy. Her face looked haggard and white. She pursed her lips at Izzy. Fear gripped Izzy's heart, and she froze in her place; her mind went blank.

"Mrs. Goldstein, you have said enough for today's purposes." Then turning her attention to the committee before her, Ms. Hitchcock apparently felt a few words of explanation were needed. "I value open communication with my staff here at Overbrook Elementary School. If they have concerns, we try to work through them together. I can see that the Board had certain expectations which we did not anticipate, and I am sorry. So we will work with you to make some changes."

Izzy looked at Laura, who was wiping away a tear from her cheek. *I feel so powerless to protect her. Will she be able to keep her job?* Izzy tuned into what Ms. Hitchcock was sharing.

"To this point, we have given parents the choice as to whether they want their children to have access to the gender education books. And we know which children have been given access to the books by their parents. But the problem which came to light is that the children are made to feel singled out by the use of envelopes for the books. Therefore, let me suggest that we discard the use of the envelopes. The children will take the books home in their bookbags, with no other stipulations." Ms. Hitchcock smoothed out her paper on the table and folded her hands.

What a wonderful principal. She is standing by us. I felt like a fish thrown to the sharks back there.

"As I have said, we are not operating under the premise that parents have the say-so in their children's education. Children these days are aware of stereotypes. They need to be liberated to choose who they want to be. I believe the gender education books belong on the new-books table in the library where all the children who have an interest can read them." The lady in black stood up. "If anyone of your staff feels differently, maybe they need to find a job elsewhere." She raised her eyebrow in Izzy's direction.

Oh, my poor babies. What kind of propaganda and perversion are they going to be exposed to?

The principal's voice once more drew Izzy's attention. "I understand that this is your view. But I will take this issue of parental rights to the next Board of Education meeting. I don't believe any more discussion here will be fruitful. For the time being we will continue to honor parents' wishes, and we will discard the use of the envelopes." The principal stood. "Are there any questions?"

Izzy glanced at the lady in black. Her eyes looked even darker than before. *It looks like we have a fight ahead of us.*

"We will be bringing your case up before the Superintendent, Ms. Hitchcock. We are not finished here." The sinister woman loudly stuffed her bag. Others murmured, but no one seemed to have any questions.

"If there are no other questions, then we will take the matter up with the Board. Thank you all for your time." Ms. Hitchcock breathed deeply and stood at the door to see them off.

The committee filed out without another word.

Laura and Izzy lingered behind. When Ms. Hitchcock returned to her seat, she looked up and smiled weakly. "Izzy, you were fine. It just put me on the spot, because nothing happens at a school without the principal's support. It is what it is. I, for one, hope the Board of Education here has not dispensed with teaching children to honor their parents' wishes.

Later that evening, Izzy lay her forehead on Marty's shoulder and her tears started flowing, dampening his shirt. She ran through a whole box of tissues retelling her harrowing experience. Finally, she angrily mimicked the chairperson in black—her fingers flashing the quote sign—"'Children these days are aware of the stereotypes. They need to be liberated to choose who they want to be.' Well, not in my classroom! Leave the children alone to explore the world, colors, numbers, and imagination! Why confuse them with unnecessary questions of gender? Uhh!"

"I am proud of you, advocating for the children, Sweetheart. I prayed for you today." Marty stroked Izzy's head as she curled up in his lap in the cushy recliner.

He prayed for me. Of course. Izzy sat up, and looking Marty in the eye, took a deep breath. "I owe you an apology, being so impatient yesterday, refusing to pray with you. It could have been a whole lot worse today. But I did feel the support of my principal. I know the battle isn't over. That's what scares me. But..." Izzy smiled. "Your prayers made a difference. Thanks."

"I'm out of the doghouse, then?" Marty made a forlorn puppy face.

"Of course, you old hound dog!" She pushed his droopy face away. "Just, next time, maybe listen longer before suggesting we pray. I just needed to be heard."

The next morning, Ms. Hitchcock called Izzy and Laura into her office.

Izzy stopped by the library to meet Laura. "Looks like the Board is not wasting any time with this case."

"Do you think ours is the only school to take issue with these books?" Laura supported her back with one hand. She wore a pinstriped sundress topped with a light-yellow sweater—the dress displaying a string of baby ducks following the mommy duck embroidered across her big belly.

Izzy smiled at her friend. "Laura, you look adorable." She gave her a hug and rubbed her shoulder. "Don't you worry. I think Ms. Hitchcock has our backs."

In the office, Ms. Hitchcock welcomed the couple to sit down in chairs around her table, and she settled into her chair with her tablet. "I have some news from the Superintendent's office. They have laid down an ultimatum. It seems that ours is the only school which has not complied by putting the books out on display."

Izzy and Laura exchanged uneasy glances.

"Some schools have already arranged for drag queens to come in and read the stories to the children." Ms. Hitchcock held up her tablet to read, "By your non-compliance you hinder progress toward dispelling gender dysphoria at Overbrook Elementary School. We will send a representative to inspect next week, when the gender education books should be displayed openly on a table in the library, one that is accessible to every child. Thank you for your cooperation."

"There goes my job." Laura looked down at her hands folded in her lap. "I just can't do that in good conscience. I have read through all of those books. Some are very graphic. Many are sympathizing with children and youth who have made that choice. But to me it sends the wrong message. The Bible says that God created man, male and female. There are no other healthy choices." Laura looked up, her face flushed. She took her glasses off and dabbed at her eyes with a tissue.

It's not fair. Laura is an excellent teacher who cares for her students. Why are they pushing this agenda on this community? Izzy clasped Laura's hand and looked to Ms. Hitchcock.

The principal sighed. Usually one who presented as very much in control, she sat silent for a moment, looking at some distant fleck on the wall. Finally, she spoke. "Ms. Chen"—Laura's married name—"I don't want you to leave. If I could give you any other position teaching here at Overbrook, would you stay?"

Izzy squeezed Laura's hand. *Is there hope we can save her job?*

Laura sat up and straightened her shoulders. "Thank you, Ms. Hitchcock, for your support. And thank you Izzy, for your encouragement. My husband, Brad, and I have already discussed the issue, and we feel that with this kind of education coming into Overbrook Elementary School we should just trust the Lord to provide another place of employment." She looked down and put her hand on top of her belly. "I'm going to be having a baby soon. I don't want to expose the baby to such confusion, and I, frankly, don't need that kind of pressure right now." Laura reached across the table and grasped her principal's hand. "Thank you."

Sadness hung in the air.

My friend and confidante, leaving! Oh, God, what am I to do? Suddenly a word lodged in Izzy's mind—"Advocate."

Back home, Izzy shared the news with Marty and Aunt

Anna. Then she sighed. "It all makes me so tired. But I've decided to stick around Overbrook to advocate for my students as they are exposed to those lies. God forbid they bring any drag queens in to read in the library. But, regardless, there are so many wholesome traditional family-oriented books. Mrs. Goldstein's reading circle is going to be a haven of peace in the midst of the storm."

"Oh, Sweetheart, your mother would be so proud of you." Aunt Anna leaned over and kissed Izzy on the forehead. Then she walked out to busy herself tidying the kitchen.

"I am proud of you." Marty picked up his phone. "And I have some good news for you. Guess what?"

Izzy sat up expectantly. "What?"

"Uncle Amos tells us to buy our tickets, his treat—a late wedding gift, he says—to attend the dedication of the temple in another year."

"Ahh!" Izzy said excitedly. "Just what we were hoping for. You'll get your chance to walk where Jesus walked, Marty. Aunt Anna, too!" Then her face clouded over.

"What's the matter, Dear?" Marty grabbed Izzy's hand.

"Remember Pastor Michaels talking about the temple being rebuilt? How it's a sign of the Beast…and of Christ's return? I'm more than a little worried about what Mr. B will be doing by then. Aren't we just counting the days? I mean, we do not yet have the mandate to get his mark in order to be free to buy and sell. But we are preparing for it. We are stocking the basement with food." Izzy's hands covered her face, and she started crying. *Wouldn't it be wonderful if it were all just a bunch of baloney and that this Mr. Bandar really is a nice guy?*

"Hey, don't." Marty took his handkerchief and handed it to Izzy. "It's clean." He hugged his wife. "I can't help but believe that Uncle Amos has everyone's best interests at heart. So if he says rebuilding the temple will be a Jewish dream come true, I think we have to trust him. Besides, if it's a sign of Christ's return…I want to be there for that adventure!"

Izzy smiled, wiping her nose. "Maybe you're right. I guess I shouldn't borrow trouble from tomorrow. It's awfully nice of Uncle Amos to invite us. And I would love to go and meet the family. I'm not sure what this year at school will bring. But by that time, it's likely we'll be ready for a vacation!" Izzy lowered her voice. "Maybe we shouldn't share this news just yet with Aunt Anna."

14. TWO YEARS LATER

Saturday morning breakfast, again! Izzy crept up on Marty and hugged him from behind. "How's my favorite pancake flipper?"

"I thought I held that title." Aunt Anna's raspy voice came from the dining room where she sat reading her Bible, a gaunt shadow of the Mrs. Claus she used to be. An oxygen tank on wheels sat by her side. That and the faint hiss of oxygen entering her nose tube had become her regular companions.

Izzy's smile dissolved into a pouty face as she went over to give Aunt Anna a kiss on the forehead. "Oh, dear Aunt Anna. Of course, you'll always be my favorite breakfast chef. But you have to admit, Marty has become adept at flipping pancakes. You taught him well." *You dear, sweet woman. I hate seeing you so frail.*

After pitching in to get breakfast on the table, Izzy sat with her napkin spread on her lap, looking to Marty to say grace.

"Why don't you pray this morning, Sweetheart?" Marty placed his long fingers across her wrist and winked.

Marty Goldstein, you get me every time. Izzy dutifully

bowed. "Thank you, Father, for this beautiful spread of delicious food, and for another Saturday morning breakfast together. Please strengthen our bodies, especially Aunt Anna's lungs. In Jesus' name, Amen."

Marty squeezed his wife's hand, leaning over to kiss her. "Thank you, Sweetheart. Now, do you know what day it is?"

She shook her head. "I am just kind of looking forward to resting. What's up?" She noticed Aunt Anna sawing at her pancake and got up to help her cut her food.

"It's been a while since we checked the news. But I heard at work that a deadline has been set for receiving what could possibly be the Beast's mark. I think we'd best keep our schedule of grocery shopping to stock the pantry."

"When is the deadline?" Izzy sat down hard.

"Year's end. That gives us another half a year." Marty took a quick sip of his coffee. "We will have gone to see the dedication of the temple by then. Wonderful timing, really, since otherwise, we could not travel."

"You are always so positive, Dear. Thank you. Yes. I need your habit, always counting your blessings!" Izzy buttered her pancakes and smothered them in syrup.

Aunt Anna's face broke into a grin. "Surely this means that Jesus is coming back soon. I am so surprised we waited as long as we have." Anna coughed into her napkin and paused. "Why, last year they postponed the finish of the temple for another year, and still, no mark of the Beast." She closed her eyes, holding her napkin to her chest, breathing loudly.

"Yes, three years ago when His Highness B miraculously survived that knife attack, we knew the clock was ticking down to the mark." Marty reached over to hold Izzy's hand. "The whole world began following Mr. B and his partner, Mr. Khalil Yasin, The Prophet. It's no surprise that they married and adopted that son of theirs. I'm afraid we have all slipped into a false sense of security." Marty tried to smooth out the worry gathering on his wife's face. "Sweetheart, keep looking up, because the Lord Jesus is coming soon!"

Oh, God! I hate these developments. Frankly, I have enjoyed the security, even though it's been a battle at school. Hard to watch the little ones struggle. But home has always been my safe place. Izzy suddenly didn't feel like eating. She looked up to Marty and asked, "What's going to happen to us?"

Marty stood up and tenderly lifted his wife from her seat. He gave her a kiss and drew her in for a long hug.

Oh Marty, just hold me close, and I'm okay. Izzy relaxed in his arms.

"Honey, God doesn't want us to worry. He wants us to trust him." Marty whispered, cradling Izzy's head against his chest.

It's easier to trust when you are holding me, Marty. Just never leave me.

After breakfast, the threesome settled before the screen in the living room listening to the news channel. Julie Quespie and Rod Rogers were interviewing Mr. B and The Prophet.

> QUESPIE: We now bring you this latest press conference with His Highness Mr. Bandar, and the Vice Premier, Mr. Khalil Yasir Hamaz. Your Highnesses.

> BANDAR: These have been difficult days for us all. Let us all stand together as one man.

> HAMAZ: Everyone knows that a divided house

cannot stand. So, for the sake of peace, get the mark. Together we will stand strong.

With those words, Mr. Hamaz, The Prophet, offered his hand to a crippled man whose caregiver had stopped to listen. Everyone held their breath as the octogenarian leaned forward. Strength returned to his useless legs. "I can walk! Look at me, I'm walking!" His caregiver screamed and hugged the old man.

ROGERS: Unbelievable, except that lately miracles have become commonplace. Just last week, let's not forget, Mr. B brought sight to the blind and hearing to the deaf! Many are saying, 'This has to be the second coming of Christ with one big surprise for some of the people who call themselves Christians—no rapture.'

QUESPIE: That's right, Rod. On another front, scientists are watching for the ethereal culprits who seem to be connected with the disappearances of cows.

ROGERS: Come again. Did you say cows?

QUESPIE: Yes, Rod, you heard me right. Take a look at these shots. You see the blur of light there? And there. And there. These farms in Nebraska, belonging to one of the biggest dairy conglomerates, have begun to lose their most important commodity—cows. Listen to CEO Tom Newquist...

NEWQUIST: We have lost about fifty cows in the last week alone. It's a very troubling trend. Especially when it is paired with the appearances of the strange lights over the range at night. The cows seem to disappear directly from their stalls at night.

ROGERS: Surely there's an explanation, Julie. I mean, with AI, theft seems to have skyrocketed with the development of very sophisticated tools.

QUESPIE: So true, Rod. The authorities are talking with the experts to try to solve this mystery.

ROGERS: On another note, with the rash of meteor strikes over the last year, over fifteen percent of the world's fresh water has been poisoned. Listen to what spokesman for the WCEP—Bill Toliver—has just announced from the steps of His Highness B's office in Ramle…

A stocky man wearing a blue dress shirt and sporting a thick black moustache stood in front of the stark cement building in Ramle—formerly the headquarters of the Green Earth Movement but taken over by Mr. Bandar's regime.

TOLIVER: His Highness Abdul Mutakabbir Asahd Bandar's WCEP has spent grueling hours trying to come up with a solution to the world's deteriorating water supply. They just published this mandate, as follows—'According to the authority vested in me and the World Council for Emergency Preparedness —now called the World Order for Peace—I ordain the ten-day workweek, which is to be commenced immediately. This will increase the speed with which the water recycling and remediation can take place across the globe.' Signed Mr. M.A. Bandar and the World Order for Peace. We of the WOP regret the inconvenience to the great peoples of the earth, but we know that you will have the heart to sacrifice for the needs of all to be met. Thank you.

Izzy grabbed the hands of her spouse and aunt. "World Order for Peace? What's going to happen? How will they enforce a ten-day workweek?"

As if in reply, Julie Quespie elaborated—

QUESPIE: Listen, folks. This has just come down from the Governor. If your last name begins with A to K, please report to work tomorrow to do the paperwork for this transition. Otherwise, report on Monday. Tuesday will be a day of rest for all. Thereafter, the first ten-day workweek will run from Wednesday through Friday. Then, brace yourselves folks, you will have one day off before the next ten-day cycle begins.

ROGERS: This sounds like a prescription for chaos and sickn...

Rod Rogers stopped, put his hand to his ear, and said, "Yes Sir, yes Sir, yes Sir." His face suddenly pallid, he began again.

Marty and Izzy looked at each other in surprise.

ROGERS: Certainly, um, the ten-day workweek is a brilliant remedy for the world's water crisis. Stay tuned for more information after this break with our sponsors...

"Our man Rogers got himself into trouble, I'm afraid. Didn't Pastor Michaels say something about the Beast tampering with the calendar?" Aunt Anna coughed as she began to speak, holding up her hand to continue while she covered her mouth with the other. Her head down, she wheezed as she waited for her throat to calm down. She took a sip of water, then ventured to talk again. "Look up Daniel 7:25." She began to turn to the page in her Bible, then pushed it over toward the edge of the table for Izzy or Marty to retrieve. Marty picked it up and read—*"He shall speak words against the Most High, and shall wear out the saints of the Most High, and shall think to change the times and the law; and they shall be given into his hand for a time, times, and a half time."*

"Wait, wait, let me read that again." Izzy stood over the open Bible, trying to make sense of the words. "It sounds to me like the Beast will be on a vendetta to make things tough for the saints. So do you think the ten-day workweek is aimed at Christians and the Church?"

"Yes, indeed. That, and mandating we receive his branding to buy and sell." Aunt Anna patted Izzy on the arm.

"Speaking of buying, I think it best we head on out to the grocery store. It's bound to be busy, seeing it is Saturday." Marty looked at Izzy. "You ready?"

"Aunt Anna, can we get you anything before we go shopping for a little bit?" Izzy checked the oxygen tank to make sure it had enough supply for a while.

"I'll do just fine. Just me and my Bible, and the Lord, of course!"

"Good-bye, Aunt Anna. You guard the house while we're gone," said Marty.

"Me and my guardian angels." Aunt Anna patted the backs of Izzy and Marty who stood on either side. "Take care. I trust you will get your shopping done without any hang-ups."

Izzy chose to drive their silver Toyota van, as it afforded more space for the groceries. "Do we have a list?" Izzy looked at Marty as he buckled up on the passenger side.

"Some of our canned goods have expired, I'm afraid. So, we will try to restock. Plus, let's pick up about five gallons of water, if we can. They ran out the last time." Marty spoke, looking ahead at the road. As they drove into the parking lot, he said, "Look at all these cars. And there's a crowd outside the store."

Izzy saw tables with signs that read, "World Order for Peace, Authorized Branding Station."

After finally finding a parking spot, the Goldsteins linked arms to approach the store together. They lined up behind the crowd. Five people poised for action like a paramedic's squadron sat behind the table.

"Get your mark before the deadline and you'll be awarded an extra one hundred dollars in your account, compliments of our Prince of Peace, Mr. B himself!" hawked one of the WOP forces.

Izzy tugged at Marty's arm. *Two hundred dollars is nothing to take lightly. And wouldn't it be lovely not to have to worry about buying and selling in the future? Oh, God!* "I wish so much this Beast nonsense was all a big lie and that we could go on with our lives!"

"We both know better, Sweetheart," said Marty shaking his head, his arm wrapped around her in a protective embrace. "Let's just trust the Lord together."

One of the men behind the table picked up on Marty's words and snarled, "Come on, Miss, get your extra hundred while you can. No one will be doing business without the Brand, so it's the best choice you can make for a secure and healthy future."

Marty squeezed Izzy around the shoulders and marched her into the store.

Izzy noticed a sign which read—'Water ration, one gallon jug per person.' "Oh, dear, Marty. Our family could easily drink a gallon a day. How will we be able to stock the pantry?"

"So long as supplies last, let's come back every day." Marty lifted two gallons from the shelf to the cart.

"I suppose we could bring Aunt Anna out in her wheelchair next time." *That is, if the air quality improves.*

Their shopping cart full, Marty and Izzy made their way out of the store. Shouting drew their attention toward the entrance to the left.

"We do not need your hundred dollars! Our liberty is in jeopardy here. Who is this Mr. B, anyway? Some Iraqi guru!"

That voice sounds vaguely familiar. Izzy craned her head to see through the crowd gathered at the table at the entrance. "Oh, no. It's Jamie. And poor Max is with her, hanging his head."

"Should we go help?" Marty turned to see.

"What? How could we help? I wouldn't help that woman after what she did to me." Izzy pulled Marty back to go to the car. He resisted at first, but then followed her to the car and got in.

"Izzy, I remember the pain she caused you, and Laura, and even Ms. Hitchcock. The Board, and the Superintendent, could not understand the efforts you all made to shield the innocent children from too much sex education too soon. Laura chose to leave when they insisted she display the books prominently for all the children to see. That hurt you dearly, and…"

"And I lost tenure, and I have been on trial ever since!" Izzy's blonde curls hid her face as she leaned over the steering wheel. She grabbed a tissue and blew her nose.

Marty got out of the car and walked to Izzy's side. Opening the door, he coaxed, "Take a break. Let me drive home."

Just then, Izzy looked up to see Jamie and Max coming away from the store in a huff, each carrying only a bottle of water. "Oh, no, no, no. Get in. I don't want to talk to her."

"What?" Marty looked over his shoulder and saw Jamie and Max. Turning back, he said, "Just let me drive, okay?"

"No! Let's go now! Please, get in!" Izzy screamed louder than she intended. *Doesn't he care how I feel?*

Marty started for the passenger side and nearly ran into Jamie. She and Max stood with their heads down, not saying a word. "Excuse me. Excuse us. Having a bad day."

What? Because of that person I'm having a bad life! Izzy squealed out of the parking lot as soon as Marty closed the door.

"This is why I wanted to drive!" The words exploded from Marty's mouth. He struggled to buckle his seatbelt. He closed his eyes and leaned his head back on the headrest, turning his face away from his wife.

Izzy seethed in silence all the way home. *This is all Jamie's fault.*

Then, at home, when Marty emptied the car of the groceries without saying a word, avoided eye contact with her, then silently slipped into his bedroom without a glance, Izzy felt devastated. She walked, steel-faced, by Aunt Anna.

"Hey, what's going on? Something happen between you two at the store?" Aunt Anna spread her arms out, her brows drooping in dismay.

Izzy swung around to see her aunt's consternation and expelled a deep breath. She sat down with Aunt Anna at the dining table and held her head in her hands. *Bummer. Poor Marty, I know I embarrassed him back there. I should have let him drive, but then I would have come face to face with that monster.*

Finally, Izzy confessed to her aunt what happened. Then she hung her head and asked, "What do I do?"

Aunt Anna used both hands to push Izzy's hair out of her face. "Darling, you tell me something. What did you vow when you married Marty?" She let her arms rest on the table, tilted her head, lips pursed.

Marty, you deserved my respect today, but I blew it. Please forgive me.

Izzy leaned over and kissed her aunt on the cheek. "Thanks, Aunt Anna."

Then she went to apologize to her hubby in the bedroom.

Supper was light that night. Marty buttered his toast, deep in thought.

"Penny for your thoughts." Izzy still felt insecure after her blunder that afternoon. *Are we okay?*

Marty looked up and smiled, reaching over to grasp Izzy's hand. "Today you took me by surprise when you entertained the possibility that we could receive the branding of Mr. B. We have all been sucked in by this supposed Prince of Peace. He's been a good guy, done a lot of good." Marty put down his food and took both of Izzy's hands in his, looking her square in the eye. "Izzy, I love you. I know you wish that all of this was just nonsense with no basis in the truth. You wish we could get the mark and go on with our lives. But I look forward to being with you in heaven someday. Our marriage might just last until the rapture, but I want to be with you, together, when we see Jesus."

Tears dripped down Izzy's nose. She looked down at her hands. *I'm so afraid of the future.*

Aunt Anna put her food down and looked up to Marty as she wrestled Izzy's hands from his with an amazingly strong grip. She turned loving eyes to her niece. "Oh, Izzy, I didn't know you were still struggling. Now we have overwhelming evidence that Mr. B is, in fact, the beast that we have been looking out for. Let's listen to what Pastor has to say about the Beast's identity." She briskly rubbed Izzy's hand, searching Izzy's face for an answer.

"All of Pastor Michaels' classes and sermons have been recorded to help those of us who work on Sunday." Marty took a sip of water. "I know just where to find them. Let's watch one of his recent classes we haven't seen, as soon as we finish eating."

Izzy reached over for a hug from Marty, then squeezed Aunt Anna's hand. "Thanks, I love you both."

After supper, everyone gathered in the living room to listen to what Pastor Michaels had to say about the identity of the Beast.

Marty found a message entitled "Who is the Beast?" and put it on.

Pastor Michaels, looking a little heavier than before, spoke. "Of course, we know from Revelation 13:17-18 that the mark is the name of the beast or the number of his name. I understand the Chaldeans, or forefathers of present-day Iraqis, assigned numbers to names based upon the date of their birth. So that it is conceivable that the same name can have a different number for different birth dates, and even different times of birth. Now we have been following developments with His Highness Bandar of the WCEP. This is the man who suffered a fatal wound and miraculously survived. And he also signed a contract with ten nations of the world for a seven-year period. Under his regime the Jewish temple is being rebuilt, and soon will be dedicated. So, this evidence is overwhelming that the beast coming out of the sea in Revelation 13 is, in fact, Mr. B. Now Chaldean and Chinese numerology experts have assigned a number to His Highness Bandar's name—666. Read it for yourself from Revelation 13:18—*This calls for wisdom, let the one who has understanding calculate the number of the beast, for it is the number of a man, and his number is 666.'*

Pastor Michaels continued, "I am not a man with understanding when it comes to calculating numbers. As a matter of fact, as a Christian I shy away from numerology just as I don't dabble with astrology. These studies may lead us into the occult. Yet we know that God used experts who watched the stars to follow a star in search of the newborn King of the Jews. So friends, Brothers and Sisters, leave it to the people with understanding—they have identified Mr. B as the man whose name has the number 666. So I beg you, trust in your God to be with you and save you in times of trouble; someday He will come to take you home to Himself—either through the rapture or through death. Don't fear. Trust in Him. Run from receiving the mark of the beast. I want to see each of you in Heaven someday. Those who receive the mark seal their fate to the fires of hell, forever cut off from the love of God. But those who trust in Christ have a place prepared in heaven for them. May the peace of God which passes all understanding bless and keep you."

Izzy looked into Marty's and Aunt Anna's expectant faces. *I still don't like it, but I can't disappoint them.* "Yep. He's the Beast, no doubt about it. Thank you for making me face reality." She yawned and stretched, looking at her watch. "Oh, my goodness, I'm exhausted, and tomorrow Marty and I need to check in to work to transition to the ten-day workweek. I don't know how we're going to do it."

15. PREPARATIONS, FOR WHAT?

"Whew! I'm beat." Marty sat down to the roast pork Izzy had put in the crockpot before going to school that morning. "Mm, mm. I love your roast." He leaned over to kiss Izzy on the cheek she offered. "Roast pork, carrots and onions, with gravy over rice. It's got to be my favorite."

"Yeah, like Mom used to make. It sure is easy to fix, and nice to come home to. This is only the seventh day of our ten-day week, and I'm feeling a little ragged." Izzy stretched and joined Marty and Aunt Anna at the table.

"For this food, we give you thanks, O Lord. Strengthen our bodies, and give us grace to keep going, especially the young'uns." Aunt Anna squeezed the hands of the two 'young'uns' at her table. "I pray for you every day, for grace to keep going. I can tell this ten-day workweek isn't easy."

"Thanks lots, Aunt Anna. That means a lot. We just hate leaving you here alone. So grateful for your friends who drop by." Marty took a big bite of the roast with carrots. "Hmm. That's tasty!"

"Marty, how is it at the university for you? You seem to have non-stop meetings with everybody on campus." Izzy fingered the simple gold band on Marty's left hand.

"Well, not quite everybody. But there is the Health Education Department, my grad assistants, and the grad students assigned to me." He snarfed down a buttery hot roll. "And how about you, Sweetheart?" Marty could hardly get the words out.

Izzy smiled and shook her head. "Who taught you manners, Marty Goldstein?"

"You did," he accused.

"Well, today I read from *The Berenstain Bears Forget Their Manners*. I'll have to check it out for you." She gave him a little shove.

"I got a sweet message from Uncle Amos today. When we've finished eating, I'll read it to you all." Marty took his phone out and laid it on the table.

After the dishes were cleared and the table cleaned, Marty, Izzy and Aunt Anna gathered there again. Marty picked up his phone and sat down, pushing back from the table to rest his foot on his knee. He leaned back and started reading. "Dear Marty, Izzy, and Aunt Anna. The day for the dedication of the new temple is almost here. I must say the whole family is counting the days to your coming. It's just another month away. We trust that all your papers are in order, and your bags ready for packing."

Izzy asked, "Do we need a visa? What kind of papers do we need to process?"

Marty scratched his head. "None that I know of. Thankfully, we won't need the mark to fly but will almost as soon as we get back."

"That's kind of scary." *I'm petrified.* Izzy pulled her knees up to her chest, but realized she couldn't hold that pose for long and put her feet back on the floor.

"To continue." Marty cleared his throat. "Our family is to present the grain offering as part of the dedication ceremony at the temple. And so we took young Benjie out to a traditional threshing floor to give him a new experience. There I taught him how I used to thresh grain for my parents when I was a youngster. After a few failed attempts, I found the rhythm for tossing the grain in front of the fan. But I don't think I'll do that again. It was quite a tedious process picking the chaff from our clothes later. Here is a picture of Benjie."

Marty shared the pic with Izzy and Aunt Anna, and they both burst out laughing.

Benjie, chubby cheeks beaming with his grin, looked like a scarecrow, standing with a pitchfork in his hand in front of a pile of grain.

"There's more," said Marty holding up his finger as he continued reading. "Abigail and I were so proud of the children, asking for a part in presenting our sacrifice. They even wanted to contribute toward the cost. What a blessing it is to see that they have grateful hearts. So Mama and I will present one basket of grain, and Daniel another. Our Hannah will carry a crystalline cruet of oil, and, last but not least, Benjie will present the salt. Daniel thought that very appropriate as he said to his brother, 'Benjie, you always add spice to our lives!'"

Everybody chuckled. Then Marty shared a photo of the whole family holding their gifts lined up before their stucco home. Uncle Asher wore his robes with tassels and a large headdress. The boys wore robes and yarmulkes. Abigail and her daughter wore simple dresses to the knees.

"So lovely," said Aunt Anna, wiping away a tear.

Oh dear, she knows she won't be coming with us. Izzy looked up to Marty for support.

"Aunt Anna, I really expected you to be coming with us this trip." Marty put his hands on Anna's shoulders and gave a gentle massage.

Izzy lightly rubbed her elbow. *You are much bonier than*

you used to be, Dear. "Aunt Anna, it kills me to be leaving you here. The doctor…"

"Now you two don't have to worry about me. I'll be alright. My friends from the Ladies' Fellowship are going to drop by every day for a time of Bible Places and Customs. I have told them your itinerary, and the young'uns are preparing slides and activities to help me follow what you're doing. I'm looking forward to it. And the day of the dedication, Pastor Michaels will come with the gang and we will share a Sader feast, remembering the Passover and celebrating Christ's sacrifice for us."

"Wow. I almost feel like we're the ones who will be missing out." Izzy gave her aunt a long hug. *Aunt Anna, two more weeks, and we'll be flying. We'll see you when we get back. Surely, we'll get back. If it weren't for the family, we would be running away from the beast, not toward him.*

One by one, people around Marty and Izzy got the branding of His Highness Bandar. It appeared as a slight rise in their skin, either on their foreheads, or on their right hands.

"Does it hurt?" Izzy asked Miss Karen, the third-grade teacher.

"Well, itches a little. But it's not too bad." Miss Karen looked like a model, thin and shapely. She held out her hand to let Izzy inspect her mark. Her nails were dazzling. "What about you? Are you going to get it? The deadline is coming up fast, you know."

Izzy looked around. Many eyes were upon her. "I, um, am aware. My husband won't get the mark. I…I'm with him."

"Are you all Jesus freaks? Do you expect the rest of us to go to hell?" Mr. Bart, the fifth-grade teacher addressed her from a table on the other side of the room.

"What? What are you saying?" asked a young P.E. teacher, Mr. Arnez.

"Yeah! You didn't know?" said Mr. Bart. "Christians believe that anyone who receives the branding of Mr. B— fine, law-abiding individuals—will go to hell. Ha! It's unbelievable! So egocentric."

I do not want to have this conversation. Izzy looked up into the confused face of Mr. Arnez. She noticed the red mark on his forehead, and her heart sank. "Excuse me, I'm sorry. But I've got to get to class." She escaped to her classroom and had a good cry before her students returned.

On another day, the new principal, Mrs. McClean, sat down next to Izzy.

"Mrs. Goldstein, I notice that you have not yet received the branding. You will need to do that as soon as possible to keep your job here at Overbrook."

Izzy swallowed her food, grasping for words. She cleared her throat and took a sip of water, her face drained of color. "I, uh, of course. I understand. It would be difficult for you to pay me." She forced a smile.

"Do you plan on complying soon? You just have a few weeks." The principal peered intently at Izzy through gold-rimmed glasses, her dirty-blonde hair frizzing around her face like puppy ears.

"We are planning a trip for the dedication of the temple in another two weeks. I…"

"No, no you're not. Didn't you get the notice that your request for vacation time was denied?" Mrs. McClean gently touched Izzy's arm.

"What?" Fear tightened Izzy's throat. "How can this be? We have had our tickets forever. I thought this was on the calendar over a year ago."

"Ms. Redding had priority over you in the scheduling, we

discovered. She already has tenure. Tenured teachers have the first choice. I'm sorry. There're just not enough substitute teachers to go around."

Izzy blinked back tears; she was incredulous. *I hate Jamie. If it weren't for her, I'd already be tenured. I came into the system a year before Ms. Redding!*

Izzy lay back, eyes closed, clasping Marty's hand in hers, counting back through the whirlwind of activity that had landed them on the plane bound for Israel. They had just taken off, and the pilot turned off the seatbelt sign. A stewardess came by with towelettes for their hands.

"It was so hard saying good-bye to Aunt Anna. She had hoped she could fly with us, but the doctor said, 'No.'" Izzy turned her head on the pillow in Marty's direction.

"Yes, it did not seem right leaving her there. She has been our guide through the Bible these many months. I would have loved pushing her through the streets of Jerusalem." Marty cupped Izzy's hand in his.

"Me, too! Do you think she will be okay? It is so nice her friends volunteered to take care of her while we are away and even lead her on a daily trip to Israel via power point." Izzy chuckled and shook her head. "Could you believe her last words to us?"

"See you here, there, or in the air!" Marty laughed.

"I sure am counting on seeing her there when we return." *How can the rapture possibly happen? It seems so unreal.*

Marty sat up and brought Izzy's hand up to his lips. "I am sorry I have not done a better job of managing our time together these weeks and months. It has been all I could do to dig myself out from the pile of papers and exams produced over the ten-day weeks. That, and keeping hours for my students as well as for the department."

Izzy nodded her head. "Hey, I know a teacher's work is never done! Let's put that all behind us and soak up the moments together this trip. I almost didn't make it!"

"It's a miracle we could both keep this vacation time together. The powers that be seemed determined to deny your travels…"

"All because they refused to give me tenure over my involvement in the gender education debacle. Therefore, I did not have seniority when it came to taking time off." Izzy held her head in her hands.

Marty's dimples appeared, and his eyes twinkled. "But God heard our cry for help. One dark night, while all the students slept, not a creature was stirring—"

"Not even a mouse!" Izzy sat forward with anticipation.

"When out on the lawn there arose such a clatter, I arose from my bed to see what was the matter." Marty smiled as he recalled the events of that fateful night when a meteor went down with a burst of light, landing in the woods just beyond the playground at Izzy's school. "And wouldn't you know that the windows all shattered? School closed for repairs, so the teachers could scatter." Marty wriggled his fingers in the air, representing the missing teachers.

The muffled quietness of the plane cabin, Marty's animation and joy after the rush and bother of boarding, made Izzy just want to laugh out loud and snuggle under Marty's arm. *I cannot believe I am here, safe and sound, enjoying these moments together. Well, God, you did do this one right. I had almost given up believing when they nixed my travel plans for someone with seniority—someone who entered the system after I did.* Izzy frowned.

"Hey, why the long face?" Marty's thumb swiped up at the corner of Izzy's mouth.

"Just remembering disappointments along the way. I

almost lost my faith in God altogether! The ten-day week had already left me frazzled, and you were almost nowhere to be found. You wouldn't even answer your phone the day I got the news!" Izzy searched for a tissue in her pocket. *I didn't know I had any more tears left!* "Ah, no. No more of this pity party. The sad face must go. We have this time together, so let's not spoil it with tears, Izzy Goldstein!" She leaned over to receive Marty's embrace, wishing this feeling of security would never end.

"Yes, it has been a crazy time. Life was busy before Mr. B ordered the ten-day week. By messing with everyone's internal clock, and robbing us of rest and recreation, the human race seems more short-tempered and aloof. I really appreciate Pastor Michaels' being proactive and maintaining a regular routine of Sunday church—even though we had to add it to our workday."

"Hmm. Routines are what make the world go round. Which is why I find it unnerving that the deadline for receiving Mr. B's branding is here in just two weeks. No more life as usual. Life would be so much easier if we could just bend and bow with the forces that be.

"I know God will show us the way. Try not to worry." Marty leaned over and kissed Izzy's head, drawing her close with his hug.

The screens before them flickered on, showing crowds of people moving through the gates of Jerusalem. CBS's broadcasters—Dan and Val—bantered back and forth.

> DAN: The dedication of this new temple has drawn people from all over the globe.

> VAL: That's right, Dan. His Highness B's newly commissioned World Order for Peace troops can be seen all over the city keeping order.

DAN: There are some tensions in the air over the speculation that the Jews want to bring back animal sacrifices. Quite a few animal rights activists are carrying placards with sayings like, "PEACE BUT NOT AT THEIR EXPENSE" and "THEIR BLOOD CRIES OUT." So what is the significance of animal sacrifice in temple worship for the Jews?

VAL: I believe the blood was used for cleansing and to denote forgiveness of sins. Back in history, Jewish people would bring lambs and pigeons to the priest to atone for their sins. That practice ended with the destruction of the temple in 70 AD.

DAN: Well, then, that was the end of an era. Does God still require bloody sacrifice?

VAL: We shall see. The clock is ticking down to the dedication of this third of the Jewish temples. Quite an elaborate program is planned.

DAN: Will we see His Highness B and Vice Premier Hamaz come and bless the whole affair?

VAL: I saw them both visiting with the crowds earlier today. Mr. Hamaz, also known as The Prophet, even healed some of the sick. I believe the anticipation is high. After all, without His Highness's finesse, this temple would not be standing today.

DAN: Truly, Val, this temple stands as a testament to Mr. B's honor and brilliance. He has been a broker for peace and a whole new world order.

Marty leaned over and whispered into Izzy's ear. "Let's not forget we only came to celebrate with Uncle Amos and his family for doing their part in the dedication of their long-awaited temple."

"That's right. Stay out of politics. And hope for no surprises. Let's just enjoy ourselves. I can't wait to meet Uncle Amos' family, finally!"

16. <u>LESSONS AND SURPRISES</u>

Benjie's pudgy soft hand held Izzy's. His teeth gleamed as he proudly led his cousin Izzy and pointed to the huge white marble building with golden doors across the street. "Look, isn't it magnificent?"

"That it is! You must be very excited about the dedication ceremony. I am so glad Marty and I could be here to help you celebrate." Izzy had to blink at the brightness of the morning sun reflected from the massive golden doors and towering white walls. She grabbed her sunglasses from the purse slung over her shoulder.

"So, this is the east gate only?" Izzy craned her neck to take in the width of the whole compound they called the temple square.

Uncle Amos wearing a light-gray suit and Abigail wearing a modest light blue dress and scarf led the way with Marty. Izzy happily took Benjie's hand when he offered it. Daniel and Hannah followed close behind, keeping an eye on Benjie and an ear open for questions.

"This gate faces east, and will stay shut until the Messiah comes," volunteered Daniel.

"Oh? His second coming?" Marty asked, putting his hand on Daniel's shoulder.

"I only know that Ezekiel the prophet says that the eastern gate will remain closed until our Messiah comes in victory." Daniel squinted and looked up at Marty.

"This is something I will have to explore more. Speaking of exploring I would love to walk where Jesus walked while here in Jerusalem." Marty turned around to look for Izzy and laughed to see her with her student in tow. "I would say we came to the right place! Are you happy?"

"Yes." Benjie nodded vigorously, a big smile lighting up his face.

"Absolutely!" Izzy tousled Benjie's hair.

"Just the size of the gates to the compound makes it all very impressive. I can't wait to get inside. Will we be allowed in tomorrow during the ceremony?" Marty looked to Daniel.

"Papa got you tickets." Daniel nodded proudly. "Our family is part of the privileged few who will be allowed in tomorrow—only three thousand will participate in the ceremony. After tomorrow, about twelve thousand pilgrims will be allowed onto the temple square daily, except for the Sabbath."

"That's right." Uncle Asher turned to join their conversation. "Pilgrims will progress through the North gate, and will depart by way of the South gate, or vice versa. They will be allowed access to the outer court, and to make offerings of grain or oil—but no animal sacrifices. Instead, dining rooms line the outer court, providing for pilgrims to share meals together before departing."

"I heard you mention the Sabbath. Aren't you all affected by the ten-day week?" Marty stood with his hands on his hips. Izzy smiled to see nine-year-old Benjie take the same stance.

"Regardless of the ten-day week, we continue to observe the Sabbath." Amos Asher answered so quietly that Izzy strained to hear.

Izzy glanced up at Marty, who said, "I respect your convictions. So far, Mr. B, also, respects the nation's boundaries?"

"So far."

That afternoon, Uncle Amos arranged for a Christian Arab to guide his guests on a tour of Jerusalem. "I am afraid you won't have time for a broader tour of the Holy Lands this time." He talked with Marty and Izzy as they gathered at the front door.

"That's fine. I just want to spend some time with Yeshua Ha Mashiach—or Jesus the Anointed One, my messiah— walking the roads he walked. Thank you for arranging this."

"My pleasure." Uncle Amos sighed, looking haggard. "I would join you, but I need to be in the office today. Tomorrow is a big day."

Their guide arrived, tan, clean cut, wearing sunglasses and dressed in a beige polo shirt, tan pants, and running shoes. "My name is Andrew. Like Andrew in the Bible, I like to bring people to the Savior. I trust your tour of Jerusalem will bring you closer to Jesus today."

"Thank you, Andrew. Will we be driving today, or walking?" Marty asked, putting his hand on Andrew's shoulder.

"We only have time for a walking tour."

"Ah, excellent." Izzy ran in place and stretched. "I would love to walk the streets of Old Jerusalem!"

"Well then, may I lead us in prayer?" Marty stepped back and clasped his hands together. Then he looked at Izzy, winked, and bowed to pray as they stood in the walkway before the Asher home. The sun warmed the little trio, and Izzy removed her sweater before Marty could say, "Amen."

Andrew led them from municipal Jerusalem to the Jaffa Gate. "I am sure you will want to visit the Western Wall, also known as the Wailing Wall. That is part of the remains of the second temple."

"Yes, I have some memories as a naughty little boy—a little younger than Benjie, maybe five years old—at the Wailing Wall." Marty smiled.

"Your folks brought you back for a visit? So, what kind of memories did you make?" Izzy grabbed his hand and grinned.

"Oh, I loved to dig out the prayers already stuffed in the crevices and replacing them with pictures I had drawn of my dream home."

"Your dream home?" Izzy cocked her head, skipping to keep up with Andrew and Marty.

"Yes, up to that point, I had grown up in the back of the clinic on the mission compound. Other kids lived in spacious homes with gardens and trampolines in the yard. But Mom and Dad liked it simple. Then one day, I got my dream home, in Chicago."

"And that's where you grew up for a while with Uncle Asher."

"Exactly." Marty winked, brushing his hair with his hand.

"Would you like to pray at the Wailing Wall, or leave a prayer?" Andrew asked.

"No, please take us to the Church of the Holy Sepulcher. I understand that it houses the place where Jesus was nailed on the cross, as well as the cave where he was buried."

"I will take you there, but it is bound to be very busy now. How about I lead you to the Garden of Gethsemane on the Mount of Olives, where Jesus went to pray before he was betrayed? Then we will walk back by the Via Dolorosa— The Way of the Cross—to the Church of the Holy Sepulcher at closing time, when the crowds lessen."

Marty took both of Izzy's hands in his. "Sound like a good plan?" He brushed blonde hair back behind her ear. "You're beautiful, Izzy. I hope you enjoy this pilgrimage as much as I do."

"Oh, totally! With you, wouldn't miss it." She gave him a peck on the cheek.

Andrew led them at a quick clip. At the Garden of Gethsemane, they discovered a church with a huge boulder cordoned off and kneeling pads provided for prayer. Izzy left Marty there and meandered around the garden. When Marty emerged, he pulled his journal out and found a bench for collecting his thoughts. They sat another ten minutes until Andrew coughed, and said, "The sun will be setting, so we had best follow the path Jesus took with his cross."

Marty finished the sentence he was writing, pulled the ribbon into place, and closed the book and returned it to his inner coat pocket.

"My mom used to say, 'A penny for your thoughts?' Do you want to share your experience?" Izzy hooked elbows with Marty and followed Andrew through the lane known for Jesus's final trek.

"When the soldiers came with Judas to capture Jesus at the Garden of Gethsemane, the first place they took him on the Via Dolorosa, or Way of Sorrow, was the high priest's house. There the soldiers mocked, blindfolded and struck him, asking, 'Who hit you?' There were many false witnesses to accuse him, but finally it was his own words which condemned him before the Jewish Council." Andrew relished his role as tour guide.

So Marty whispered in Izzy's ear, "Let's listen for now, and share later," kissing her on the cheek as he pulled away.

"Ah, excuse me, Andrew. What did Jesus say which condemned him?" Marty's brow knit in interest.

"He said, 'From now on the Son of Man shall be seated

at the right hand of God.' And when they asked him if he was the Son of God, he did not deny it, but said, 'You say that I am.'"

Andrew continued speaking. "The Jewish priests and scribes then took Jesus to Pilate's palace, and the judgment seat. Today, it is a school, but the stone courtyard is the same place Jesus was tried. There they mocked him again, dressing him in a purple robe, pressing a crown of thorns into his scalp, spitting in his face and plucking his beard. At first Pilate, the governor, declared him innocent. But the Jewish leaders roused the crowd against hm. They cried out, 'Crucify him. Crucify him.' So Pilate had him flogged, giving him thirty-nine lashes using leather strips with sharp stones and shards attached. So his body became a mass of lacerations and blood. Then the governor washed his hands of the matter, saying he found no fault in him. And the mob replied, 'Let his blood be on us and our children.'

Marty pointed to himself, his eyes filling with tears and his mouth quivering, and whispered to Izzy. "That's me. We Jews sent Jesus to the cross. Yeshua, I am so sorry."

Andrew kept forging ahead. "So, then Jesus was led out through these narrow streets we are walking today. Tradition says he fell three times. The first time, the soldiers forced a traveler called Simon the Cyrene to carry Jesus' cross for him, because he no longer had the strength. It is no wonder. From his capture at the Garden to the cross at Golgotha eighteen hours had elapsed. The day before, Jesus had not slept. The flogging left his skin raw and bleeding; he'd lost a lot of blood."

Izzy and Marty walked briskly to keep up with Andrew through narrow cobblestone streets lined with wares, and up and down steps. They did not talk much, but listened, and thought.

Jesus suffered so much here. He was God who became

man for us and suffered and died. So awful. Izzy walked behind Marty and wondered if he walked a little more bent over as he walked the path that Jesus walked.

Finally, Andrew brought them to the Church of the Sepulcher. "Here Roman soldiers stripped Jesus and nailed him to a cross. There were three who died that day by crucifixion—Jesus was nailed between two thieves. One thief asked Jesus to remember him when he got into his kingdom; Jesus promised him, 'Today you will be with me in Paradise.' When Jesus died, the sky grew dark in the middle of the day, and a mighty earthquake broke apart the rocks you see here." They followed Andrew to the upper floor of the Church, where a large white stone lay on display, cracked in two. "The veil in the temple, also split in two, from top to bottom, like the finger of God had cut a way for us sinners to come to him in the Holy of Holies."

"So powerful!" said Marty to Andrew as he shook his hand at the door of the Ashers' home much later. "You gave us a very meaningful experience, actually walking where Jesus walked. I feel a bit speechless right now."

"Yes, absolutely, thank you. I will always remember this." Izzy wiped away tears. "You are a wonderful tour guide."

Once indoors, Marty and Izzy knew that everyone was already in bed preparing for the dedication the next day. Marty suggested they each share just one of the significant lessons they learned that day. They sat down on the sofa in the living room.

"My feet are sore." Izzy took her shoes off and rubbed her feet. Seeing the disappointment in Marty's face, she added, "That's not my significant lesson. Sorry." Izzy broke into a wide smile and hugged his arm.

"Ok, I'll share mine first." Marty began. "The judgment seat at Pilate's castle really gripped me. That's where they flogged Jesus, giving him thirty-nine stripes which tore away his flesh. He did that for me." Marty's eyes shone in the low light. "And he did that for you. And I'm so glad he did." Marty wiped away a tear. "And yours?"

"The fact that Jesus became so weak that they had to force a passerby to carry his cross, that really struck me. Trying to wrap my mind around God becoming a weak human being so that we could know him."

Marty's smile grew wider as he listened to his wife. Then they both agreed it was time to sleep.

Izzy arose with the sunshine and put on the special outfit she had prepared for the occasion. Marty woke up and whistled at her picture-perfect presentation of white on white with black accents in her belt, shoes, and hat. "You are just so easy to please," she said as she gave him a kiss.

As Amos and family gathered for breakfast, they held hands to pray and encouraged Izzy and Marty to join in. "Why don't you ask the blessing, Marty?"

"I'd be honored." Marty bowed his head and closed his eyes.

Seconds passed by. Izzy opened her eyes and caught Marty wiping away a tear. She mouthed, "You, okay?"

Marty nodded. Then he closed his eyes. "Almighty God and Father, may your presence bless this day of dedication of the temple. Hasten the day of our Messiah's coming to bring his kingdom and peace to earth. Amen."

Everyone responded with a loud "Amen!"

The excitement in the crowd was palpable as they headed to the ceremony. Izzy held onto Marty's hand so as not to lose him in the crowd. They made their way to the stands opposite the outer Northern Gate of the temple square. "Do they expect twelve thousand pilgrims today? Because I think they are already here." Izzy yelled to make herself heard.

"Not until after the dedication ceremony. How is it that you and I should be so blessed to witness this historical moment?" Marty put his arm around Izzy as he tried to keep pace with Uncle Amos and the family.

Finally situated in the bleachers, Izzy noticed that the Asher family sat with others behind a cloth-covered table. Their grain, oil, and salt sat on the table before them. Benjie noticed her gaze and waved, his face all lit up with a smile. *Shine, Benjie, shine!* Izzy gave him a thumbs-up.

Marty touched Izzy's arm and nodded toward the opposite end of the platform; she noticed a ramp going to the outer Northern Gate of the temple square. His Highness B and The Prophet stood there for opening remarks. Their son, Richard, sat with them, his gaze focused on his hands in his lap. *I wonder what it is like for him? Poor boy.* Izzy smoothed out her skirt and reached for Marty's hand.

Rabbi Arthur Shmuel—dressed in the dark robes of the Hassidic Jews—introduced their honored guests and benefactors. "Thanks to the encouragement and support of His Highness Bandar, Premier of the World Order for Peace, this day has become a reality. Your Highness."

Premier Bandar came to the podium with great applause from the audience. Clearing his throat, he said, "Father Abraham deserves the applause, giving this great planet many nations, most of whom have sworn their allegiance to World Order for Peace." He looked to the Jewish dignitaries. "I'm confident we can count on your allegiance. As you offer prayers in this place, remember me. Thank you."

Izzy noticed Amos cast a worried look at Abigail. *How shall they ever receive the mark?*

Rabbi Schmuel dove right into the program. "Blessed are you, Lord our God, king of the universe, who has brought us to this occasion…"

The dedication of the temple proceeded with the Torah reading, and singing, and even dancing with the Torah and the blowing of the shofar. The Asher family came forward to retrieve their gifts for the offering and proceeded through the Northern Gate to the outer court within. Izzy sat up with anticipation, watching the big screens placed at the gate to see what would happen inside. Izzy caught a glimpse of each member of the family as they placed their gifts on the altar, Benjie adding an extra pat to his container of salt with obvious pleasure.

Many prayers were said for the watching world. "O LORD, for those in authority in every place we pray for wisdom and love to guide their decisions. O LORD, hear our prayer. For those affected by world disasters, have mercy upon them, and guide them into safety and peace. O LORD, hear our prayer…"

Izzy grew restless and opened her eyes. In that moment she caught the icy stares of Mr. B and The Prophet, faces raised, their fists clinched. Their son, Richard, lay in a fetal position at their feet. Izzy's heart stopped. *What do they see? Who do they see? That poor child, is he in trouble?* Izzy looked around to see if anyone else noticed. Marty's head was still bowed in prayer.

Izzy tugged on Marty's hand and glanced back toward the mysterious family.

They were gone!

17. <u>DISAPPEARING ACT</u>

Marty opened his eyes and seeing the fear in Izzy's eyes, immediately put his arms around her and whispered, "What's wrong? You look like you saw a ghost!"

Izzy looked up into her husband's face, then riveted her head to point toward the scary spot. To her surprise, Izzy saw His Highness, The Prophet, and Richard sitting as if nothing had happened! *Am I seeing things?*

"I, I, I don't know. Maybe I did see a ghost. I opened my eyes during prayers because I felt restless, and immediately saw a hateful, evil look on both Mr. B and The Prophet. It made my heart stop. And their son lay on the ground at their feet, in a fetal position. I tried to get your attention, and then they were gone. Vanished! B-but now, there they are! How could that be?"

By this time, Amos and Abigail glanced over toward the bleachers to see what was going on. They saw Marty hugging Izzy's head to his chest. Marty, not wanting to disrupt, pointed to the sun and made motions to escort Izzy out.

He whispered to Izzy, "I'm taking you out of this sun. Let's get you someplace where we can talk. You okay to walk?"

"Hm-mmm. Yeah, get me out of here." She looked up at Marty and smiled weakly.

When Marty and Izzy stepped down from the bleachers, they saw Amos with Abigail and their three children waiting for them.

"Follow us," said Uncle Amos.

The little family wound their way beyond the bleachers, then down into a shaded alley. There they found a pizza shop and sat down together.

"I told them we needed covered bleachers. But with fall weather coming on, my recommendation went ignored. I am so sorry about your discomfort, Izzy. Are you okay? Quick, let me order a drink for you."

"No, no, you all don't understand." Izzy felt faint. She closed her eyes and regrouped her thoughts. "I saw Mr. B and The Prophet with hateful faces looking at something ahead of them. They were scowling. And, and, their son lay at their feet, in a fetal position. Something terrible was going on. I know it! But then, they disappeared." Izzy grabbed the cup of water brought by the server and gulped it down. *Am I going crazy?*

"It could very well be heat stroke, for both you and the boy. Try not to worry about it. Let's get you home where you can rest." Abigail spoke, looking up into her husband's face.

"Oh, but we can take a taxi back to your house. This is your chance! Your family should be among the first to tour the newly built temple. Please, let us just take a taxi home."

"We could not do that, Miss Izzy. We will take care of you." Benjie had Izzy's hand in his, and he was rubbing it back and forth, looking pensively into Izzy's face with big brown eyes.

Izzy broke into a grin, and everybody laughed.

That night the Ashers and the Goldsteins talked around

the dinner table until late. "This has been a gift from God, being able to spend this time together. Now may God bless and keep each one. These children need to go to school tomorrow." Benjie let out a groan. "And you two have an early-morning flight, correct?" Amos stood at his place at the table, folded his hands on his belly and looked fondly at his family.

"So sad, it is time to go. It was lovely. Thank you for your hospitality." Izzy gave Uncle Amos and Aunt Abigail big hugs. Then Benjie, Hannah, and even Daniel lined up for their hugs.

Within five hours, Izzy and Marty crept to the front door with their luggage. Both Amos and Abigail were there to see them off in the taxi they had called.

"Marty, thank you for sharing your relationship with Yeshua. You have given us much food for thought. We certainly do not want to miss the rapture."

"And neither do you want to receive the mark!"

"Very well. Shalom!" Uncle Amos gingerly closed the door to the taxi.

"Do you think, Marty, peace is possible anymore?" Izzy held tightly to her husband's arm and rested her head there.

The taxi pulled away from the curb, as Marty pulled away from Izzy to look into her eyes.

"Sweetheart, I have peace in my heart, even though Jesus has not yet come for us, and the Beast's deadline is right around the corner. I trust him. He will take care of us." Then Marty pulled Izzy into a hug.

"Oh, Marty, I hope so. It's just hard to anticipate what life will be like when we step off the plane."

It started with a wail of despair which awakened Izzy from her fitful sleep on the airplane. Pushing herself to a sitting position from her perch on Marty's shoulder, Izzy gasped for air and looked around.

A distraught woman, blonde hair pulled back in a ponytail, face flushed, stood holding a bunch of clothes to her chest. "My husband, my husband is gone! What is going on? Steve! Steve! Where are you?" She buried her face in the pile of clothes—some dark jeans, a leather belt, and a red plaid flannel shirt.

Then another scream went up. "Laura! My Laura, what is happening?" An elderly man moaned from a few rows back.

Marty! Has it happened? Did Jesus really come? Izzy turned to grab Marty's hand. *Oh, my God! Where is Marty? My heart, oh, this can't be happening!* There on the seat were her dear husband's clothes—her favorite yellow polo shirt and dark tan khaki pants.

Suddenly an announcement came from the bridge. "This is lead flight attendant Candice. There is a situation on board which will require everyone's cooperation and patience. If you are traveling with someone who has disappeared, please push the service button, and the crew will come to take your report. For the safety of this flight, and for your own safety, please do not wander around the cabin looking for your loved one. Please, unless you need to use the restroom, please remain seated. Thank you for your cooperation."

Marty! You can't be gone! You can't be! Izzy pushed her fists into her eyes. Tears drenched her hands and sleeves.

"Excuse me, Miss. Did you lose someone?" A friendly voice spoke beside her. Izzy looked up to the stewardess who put her hand gently on Izzy's shoulder and leaned over in concern.

"I, I, don't know. But here are my husband's clothes." Izzy gathered them up and hugged them to her chest.

"And these, do these also belong to him?" Marty's overcoat and briefcase were in the overhead bin. "The airline will do everything we can to find your loved one. Our records show his name is Mr. Martin Goldstein. Is that correct?" The stewardess finished her records for Marty and prepared to move on to another panicking passenger. She put her hand on Izzy's shoulder and said, "Mrs. Goldstein, if I can get you anything, please let me know."

Izzy nodded numbly and closed her eyes as she sank back into her seat for a fitful sleep. Once on the ground, Izzy looked at her phone, where she saw a text from Uncle Amos.

AMOS: Dear Marty and Izzy, Our family almost lost Benjie today, but then the whole world has lost countless souls, I believe, to the rapture. Because you shared your faith in Yeshua with us, hoping that we would not miss the rapture, we regret not receiving him as soon as we heard of his great salvation. And I hope that you are no longer here to receive this message, but just in case—before I lie down to sleep—I write.

When Benjie was on his way to school, he heard a beautiful song in the air—a beautiful chord as from an acapella choir. He said he stood still to listen and locate the source, when the blow torch fell directly before him! How we thank God for that mysterious song which saved his sweet soul! Our family all bowed our heads tonight in gratitude for God's great love and mercy.

God spared our son's life today. But there is a Son who was pierced for us, one whom we as a nation have despised—Yeshua HaMashiach. How I wish we had prayed with you to receive him into our hearts. Today Hannah's friend, Amelia, and Abigail's two friends, Paula and May disappeared, their clothes left in a heap where they were. They were all Christian, so Jesus took them. Today we heard loud booms and crashes on every side. I ran out, and had to shield my eyes, the sky was so bright. And there, in the clouds, I saw the form of one sitting on a throne, his pierced hands raised in blessing over the city. I could not shake the warmth in his eyes for me. Startled, I dropped to my knees. Could this be the Messiah? When I looked up again, he was gone.

I did not see him again, but I felt his presence with me. The bedlam around demanded my attention; as I turned to respond to the cries around me, I discovered the Lord sent his helpers!

There were young men out in the crowd, all dressed in jeans and flannel shirts, handsome and strong, helping the injured and forlorn. One, named Reuben, sat me down on a bench and shared how he and his comrades—sent by Yeshua—came to teach us of our Messiah and his ways, but that time was short. So all of Jerusalem today gathered with them in homes and offices, shops and parks, reading through the New Testament. Even though we missed the rapture we cling to this hope from John 3:16-- God so loved the world that he gave his only Son, that whoever believes in him should not perish, but have everlasting life!

Please respond if you are still with us.
Shalom.--Uncle Amos

Izzy typed a quick message back.

IZZY: Marty is gone, and I just landed at the airport. I don't understand why I got left behind. I thought I was a believer. Now, I don't know. Please keep in touch. It's just that in a few more days we will lose service if we don't have the mark. I love you ALL! –Izzy

Izzy moved and looked like a zombie all the way home from the airport. Everyone in the Philadelphia International Airport seemed equally dysfunctional. Service personnel were missing. People cried and shouted. Headlines in the Inquirer said, "UFOs Spotted Before Grand Abduction!" and "Millions Missing!"

Do I dare leave my checked bag? I only want to go home and check on Aunt Anna. But she is certainly GONE. Izzy called, but there was no answer. An hour later, she had one huge suitcase—full of keepsakes and souvenirs—and two carry-ons piled up on an airport cart, heading toward her car parked in the long-term parking lot. Getting there required a shuttle ride, which took another hour and a half! She no longer cared what she looked like. Tears washed down her cheeks in sheets as a question bore into her mind. *Why did I get left behind?*

Marty, I feel so alone, and so extremely sad. Izzy contemplated not driving home because of the snake of cars she needed to wait for just to get out of the parking lot! *But I need to go home to check on Aunt Anna.* Izzy moaned as she saw one car pile-up after another pushed over to the side of freeway I-95. In many places all the traffic funneled down into one or two lanes. Broken glass and clothing littered the landscape. Some cars had careened over barriers into on-coming traffic, exploding on impact or flipping and landing upside down, wheels up. Izzy closed her eyes so many times trying to avoid seeing human carnage. Four hours later when she finally reached Wynnefield, and home, Izzy felt shell-shocked.

She turned off the key in the ignition and leaned back, balling. *Oh God, I cannot do this! Marty, I need you so much. I miss you so much.* She struggled to open her door, and stand up in front of her home, keys dangling in one hand.

Aunt Anna? Will I find you? Izzy decided to leave her luggage in the car, and stumbled toward her home, Aunt Anna's home—hers and Marty's home.

Her hands trembled as she turned the key in the door. Izzy stopped breathing as she pushed open the door and quickly flipped on the lights. The chimes of the clock sounded nine. *Home. Aunt Anna?*

Izzy looked over to the recliners. No Anna. The kitchen table held an open Bible—Aunt Anna's Bible. Her glasses rested on the open pages. Izzy peered at the print, wishing that Aunt Anna were there to give her a shoulder massage and a big hug. "God is love" written in Anna's hand jumped out from the top margin. *God does not love me.* A sharp pain jabbed at Izzy's broken heart.

Exhaling slowly, Izzy walked down the hall to Aunt Anna's bedroom. She opened the door, flipped on the light, and stood in the doorway looking in. There she saw the oxygen cord lying on a crumpled pillow, and her aunt's favorite flannel gown poking out from under the Pennsylvania Dutch quilt with a sleeve resting where her arm had been. *Gone, too! I'm all alone!*

18. <u>ANXIOUS FOR OTHERS</u>

Izzy found herself hugging Aunt Anna's flannel gown early the next morning. She lay there, dazed. She couldn't remember where she was, or what had happened. *Marty?* She sat up and looked around. *Marty, how can this be happening to me? Will I ever see you again?* Izzy cried into Aunt Anna's flannel gown. *Oh, Aunt Anna. How I need you!*

Suddenly, a heavy weight of fear gripped Izzy's gut. *What day is it? Do I have any more time before the mark takes effect?* She got out of bed and went to check the calendar in the kitchen. The deadline for receiving the mark fell in another three days. *What would Marty do?* Izzy's palms pressed in upon her eyes as she raised her head heavenward. *Pray.* That man always prayed. *Dear God, I do not feel like talking to you right now, because I don't understand why you did not take me with Marty and Aunt Anna. But, God, I am scared stiff, and I do not have a clue what to do. Please give me wisdom to know how to survive. In Jesus' name, Amen.*

Izzy peeked out the window and saw the car at the curb. *The luggage!* She ran out, noticing for the first time a burned-out car which had crashed in a ditch about a block down the hill. So many people disappeared, even from behind the driver's wheel! Izzy shuddered to think of the horror of being stuck in a car careening out of control without a driver. *God, I guess I should thank you for not taking the pilots yesterday. But I am still angry with you. Why, oh why did you desert me?* Tears unbidden streamed down her cheeks as she angrily lifted the luggage out of the trunk.

With the luggage back in the house, Izzy decided to begin unpacking Marty's suitcase. As soon as she flipped open the lid, Marty's journal slid out. She grabbed the book and retreated to her favorite recliner. *Oh Marty, how I wish you were here.*

She wiped away the tears which trickled down her face and settled down to read.

The inscription in Aunt Anna's hand—on the first page— read: *Dear Marty, "Therefore, if any man is in Christ, he is a new creation. The old has passed away; behold, the new has come." (II Cor. 5:17) As you embark on your new life in Christ by following Him in baptism today, I am giving you this journal to accompany you on your journey.*
Use it to talk to Jesus. Then God will speak to you.
Love, Aunt Anna

Izzy blindly rubbed Aunt Anna's signature. *Love. I am unloved, rejected.* She slammed Marty's journal shut and threw it on the coffee table. *I have no life in Christ. He has left me. I'm all alone. The best thing I could do is take the mark. Then I won't have to worry.* Sorrow plunged her into a fit of anger; she got up and turned over every Bible promise on display on Aunt Anna's walls and tabletops—

"Casting all your anxieties on him, because he cares for you." (I Pet. 7:7) "You do not care!" Izzy yelled and pulled her hair.

"God is love." "Ha!" she spit out angrily. "You have taken away my LOVE!"

"And we know that for those who love God all things work together for good..." "Prove it, plea-ea-ease!" Izzy bawled uncontrollably. Curling up in Marty's recliner, she fell, exhausted, into a deep sleep.

Izzy saw Mr. B and The Prophet robed in black, hoods pulled forward, talking.

"Our Lord Liege is not pleased. Praise and power belong to you, you alone. Your image stands ready. Now you need to give it life. You know what to do. Only you can do it." The Prophet clutched Mr. B's arm, head bowed in silence. Then released him.

The travesty happened in a hidden place beneath the city. Izzy saw in a flash the temple square, and the dark hall below. *Am I seeing things?*

Hooded figures garbed in black moved in waves, pulsating around His Highness B. He stood behind the stone altar, knife clinched between his two hands, waiting to plunge it into the writhing form of his only son draped in black on the table before him.

Izzy heard a deep sinister voice reverberating off the walls. "Life is in the blood. New life, new power for you to fulfill your call. You will be invincible! You will be king of all! All will bow the knee to you!" Evil flowed around the robed beast like a vortex, compelling his raised hands clutching the knife to forcefully descend and sever flesh. *That poor boy.* A scream caught in Izzy's throat.

Izzy tossed fitfully in her sleep. The dream continued.

A roar resounded around the room, shouts of "A god, and not a man!"

"Worship the King!"

"Hail, King B!"

"Glory be to our king of kings! Let every knee bow!"

With a woosh suddenly all went down on their knees. A surge caused the lights to flicker on and off revealing paranormal intruders in the ghastly glow of torches. In a prominent portico of the temple, Izzy saw the image of the god open its eyes.

Izzy sat up with a scream. But the dream persisted. She saw three people silhouetted against an open window in a stone frame—His Highness B sat, arms raised. On either side of him stood The Prophet and a young man, both holding up Mr. B's arms. Izzy could see through the window the pleasant blue sky morph into a dark ball of angry clouds splintered by lightning. Flood water came.

Suddenly, there was Uncle Amos, arms raised in prayer in the midst of the storm. Izzy saw water rushing down on him and his family. She screamed.

Izzy woke up and looked around the darkened room. She huffed, her heart beating wildly, sweat pouring down her face. She sank back into the chair and closed her eyes.

Surely it was just a dream, a terrible nightmare.

Izzy needed a shower. She shuddered. The dream seemed so real, so vivid. *Did Mr. B kill his own son? Are Uncle Amos and his family alright? Maybe the News will give me some answers. I hope I still have cable.* She thought for a moment as she washed her hair. The warm water felt so good, and she realized she had not showered since getting on the airplane.

Dressed and refreshed, Izzy looked at the clock. Seven-thirty, just in time for the evening news. She grabbed the remote control off the table and turned on the news. Rod and Julie were on.

ROGERS: The world is still reeling from yesterday's Grand Abduction of millions of people from the face of the earth. The WOP government headed by His Highness Bandar has set up a hotline to allow people still here to let their loved ones know they did not disappear. You can find the number at the bottom of your screen.

QUESPIE: The theory is that the AI circuit stealing cows had been practicing for this feat of abducting millions at once. This is a mystery that is still under investigation.

ROGERS: The clean-up from the Disappearance is on-going. If your vehicle, or the vehicle of a loved one has been reported disabled, your case has been assigned a number. Authorities will contact you when they are ready to move your car.

QUESPIE: Our correspondents in Israel continue to surprise us with developments there. The long-awaited dedication of the Jewish temple just happened forty-eight hours ago. On the first day alone over twelve thousand people milled around Jerusalem, considered holy ground by Muslims, Christians, and Jews. About three thousand got to tour inside the Temple Square after the dedication ceremony.

ROGERS: This just in, breaking news—the body of Richard Bandar, adoptive son of the Premier and Vice Premier of the World Order for Peace government, was found dumped in the Kidron Valley. His death is under investigation, and likely the result of a kidnapping for ransom.

Oh my goodness, Richard, you poor child. I saw you murdered by your own adoptive parents! It was more than a dream! But why would God reveal this to me? And what of Uncle Amos and his family? Are they gone, washed away by the flood? Izzy covered her face with her hands. "Oh, God! Save Uncle Amos and Aunt Abigail. Poor little Benjie, Hannah and Daniel! Oh God! Please save them."

ROGERS: More breaking news coming to you from our correspondent in Jerusalem, Farar Emanuel. Farar.

EMANUEL: All of Israel's WOP Force was placed on high alert following the disappearance. Jews were seen congregating all over Jerusalem, and rumor had it they were plotting to overthrow His Highness Bandar and the WOP regime. The Prophet immediately called down fire from the sky to denounce the coupe. He then placed an image of His Highness Bandar in the North Gate, and demanded all prove their allegiance by bowing down to it,beginning with the Jews.

But in a strange twist of fate, during the night many Jews made their escape. Hundreds, even thousands, exited the city in the dark of night to one of two places—Qumran National Park and the fort at Masada.

ROGERS: Hold on a minute, Farar. How could so many people leave the city in the dead of night without being stopped by the World Order for Peace forces?

EMANUEL: Unfortunately, twenty-nine WOP Force members, including Commander Ehud Halil, died before a firing squad in the Kidron

Valley for sleeping through the exodus of the Jews. It is a mystery how this could have happened, Rod. The Jews began their flight in the middle of the night and fled the sixty miles to Masada by bike, motorcycle, car and on foot. Some even got there by private plane.

Izzy stood up waving her hands nervously, pacing back and forth before the TV screen. *Come on, come on. What happened to the Ashers? Uncle Amos, are you all alright?*

> QUESPIE: You've got me on the edge of my seat. So are the Jews suspect of treason? Isn't there some recourse?

> EMANUEL: There's more to the story, and it is ongoing. For His Highness B and The Prophet can be seen here calling down rain to stop the Jews' escape. The Wilderness is renowned for flooding, especially the mountain pass below Qumran. The torrential rain came barreling down, and would have overwhelmed the Jews, except for the earthquake…

> ROGERS: Earthquake? Let me get this straight, Emanuel…

Izzy could not stand the suspense anymore. She dropped to her knees and yelled, "So, what happened to the Jews? Please, they weren't overcome by the flood, were they?"

> EMANUEL: Yes. The whole mass of traitors, estimated at about three thousand Jews, were saved by a powerful quake which split the earth open and swallowed the flood waters!

QUESPIE: You've got to be kidding.

EMANUEL: I would not dare fabricate this story. His Highness's WOP force retaliated by shooting missiles into both hiding places—the Qumran National Park about twenty-eight miles east of Jerusalem by Highway 1, and Masada, another thirty-four miles south down Route 90.

No! No! God, no! Izzy broke down crying again for Marty's Uncle Amos and family.

The correspondent continued, dumbstruck.

EMANUEL: It's like there was a protective barrier over each place. Missiles exploded in mid-air, leaving no ground damage.

Oh, God! Thank you! You heard my prayer. Surely the Ashers are safe. Father, thank you. Izzy felt exhausted. She turned off the TV and retreated to Aunt Anna's bed where she hugged her aunt's flannel gown, wrapped up in the familiar quilt, and dropped off to sleep.

Izzy slept soundly. When she woke up, the sun had not yet risen. She heard the birdsong outside her window and stretched. "Thank you, Father, for the good rest last night." She sat up, looking for Marty. Then she fell back onto her pillow, shocked and disappointed. She wiped away a tear as she remembered that Marty wasn't there.

Marty, I miss you terribly. It still doesn't feel right that I am here without you. Operating on autopilot, she brushed her teeth and showered. As she washed her hair, she thought about her last few days with Marty. She remembered her trek along the Via Dolorosa, and blinked away tears reflecting on how much it meant to her husband. *The journal! I wonder what Marty wrote that last day.*

Izzy quickly dressed and ran out to the kitchen for some breakfast. She ate some cereal with milk and found an apple in the bottom of the refrigerator. She made some coffee and found Marty's journal on the floor next to the coffee table. Then she remembered the terrible dark mood she had been in, and her temper tantrum. She went around the room returning the Scripture promises on the walls and table to their proper position.

One was cracked by her angry treatment--"And we know that for those who love God all things work together for good…" Izzy thought, "All things?"

She heard some noise outside and looked at the clock. *Hmm. It's only seven-thirty. What could be happening this time of day? But today is the last day before the deadline for taking the mark.* She crept over to the window next to the front door and peeked through the curtains without opening them—first one way, and then the next. It sounded like a truck. Seeing nothing, she decided to open the door and look down the street toward the sound.

A tow truck stood before the gutted car which had veered off into the ditch. *Poor people, no way they could have survived that—the car is completely charred.* Izzy forgot caution and tried to get a better look at the car. As she moved a little closer, two people came from behind the end of the car out into the street. *Jamie? Max?*

Without thinking, Izzy immediately turned to run back to her house, but not without looking back. Jamie saw her and took a few steps in her direction. *No, no, no, no! Please, I'm not ready to see you, Jamie.* She slammed the door shut and leaned on the door and slunk down to the floor.

Maybe she needs a friend. Izzy looked around. *Where did*

that thought come from? I could never be her friend, not after what she did to me! Izzy stood up and picked up Marty's journal to read his last entry. She snuggled longingly down into the recliner which had been Marty's.

Izzy brushed away a flicker of fear, and turned to the last entry, curious what had been on her hubby's mind in the Garden. She read—

Today at the Garden of Gethsemane I prayed where Jesus struggled with the Father, praying, "Not my will but yours be done!" It's like he had to make that conscious choice on the eve of his crucifixion to forgive us sinners and go to the cross for us. Thank you, Jesus, for making that choice for me. So, as I follow you, help me to choose to forgive others. And help me to broach this subject one more time with Izzy. She needs to be set free. Perhaps on the air trip home.

Izzy felt annoyed. She knew Marty wanted her to forgive Jamie. She flipped back in the journal to see what else Marty had to say—

I argued with Izzy today. That doesn't happen very often. We were at the supermarket. There was a table outside manned by the World Order for Peace force. As we were leaving, we heard Jamie yelling at the WOP team, adamantly refusing to receive the branding, calling His Highness Bandar an "Iraqi guru!" I wanted to go to her aid, but Izzy—who was terribly hurt by Jamie—said she could not possibly help her after what Jamie had done to her, and even said, "I will never forgive her!" When I get the chance, I must talk with Izzy about letting go of unforgiveness. Jesus chose to forgive us, so we need to choose to forgive others. Jesus said that if we refuse to forgive anyone, then our Father in Heaven would refuse to forgive us our sins. That is a scary proposition. Oh God, please forgive Izzy's unforgiveness, and enable her to forgive Jamie. In Jesus' Name, Amen.

Izzy's anger propelled her out of the recliner. She stood, fists clinched, shouting, "How could you expect me to forgive that woman after what she did to me, after what she did to us?" Then she fell to her knees and crunched up in a ball on the carpet. "No-o-o-o-o! No-o-o-o-o! This can't be happening! Ahh!"

For about twenty minutes the clock ticking from the wall in the kitchen calmed Izzy's frazzled nerves. She remembered that conversation with Marty. He had worn a light blue long-sleeved dress shirt with a lightweight beige vest. *I loved you Marty, always so sharp looking on your way out to a day full of faculty meetings, teaching, and such; I felt more than a little jealous of your time.* Izzy sighed, got up from the floor, and crawled back into Marty's seat.

Marty had said, "Honey, I wish we had more time to talk together about this morning's Scripture. But it's been on my heart to share it with you, so I'll throw it out there for you to think about."

Izzy took a deep breath, remembering.

"Matthew chapter six, verses fourteen and fifteen. Jesus has just taught the disciples how to pray with what everyone now calls the Lord's Prayer. He says, 'For if you forgive others their trespasses your heavenly Father will also forgive you, but if you do not forgive others their trespasses, neither will your Father forgive your trespasses.'"

At that point, Marty leaned forward and grabbed Izzy's hand, and asked, "Do you remember the story of the prodigal son? It's really the story of the father who waited anxiously for his wayward son to come home from a wasted life. When the father saw his son on the road home, he ran to welcome him home. He told his servants to dress his repentant son in a new robe, put a ring on his finger and new shoes on his feet, and then to throw a party for him, saying, "My son, who was lost, has been found! He was dead and now is alive!"

At that point, Marty took both of Izzy's hands in his, looked into her eyes and kissed her gently. *Oh, Marty, you knew how to melt my heart. I regret what happened next.*

The memory continued to unfold. Marty's eyes and dimples shone with a smile. He put up his finger, like Aunt Anna always did, and Aunt Anna laughed. Then he continued to make his point, "There was an older brother we did not read about. When he came home and heard that his profligate brother had returned, and that his father had welcomed him home by killing the calf and making a feast, he was furious. He refused to go in to see his brother. His dad tried to reason with him, saying that all his possessions were his, but that his little brother had lost it all, and had now been found. He was dead, and now he was alive!"

I remember you wiping away tears, Marty. As soon as you believed that Jesus was your Messiah—that he had come for you—your heart was so tender to God. You saw yourself in that little brother coming home to his father. But me? No, not me. I was the big brother—when you encouraged me to forgive Jamie, I got up and walked away.

Sadness draped over Izzy like a heavy weight, suffocating her. She curled up in her chair, grabbed the lightweight throw blanket from the back and huddled there, with Jesus. "Dear Lord Jesus, I had it all. I had your love, your forgiveness for all my petty sins, a beautiful life, a wonderful family with Aunt Anna, and then, the icing on the cake, a great husband!" Tears flowed uncontrollably as Izzy grieved her loss. "Father, do I even have the hope of heaven anymore?" Her voice squeaked. She sobbed, threw back the blanket and searched desperately for some tissue to wipe her runny nose. Then Izzy fell prostrate on the floor, exhausted with sorrow.

Within the quiet, she heard her mother saying, "God is

love, Izzy. He loves you dearly, and he wants you to trust him, to become his child. For God so loved Izzy that he gave his only son…"

Jesus.

"So that if Izzy believes in him," Mom continued, "She will NOT perish, but will have everlasting life."

Everlasting life! Father, I want to come home to you. Please, please forgive my stubborn, hateful heart. I forgive Jamie. I forgive her. Please welcome me home. I want to be your child forever.

Izzy felt a warm embrace. God whispered to her heart, "I love you, my child. Rest in my love. You are free from the burden of unforgiveness. Your sins are forgiven. Welcome home!"

What is this like the waves of the sea, gently washing over my soul? I feel so clean, so free, so…loved!

Izzy rested awhile. Then in her mind's eye, she saw Max's full head of blond curls and thought about how he had connected with a couple of friends in his class. It felt good to see him find friends. She pushed herself up out of her reverie. *Jamie. How shall I make it right with Jamie?*

She knew it was futile, but Izzy went to the door to look where she had last seen Jamie and Max. Of course, they were not there. But as Izzy turned back to the house, she saw an envelope in the mailbox by the door.

Izzy nervously examined the envelope. Sure enough, the sender was Jamie, and she left her address—1416 Garfield Street, Wissahickon. *Hmm. She seems open to contact.* She gingerly turned the letter over to open it. She prayed, "Father, help me to make it right with Jamie."

Jamie wrote—*"Dear Ms. Frank. Max misses you. He*

never had you for a teacher, except on the playground. You made a difference in his life. Thank you."

Wow. What a pleasant way to start.

"I figure you don't want to talk with me, and I don't blame you. I owe you an apology..."

What? Izzy sat up with interest.

"I was too quick to contact the Board. I saw how that devastated you and Laura, and even the whole school. Miss Laura left, and then Ms. Hitchcock was transferred to another school. I was painfully aware of how alone you felt. But I have always felt a barrier between us; I sensed you judged me harshly for the choice I have made concerning my sexual orientation. So, I did not know how to tell you I am sorry.

"I hope you will forgive me. I also need to tell you what my interest was in the books on the gender education shelf. Believe it or not, I asked Max to check out the books so that I could communicate with the Board about the unnecessary graphics. Young kids do not need that. Let them enjoy the world around them—colors, numbers, and make-believe!"

Izzy could not believe her eyes. *Oh, Lord. I presumed too much and brought all this trouble on myself. Please forgive me. Jamie and I think more alike than I could have ever guessed!* She anxiously picked up the letter to see if there was more. The last page broke Izzy's heart for Jamie.

"Carol and I broke up last year. She just would not stop talking about Jesus and the rapture. It looks like we missed it. I am surprised to see you here. Max keeps crying, wishing he had believed in Jesus when he had the chance. He's a believer now. But not me. My parents both died that day in the car you saw them towing. Carol was behind the wheel. When she disappeared, the car careened into the tree and exploded into flames. Mom and Dad didn't have a chance."

19. <u>ON THE LOOKOUT</u>

Izzy wanted to go immediately to find Jamie. *I need to apologize to her. I never gave her a chance. I'm so glad you gave me a chance, Jesus. Help me to find her.* She looked outside and realized daylight was nearly gone. *It'll have to wait until tomorrow.*

Suddenly she remembered that tomorrow was D-Day—the day everyone needed to have Mr. Bandar's mark in order to buy and sell. "Not me, Mr. Evil. God help me, but I'd NEVER take your identity on my body. I belong to Jesus now." She decided to see what the news had to say. *Tomorrow I might not have the TV or phone service anymore.*

Oh! Phone service. I wonder if Uncle Amos could have possibly written?

Izzy opened her phone. A message from Uncle Amos awaited her. *This is better than the news! Thank you, God!* She decided to read it standing, pacing back and forth for some exercise. *I've been too sedentary.*

AMOS: Izzy. Don't get the mark. That is not a solution. Let Jesus take care of you. You want to see Marty, and Aunt Anna again? Jesus loves you. Perhaps you had some lessons to learn before you were ready for heaven. Please DO NOT GET THE MARK.

No, no mark for me! And, yes, I needed to learn how to forgive. Izzy continued to read.

I hope this message finds you well. We are well! Yeshua did miracles to bring us safely through the flood. He has hidden us in the Judean Wilderness. The story is too long to tell. I don't know how long, or even if, the wifi is accessible. But by faith, I wanted to let you know we survived, and even THRIVE.

Through the years, God used the Secret Service to carve out a haven within the mountain plateau of Masada, as well as in the Qumran National Park. My Uncle Rufus, sneaky fellow, was a part of the making of this place, and we never knew it. It is unbelievable what God has prepared for us here through his hard labor, and the labor and sacrifice of many.

Praise to Yeshua.

Uncle Rufus, who is already in his seventies, revealed how when he worked for Israel's Secret Service as an engineer, for twenty years he and a team of men were commissioned to use pick and shovel to slowly but surely remove the slate, rocks and soil to fashion a bunker which could house hundreds of people. Explosives were used to prepare a tunnel system and carve out a mall under the neighboring mountain. All this was accomplished at night. Everyone who worked on location—day or night—were under the employ of the Secret Service. God used them to prepare for us the biggest surprise.

The bunker beneath, and the mall beyond, are so immense that it boggles the mind. Electricity uses solar energy. Top floors house row upon row of hydroponics. At the next level down aquariums full of various fish and seafood give us nutritious meals we could have never anticipated. We feel like we are in heaven. Our God is an ABUNDANT God and Father. Just as he promised in Revelation 12:6, he has prepared a place in which (we) are to be nourished for 1,260 days.

Dear, dear Izzy, God is taking care of us, and I am confident he will take care of you. Be on your guard. Read what Revelation 12:13-17 has to say: *"And when the dragon saw that he had been thrown down to the earth, he pursued the woman who had given birth to the male child. But the woman was given the two wings of the great eagle so that she might fly from the serpent into the wilderness, to the place where she is to be nourished for a time, and times, and half a time. The serpent poured water like a river out of his mouth after the woman, to sweep her away with a flood. But the earth came to the help of the woman, and the earth opened its mouth and swallowed the river that the dragon had poured from his mouth. Then the dragon became furious with the woman and went off to make war on the rest of her offspring, on those who keep the commandments of God and hold to the testimony of Jesus."*

Though the deadline for receiving the mark of the Beast has come upon the world, we need to cling to the promises of God. He is still faithful. If we persevere, we shall serve with him when his kingdom comes to earth, and his throne is in Jerusalem. Abigail and I, Daniel, Hannah, and Benjie pray for you every day. Please let us know you have received this. Remember his promise— "Cast your cares on him, for he cares for you." Shalom! –Uncle Amos and Family

Izzy shook her head. *What an amazing, good, good God!* And then she shook her head in sorrow that this was the first time she really believed it. "Better late than never," she said out loud. Then she looked at the clock. *Eight p.m. already. I'd better let Uncle Amos know I am alright. Who knows when I'll have another chance.*

> **IZZY:** Dear Uncle Amos, Your letter is a breath of life to me. Thank you for writing. I am amazed at the goodness of God, and his protection for you all. I am so relieved to hear your news.
>
> Thank you. I, too, have experienced the goodness of God. I believe in him with my whole heart now. I feel free now and forgiven. Plus, I have learned to forgive. I was so blind before. So truly, *"all things work together for good for those who love God."* Now I have the hope of heaven, and I know that someday I will be reunited with Marty. His love and the love of God are what will keep me going in the days to come.
>
> Please give your whole family a big hug from me. We will meet again, in God's time. I love you!
> –Izzy

Izzy stretched and looked at the clock as it chimed nine p.m. She felt strangely peaceful. *And tomorrow is the deadline. I had better pack my backpack for running from the Beast's WOP force!*

Izzy sat up in her bed, pillow behind her back. *Your pillow, Marty. I'll never change the pillowcase. It still has your scent. I found my journal today, Aunt Anna's baptism gift. I don't know where my heart and mind were then, but now I am fully on board with Jesus. So, God helping me, I hope to keep this journal daily. I love you, and I miss you. Please give Aunt Anna a big hug from me.*

November 2—This journal dedicated to the love of my life, next to Jesus—Marty Goldstein.

Dear Marty,

I can imagine you are at the windows of heaven observing all that is going on. I am amazed I can write you now without falling apart. So much happened after you were taken away by Jesus. I was so hurt and angry that I was ready to go get the mark. Not anymore. Your journal helped to talk some sense into me about forgiveness. And Jamie reached out and asked forgiveness for the grief she caused. It took me by surprise and put me to shame. Can you believe that she had some of the same concerns I did about the gender education books? If I had only given her a chance, we might have been friends. But now it is the eve of having to receive the mark of the Beast to do business as usual. It used to be so tempting, but not anymore. I hope to find Jamie and Max tomorrow. She's bound to be lonely. She lost her parents in a car accident when the rapture happened. I don't know if we can look after one another in the days to come, but it is worth a try. The WOP force may come looking for us when they realize we are not on their grid.

I have packed my backpack. Guess what I have taken for my journey? Pancakes, peanut butter, granola bars, raisins, banana chips, walnuts, chocolate chip cookies, strawberry protein powder, five bottles of water, seaweed snacks, dried green beans and veggies.

I am not at all sure where or if there will be places to wash and dry clothes. Unfortunately, it has become quite cold outside—forties and fifties, dipping down to thirty degrees Fahrenheit at night. I am glad to be young. God help us all. So I have packed two thermal long-sleeved shirts with underwear. Do not have space for many clothes—four days' worth of underwear, four cotton shirts, one pair of jeans, some khaki pants, and a skirt and leggings (you never know when they might come in handy). I'm sure I will be wearing my warm and wooly gloves, a brown scarf, and my warm hoody; hidden inside the inner pocket, next to my heart, is our wedding picture at the grove where you proposed to me. I love you, Sweetheart, and always will!

For my sanity I packed toothpaste, brush and floss, cold medicine, hair things and face wash, white bar soap, lipstick and sunscreen foundation, lotion. I might as well look and feel my best, even when on the run. God help us!

Today's verse—"Even though I walk through the valley of the shadow of death, I will fear no evil, for you are with me; your rod and your staff, they comfort me."

Izzy leaned back on her pillow. *God, I don't know what a day will bring, but you do.* Then she slept.

Morning came too soon so far as Izzy was concerned. She stretched and wanted to roll back over to go to sleep, but she knew she shouldn't. Have to be on the lookout for the WOP Force.

She kept the curtains drawn in the living room but peered out through the crack. No activity that she could see. *I wonder if I still have TV?* Izzy gathered her breakfast—toast and egg—and retreated to Marty's recliner to eat and see what was on.

To her surprise, the TV came on but with no sound. A moment later a message started running across the bottom of the screen. It read:

This contract needs to be renewed with the proper ID. Please proceed to the nearest branding station. –Greater Philadelphia World Order for Peace Force

Oh dear. I don't have any time to lose. She bowed in

prayer, then finished off her breakfast quickly. Then she washed up her plates and tidied the table. Home sweet home. *How much time do I have in this cozy haven?*

Suddenly the sound returned to the TV. The morning news blared with hosts Rick Martin and Cindy Grawley.

> MARTIN: This morning across the Philadelphia area many people are waking up to their skin breaking out with boils, red and swollen bumps on the skin which become tender, sore, and full of puss. Hospitals and Urgent Care Clinics have been overrun during the night. Some have already closed their doors for lack of beds and medical personnel. If you come down with the boils, take your over-the-counter pain meds, and apply hot compresses to the affected area. Stay home and avoid public places as the germs seem to be highly contagious.

> GRAWLEY: Even His Highness B encountered the boils. But thanks to the healing powers of his partner, Vice Premier Hamaz, otherwise known as The Prophet, Mr. B has quickly recovered and is out tending to his affairs.

> MARTIN: And tops on the list of affairs to be tended to according to His Highness is full compliance of all the great peoples of the world by receiving the mark either on their hands or foreheads. As of today, without that mark— demonstrating full allegiance—no one will be allowed to buy or sell anything anywhere.

Father, I feel like a sheep in the middle of a pack of wolves. Be my shepherd today.

Izzy looked at her backpack standing ready at the back

door. *Nylon poncho could come in handy.* She retrieved it and stuffed it into a pocket on the outside of her bag. *Won't hold much more.*

Standing in the kitchen, Izzy scanned the large open area which had become home. Her heart fluttered, and she rubbed her hands together, flexed them, and shook them out. She put on her hoodie jacket, and took one last look around the bedrooms. She found her ear buds. *If I lose phone coverage, are these any good? Maybe somewhere along the line they will come in handy.* She stuck them in her pocket.

BANG! BANG! Izzy jumped.

"World Order for Peace Force here for inspection! Open up in the name of His Highness Bandar!" Someone tried the door.

Run! Jesus help me! Just then Izzy heard a loud crash on the street. She peered out the window. What in the world? An old man, agitated by boils, had rammed into the WOP vehicle. Izzy grabbed her backpack and slipped it on as she went out the back door. She quietly pulled the door closed and locked it, then walked quickly to the gate. Looking both ways, she saw no one and turned right down the cement alley seeking her destination: 1416 Garfield Street, Wissahickon.

Izzy trudged westward and crossed the Schuylkill. The brisk air together with the rush of the water under the bridge gave her a burst of energy. She decided to start jogging, veering away from the main streets. *Surely the side streets will shield me from the eyes of the WOP Force.* Cars lined the narrow street on both sides. In places the sidewalks had cracked and split, making running more difficult. Izzy slowed to a walk, breathing deeply of the fresh morning air. Grassy lawns and shrubs, some neat and trim, others overgrown, lay before brick row homes with cement steps and iron rails. Some had enclosed porches.

How to find Jamie and Max? I had a girlfriend in high

school who lived in that neighborhood. Izzy broke into a jog and remembered the run that brought her to Marty. Tears stung her eyes. *Oh, no. I can't afford to cry and draw attention to myself.* She wiped away the moisture with her fingers. Then she put on her gloves because of the chill in the air.

The alley dumped Izzy off onto a busy street. There was a gas station across the street. *Maybe I can use the restroom there.* She crossed the street at the crosswalk and made her way to the toilet. She kept her head down and went about her business. She washed her hands and dried them, putting back on her gloves.

As she exited a female WOP officer hobbled into the bathroom. She eyed Izzy. "Miss, have you complied with His Highness's branding?

Izzy held up her gloved hand with a smile.

"Wait for me. I'll verify when I get out." She disappeared into the stall.

Sorry, Miss, but I've got an engagement to keep. Izzy walked fast and turned a corner, then she ran down an alley. *How did His Highness recruit so many for his WOP Force?*

Well, this looks familiar. I believe Garfield is at the next intersection. The alley opened out onto Garfield Street. Izzy saw a convenience store where she and her friend used to hang out up the street. "This is it."

"1416 Garfield. Hmm. 1398. Bingo. I'm on the right track." Izzy found it cathartic to talk to herself. She lifted her bag off her shoulders and resituated it as she walked. Garfield was lined with tall pines. Izzy breathed in deeply of the pungent smell. Her pace quickened.

Across the street stood Izzy's familiar hang-out. Izzy examined the doors, house after house, each with three cement steps down to the sidewalk until she finally found it, 1416. She looked up the street from which she had come to make sure no one had followed her. "Safe." Then she ascended the steps and knocked lightly on the door. "Jamie? Max? Anyone home?"

Max, his eyes big, cracked open the door. "Mrs. Goldstein!" Jamie stood behind him. "Quickly, please," she whispered, and extended her hand to Izzy, and pulled her in.

Jamie quickly locked the door and peered out the window. "So, you found us." She looked at Izzy with tired eyes. "Thank you for coming. This town is crawling with the crazy WOP Force." Her face got red. "There's been so much loss, so many died with the rapture, and now people are sick with boils." Her eyes narrowed. "You'd think that our caring Premier Bandar would be offering aid and comfort to the people, not tracking down non-compliant people. Like a sinkhole slurping down a house, yard, and car—bit by bit, chunk by chunk—the evil unleashed by that man is destroying people's lives!" Visibly agitated, she motioned for Izzy to sit down.

Izzy nodded slowly, her face sympathetic, as she found her place.

"Max, please go get a glass of water for our guest." Jamie sat down.

Izzy took her seat and looked around a neat and comfortable living room with off-white carpeting and tan leather furniture. A frameless piece of abstract art—spheres, cubes, three dimensional rectangles, and cones, all brightly colored —stretched along the wall behind the sofa like a rainbow. She looked up at her host and cleared her throat. "I had to come after reading your letter."

Max handed a cold glass of water to his teacher.

"Thank you." Izzy grinned at the child with blond curls covering his eyes. Then she reached out and put her hand on Jamie's arm. "I'm so sorry for your loss. What a horrible experience."

"Yeah, my folks didn't have a chance. Like lots and lots of people, they lost their driver. Vanished. It almost feels like a sick joke. But it is no joke, is it? You lost your husband." Jamie looked at Izzy. "I'm sorry."

"Yes. I lost my husband and my aunt." Izzy wiped away a tear. "But I'm confident I will see them again."

"How could you be so confident? God left you behind this time. What reason should he accept you now?" Jamie stood up and spread her hands out. Max sat hugging his knees, watching and listening.

Izzy remembered the day Marty questioned whether she was ready to be baptized. "I…was…blind to the goodness of God. I took it for granted. But I didn't really know him."

"Now, after he's left you behind, you know him? Because now that my parents both died in one day, I fail to see the goodness of God. How can you say God is good when you've been stranded here for the Beast to devour?" Then looking over to Max, she said, "Sorry, Max. But we're up against some pretty tough odds. We can't buy food without branding. And now we've got to run for our liberty and possibly our lives because of the WOP Force."

Jamie walked to the door and looked through the window. The afternoon sun shone on her face.

Izzy was struck with how beautiful she was. "I was surprised that you and I think more alike than I assumed. I also wanted to preserve the children's innocence and let them enjoy their childhood."

"Exactly," said Jamie. "I really regretted how that matter spiraled out of control after I called the Board."

I really judged her wrongly. I thought evil of her and refused to forgive her. That's why I'm here. "I forgive you now, and it feels good to say it." Izzy leaned over and asked, "Can we put it behind us with a hug?"

The two shared a hug and pats on the back, and Max said,

"Me, too!" and squirmed his way into a group hug.

When they sat back down again, Jamie slapped her hands on her lap. "So, what's your plan for survival? Did you see the newspaper?" Jamie retrieved the newspaper from under the table and handed it to Izzy.

"Did you pay for this? How did you get it without the mark?"

"It is the store copy for customers across the street. I pulled it out of the trash after dark." Jamie pointed at a headline—**ANGRY IDOL LASHES OUT.**

Izzy read aloud—

"His Highness A. M. Bandar's idol, placed in the portico of the North Gate on Temple Square by Vice Premier Khalil Yasir Hamaz has come to life! While people may conjecture that it is run by AI, there is no contesting the vitriol for disloyalty, saying 'How dare you bow before other gods! There are no other gods. You owe your allegiance and worship to His Highness Bandar alone. His number is six-six-six, a perfect number for a perfect man and the only true God. Bow the knee before his image, or else die!'

"To make its point, it ordered the execution by beheading of over eight hundred Jews still in Jerusalem who refused to be branded. These, also, had been implicated in a coup attempt against Mr. Bandar's regime."

"Creepy. Can you imagine an idol coming to life and spitting out poison? Even ordering the execution of eight hundred Jews in Jerusalem—a horrible loss—and right after the dedication of the temple." Izzy wiped away some tears as she resumed reading the article—

"Therefore, the WOP Force trained in every nation to serve the needs of the world in these tumultuous days stands

ready to defend the honor of His Highness B. They will behead any and all non-conformists ages eighteen and above. However, children and youth will be given the chance to reform. Regional WOP Reform Camps have been established around the world.

"Every effort must be made to bring non-conformists into conformity for the good of society. The most common reason for non-compliance by branding is religious—these people believe in the fairy tales of Jesus and heaven, of Allah, and Buddha. Others are conscientious objectors, calling His Highness B a despot, and clinging to their ideals of freedom and independence; they are deceived and need to turn from their rebellion and embrace the freedoms afforded to all who submit to receiving His Highness's mark on their foreheads or on their right hands. There is no other path to liberty."

Izzy put the paper down and rubbed away the goosebumps on her arms. She put her arm around Max. "I understand you have trusted Jesus, right?"

Max nodded. "A little late, though. But at least I can be with Dad here. He still needs to turn to Jesus." He rubbed Jamie's back.

"Now I don't need Jesus. Where was he when thousands of people died like your grandparents?" Jamie angrily pointed at Max.

Max looked up to Izzy for help.

Izzy clasped her hands, looking Jamie in the eyes. "I used to have the same question, because God seemed to turn a deaf ear to my pleas to save my mom from a brain tumor. She died, and it left me bitter toward God. But now I've discovered…"

KNOCK, KNOCK.

KNOCK, KNOCK.

Everybody froze and looked at each other. *Is it the WOP Force?*

20. FRIEND OR FOE

Izzy noticed the clock on the wall already said five-twenty p.m. A glance at the window showed dusk had come.

Izzy whispered, "Is there a back door?"

Jamie nodded. "In the basement. But let me check who it is." Then she looked at Max. "Put on your backpack. Bring me mine."

She peeked out the window and turned around. "It's okay. Our sympathetic neighbor, Vanessa. She tries to keep us informed." Jamie unlocked the door and opened it for their friend.

"Vanessa. Where have I heard that name?" Izzy stood on tip-toe to see who would come in.

A tall stocky girl with long kinky brown hair poked her head in, telling Jamie, "I almost didn't come over as it's dinner time. But I thought you would want to know."

Jamie said, "Come on in and find a seat. I'll introduce you."

Vanessa pointed a finger to Izzy and said, "I know you."

Izzy smiled, relieved that this person was not the WOP Force. "Where did we know each other? I'm Izzy Goldstein, and I teach at Overbrook Elementary School."

"Goldstein! Yes! I had a crush on your husband. I saw

you at the tennis courts. Your adorable husband bought you a cup of coffee, which I delivered while he was on the court playing a double. Remember?" Vanessa used her bracelet to pull her hair back into a bun, the way she wore it on the court.

"Oh, my goodness. I remember. And I don't blame you for having a crush on Marty. He was a keeper." Izzy shook Vanessa's hand, and Vanessa responded with a hug.

"I'm sorry I don't see him here today. Did he disappear like the rest?" Vanessa found herself a seat, so everyone joined her.

"Yes, he was raptured. Jesus took him."

"How'd it happen? Were you with him when it happened? Did you see him go? Some people built it up to be a UFO conspiracy, an abduction."

"They can say what they want. But the Bible foretells the rapture. And it happened to us just the way Jesus told it. He said in Luke 17:34, 'I tell you, in that night there will be two in one bed. One will be taken and the other left.'" Izzy wished she had taken it seriously when she heard Pastor Michaels preach it.

"You were sleeping and woke up and he was gone? Did he leave his clothes behind? That seemed to be the common experience." Vanessa looked at her with big eyes.

"Yes, but I wasn't at home in bed. I was in the airplane coming back from Jerusalem. Someone started crying, because they had lost a loved one. Then I discovered Marty, gone." Izzy grabbed a tissue. It had only been a few days, and yet it felt like forever.

Jamie spoke up. "Vanessa, did you come with some news for us? I'm getting a little nervous." She put her arm around Max who had already put on his backpack.

"Yes. I saw the WOP Force knocking door to door in the block behind us just before coming over here. I know you are a conscientious objector, so I wanted you to know."

"How about you?" Izzy wanted to know. "Are you a conscientious objector, too?" But her heart dropped when Vanessa shook her head and gave her a sideways smile and proceeded to open the hand brace she had on her right hand.

Vanessa fingered the lump and looked up to Izzy. "Not to worry. I don't believe in heaven or hell. This is all there is, so I wanted to make the most of it by getting branded." Then she put her hand on Jamie's knee. "Now this woman is clinging to her liberty and doesn't appreciate Mr. B's regime. So, unfortunately, she and Max better flee and fend for themselves. And I wish you the best." Vanessa stood up and gave Jamie a hug where she sat.

Then she looked at Izzy and asked, "Are you also a conscientious objector?"

"No, I'm a Christian."

"So am I," said Max raising his hand.

Vanessa put her hands on her hips. "Well then you three all need to make some escape plans. And I want you to know, that on Tuesday, Thursday and Saturday mornings, you can find me at the girls' locker room at Sweeney Field— at St. Joe's, of course. If you ever need a shower, or even clothes dried, come and find me."

Jamie stood up to let her friend know it was about time. "Vanessa, you're a real friend. Thank you." She gave her a hug.

"A friend in need is a friend indeed! You all take care of yourselves, and I hope to see you around." Vanessa waved at Max and Izzy and ducked out the door into the night.

The three fugitives sat down and looked at each other. Everyone hung their heads, quietly struggling with their fears and questions.

Finally, Jamie spoke up. "Our bags are packed. I figure we could get some sleep tonight and make our escape early in the morning. Does four a.m. sound about right?"

Izzy nodded. "You're a smart planner. Could I sleep on the sofa?"

"Gosh, no. I have a twin you can use."

I can't believe my nemesis has become my friend. Father, you're amazing. Please watch over her for good and lead her to a safe refuge in you. "Thanks, Jamie. Now, do you by any chance still have food left on the shelves? Maybe we should have some dinner."

Jamie brought out bread, canned tuna, pickles, and mayo to put together sandwiches. Max found some chips in the pantry, and Izzy poured up water for everyone.

"For this food we thank you, Lord. Make us strong for the days ahead. In Jesus' name, Amen." Izzy opened her eyes to Jamie, who just smirked and shook her head. Izzy smiled and said, "Someday you'll know."

They ate in silence until Izzy had finished and went to grab her pocket-sized New Testament with Psalms. She opened up to Psalm 91 and cleared her throat.

"Hm-mm. I just want to leave you with a blessing before we get started on our trek in the morning. This is a promise to lean on." Then putting her hand on Max's head, she said, "Okay?"

Max nodded with a slight smile.

Izzy sat forward and read:

"He who dwells in the shelter of the Most High will abide in the shadow of the Almighty. I will say to the LORD, 'My refuge and my fortress, my God in whom I trust.'

For he will deliver you from the snare of the fowler and from the deadly pestilence.

He will cover you with his pinions, and under his wings

you will find refuge; his faithfulness is a shield and buckler. You will not fear the terror of the night, nor the arrow that flies by day, nor the pestilence that stalks in darkness, nor the destruction that wastes at noonday.

A thousand may fall at your side,
Ten thousand at your right hand,
But it will not come near you.
You will only look with your eyes
And see the recompense of the wicked."

Then Izzy looked at Jamie, saying this promise to her. Jamie looked away.

"Because you have made the LORD your dwelling place—the Most High, who is my refuge—no evil shall be allowed to befall you, no plague come near your tent.

For he will command his angels concerning you to guard you in all your ways.

On their hands they will bear you up, lest you strike your foot against a stone.

You will tread on the lion and the adder; the young lion and the serpent you will trample underfoot.

Because he holds fast to me in love, I will deliver him;
I will protect him, because he knows my name.
When he calls to me, I will answer him;
I will be with him in trouble;
I will rescue him and honor him.
With long life I will satisfy him and show him my salvation."

Izzy closed the book and stood up next to Max, rubbing his head and smiling. "That's for you!"

"And you," said Max, hugging Izzy's legs.

"And you." Izzy said to Jamie, wishing she could give Jamie her faith.

Jamie stood up. "Alright. Four comes early. We'd better get some sleep."

The alarm rang on her phone. Izzy sat up, rubbing her eyes. "Lord, what will this day bring? Regardless, keep us in your peace." She rolled out of bed. Using her phone flashlight, she found the light and turned it on.

"Get up, Max." She heard Jamie saying.

Before long, three people gathered in the living room, still yawning and wiping sleep from their eyes. Izzy wore thermal underwear, and sleek gray nylon jogging pants with matching shirt. Jamie wore blue sweatpants and top, as did Max.

"Oh, I like your matching outfits." Izzy smiled.

"Yeah," Jamie said with a slight smile. "So that I can find him in the crowd."

They ate a quick bite of cereal. Jamie cut up and bagged fruit for each of their backpacks. Then she looked around and asked, "What're the chances we can actually come back here someday?" Then she handed Max a key to put in the zipper compartment of his bag.

"Let's head out of the basement. I think it's easier to get out without being seen. The yard opens out into a park." Jamie led the way.

The crickets chirped as Jamie locked the basement door and headed for the gate in the backyard. She opened it gingerly, waited for Max and Izzy to exit, then replaced the latch.

Oh, God, this is it. Please guide our steps and keep us all safe. But where should we go?

They trudged across the park in silence. The dew dampened their shoes. The air felt crisp and cold. Izzy shivered and put on her gloves. She craned her head to see if there were stars poking through the treetops. *Hmm. Must be overcast.* "Should we head to Independence Mall, to mix with the crowd? Or Fairmount Park?"

"Wherever we go, Max and I should wear our matching beanies. See, pull it down and one can only assume there is a mark under there." Jamie handed Max his, and they both nodded proudly.

"Good idea. I've got my hoodie and my gloves. Wear your gloves. That'll help, too." Izzy opened her eyes wide in the dark to see if Jamie and Max were wearing gloves.

After a while, the birds began to sing. Max smiled. He skipped ahead on the sidewalk.

Jamie yelled, "Stay close, Max."

Max returned, and asked everyone, "What happens if we get spotted by the WOP Force? Should we try to stick together?"

Izzy looked at Jamie and wondered how they could best answer that question. *If we stick together, we could help each other out.*

Jamie spoke up, her sharp nose pointing toward the ground. "It seems to me that we need to be wise as foxes. I'd say we split up, so that whoever is chasing us has to choose one or the other. Max stays with me. And if we get split up, then let's meet somewhere."

Yes, she's probably smart. "Where should we meet?" Izzy thought for a moment. "I know. Vanessa was so sweet to offer the use of the showers at St. Joseph's University. Why don't we regroup there if we get separated?" Izzy asked.

"Great place…especially when it's time for a hair wash." Jamie scratched the top of Max's hat, and Max groaned. "And how about making the 30th Street Station another rendezvous place, just in case?" suggested Jamie.

"Sounds great." Izzy nodded, adding, "It never hurts to have a backup plan." *It feels good to be a team.*

They decided to follow the Schuylkill River Trail down

to the Philadelphia Art Museum. The thin two-lane bike path skirted the river on the right. To the left they enjoyed mosaic art on some of the building walls. Before long stone or brick homes were replaced by warehouses and portable units, earth movers and fenced construction sites.

"I wonder if any of these warehouses are deserted? We should keep our eyes open for places to hide and rest." Izzy noticed an abandoned house with boarded up windows.

Max needed a restroom break and found a bush.

Hmm. It's not as easy for us girls. "Let's keep our eyes open for a suitable place for us ladies." Izzy said it without thinking about Jamie's sexual preference and glanced at Jamie to see if she was offended. Jamie looked away and said nothing. *This gender confusion makes me nervous about my words. I don't mean to offend.*

Izzy caught sight of a portable toilet at the edge of a construction site, just beyond an open fence. She noticed men with hard hats some distance away by a scaffolded building but nodded to her companions and disappeared into the toilet and latched the door on the other side.

The smell of chlorine and air freshener mingled with waste was suffocating. She finished as quickly as she could and made her escape.

"Hey, that's not a public toilet," yelled a man limping toward her from the building.

"Sorry, emergency!" Izzy ran after Jamie and Max who were waiting up the road.

"That was a close one. I'm going to miss the convenience of home. Where does one wash their hands around here?"

"You didn't prepare alcohol?" Jamie reached into her bag for some to share with Izzy.

"I'm sure it's not the last thing I will wish I'd remembered to prepare. What was I thinking?" Izzy said, shaking her head.

The river trail soon brought them through plush green grassy banks lined with benches under the clumps of trees. Izzy's heart jumped as she noticed a familiar ridge in the distance—Belmont Plateau in Fairmount Park where Marty had popped the question. The wind blew gently and the sun shone brightly. Izzy noticed the thin strips of a jet trail in the clear blue sky. *Oh, Marty, how I wish I'd gone with you to see Jesus in the sky. We're just getting started on the run. How long can I do this?*

"One day at a time," popped into her head. Then looking up into the sky, Izzy said it out loud. "Just one day at a time."

The trail began to buzz with people passing by, mostly on bikes. "We'd better go single file through here."

The little troupe kept moving toward the city in silence.

Where should we plan to rest tonight? We look like tourists in the day. But at night, I'd feel a little homeless. The WOP Force will certainly ask. Within two hours the Philadelphia skyline came into view. The narrow trail got harder to walk because of the many bikers. Izzy wished they could walk the streets instead. *But by now the WOP Force will be out knocking on doors.*

She motioned for a break when they came to the Girard Avenue underpass. They went to the rail overlooking the Schuylkill to talk. "I am regretting we did not have a plan for where to end our day before we came down here. It won't be long, and we'll get to the Art Museum."

Max held up his fists. Jamie laughed and said, "He likes to run up and down the steps like Rocky."

"Of course," grinned Izzy. "You can do that. It doesn't cost anything. But can we have an idea of where we want to end our day?"

"I thought about checking out the Liberty Bell, the lawn there," said Jamie. "People picnic there."

"Maybe we could stretch out and rest there during the day. But I would be afraid of drawing attention at night." Izzy did some stretches.

"Okay, I know how you feel. This is new to all of us. We've never experienced homelessness. But many have, and Philadelphia has many homeless. We may blend in more than you realize. But let's keep our eyes open as we walk around for places where we might rest this evening." Jamie stood on one leg, pulling the other leg back for a stretch.

Max stood next to her nodding. "Got it."

"You're right. God will show us the way. We can't see what's around the next corner, but God does." Izzy tried to be upbeat. *Counting on you, God. We don't know what we are doing. Please show us the way.*

And so it was that before the art museum had opened its doors, Izzy, Jamie and Max eyed the steps with ambition. "This is something Marty and I had talked about doing." Izzy shrugged. "Life got very busy, especially with the ten-day workweek."

"Shall we do this?" Jamie rubbed her hands.

"Uh, one of us should watch the bags. I'll watch them this time. If anything goes awry, I'll meet you at Independence Hall." Izzy covered her eyes in the sun.

Jamie and Max took off their sweatshirts and stuffed them into their bags. Izzy took out her stopwatch and said, "On your mark, get set…"

Jamie and Max leapt up the stairs. Izzy wasn't surprised to see Jamie leave Max behind after ten steps. But Max swung his arms, and kept pumping his legs, determined to finish the climb. Jamie stopped, leaned over and caught her breath halfway up. But when she saw Max coming, she resumed the climb. Jamie made it to the top in four minutes;

Max lagged another two minutes.

Izzy raised her fists celebrating their triumph. They did the same.

Ten minutes later Izzy greeted them with fist bumps. "You two must be so thirsty. Quick get some water."

Jamie and Max both wiped away sweat. Jamie poured some water over her face.

"I know that water feels good, but we'd better conserve, don't you think?" Izzy the conservationist spoke up.

Max asked, "Mrs. Goldstein, will you try the steps?"

"Nah. Watching you two do it was enough to make me sweat. I'll conserve my energy."

Just then Izzy saw a caravan of three WOP Force jeeps drive past the museum. Her heart pounded in her ears. "The WOP Force just drove by in three jeeps. They may be looking for parking. We had best go mingle with the crowds."

"We haven't eaten yet. Having too much fun. Let's snack as we go. You might need your energy." Jamie patted Max on the shoulder. She retrieved sandwiches and carrot sticks from her food pouch for them both.

Izzy found a granola bar and banana chips. She drank some water, trying to make do with a little.

They followed signs on the main road for Independence Mall. They passed two concession vans. The smell of fried food wafted over the breeze. Suddenly, even though she had just munched on food, Izzy felt ravenous. She rubbed her belly.

"You, too?" Jamie asked. Max nodded and wrapped his waist with both arms.

After twenty minutes Izzy said, "If I recall correctly, we cut over to Arch Street. Won't be long."

No one wore their jackets anymore, or hats and gloves. The sun beat down on them. Izzy wondered how long they could last with their water supply. She had only prepared five bottles, with the thought that she would refill at water fountains.

As they approached Arch Street, Izzy froze. Up ahead, in front of the Reading Terminal Market sat a WOP Force team manning a branding station. She was surprised to see a crowd waiting. Izzy pulled her gloves out of her pocket.

Jamie and Max put on their hats.

"Keep your heads up, guys. God's with us." Izzy marched past the station to Arch Street, keeping her eyes open for signs to Independence Mall. Her eyes and ears strained to pick up any sign that they were being followed.

Izzy let out a sigh of relief and quickened her pace as she saw the red building housing the Liberty Bell. She turned around to Jamie and Max and unselfconsciously threw her hands up in the air. *Thank you, Lord.*

"I guess we can't pay to get in." Max looked down at his shoes, then up to Jamie and Izzy.

"No, but let's go enjoy our liberty on the grassy mall. That's free." Jamie motioned toward the lawn where families had already begun to picnic.

"And the air we breathe is free, too."

"And the sunshine!" Max grinned as he found a nylon poncho in his bag and spread it on the ground.

They spent a couple of hours on the mall, resting and throwing Max's soft frisbee.

Izzy lay down with her hands under her head, looking up into the blue sky through bare branches. A few scattered brown leaves still rustled in the breeze. She thought of Marty disappearing into the sky. *I wonder what it was like. He didn't die. He lives!* Then she thought of the cold day at the cemetery when her mother was buried. *She died. But she, also, lives with Jesus.*

Izzy sat up to see Jamie tossing the disc with her son. *Father, she's got to survive to know you.*

21. HITTING THE JACKPOT

November 9

Dear Marty,

It's been two weeks since I had to flee our lovely home. The WOP Force came pounding on our door. As I grabbed my backpack a loud crash outside made me jump, but I believe God used it to give me a chance to disappear out the back alley. Later I heard an old man—agitated by a bad case of boils—crashed into the WOP Force jeep parked on the street in front of our house.

You will not believe it, but my foe has become my friend. The Father got to me through your journal. Thank you for showing me the way of forgiveness. I will always love you for your sweet and gentle ways. God's ways.

So Jamie wrote me a letter, explaining how she had lost her parents in a car crash when the rapture happened. She also revealed the reason she checked the gender education books out—to make sure they were not too graphic for the little ones! I had no idea that she and I had the same concern. But the biggest surprise was her apologizing for going to the Board so quickly.

She regretted the fallout from that. When she left me her address, I just had to find her. And we have been on the loose running from WOP together ever since.

The first night we spent on benches along the Schuylkill River Trail after a long day downtown. I was just too nervous to stay downtown with the WOP Force patrolling with their flashlights after dark. The benches along the trail were wrought iron and not too comfy to stretch out on. So I sat on the ground and laid my head in my arms on the bench.

After that first night, we found an abandoned warehouse and stayed there one night. The rats freaked us all! Needless to say, we did not sleep much that night. The last week we spent in a garage behind an abandoned house. This arrangement was the best so far. Praise God for his provision. It rained for a couple of days. So it was great having a dry place to hang out. And thank God it had a toilet—one of the conveniences of life we take for granted. There has been no water for cleaning, so we are talking about going to St. Joseph's University locker rooms next to Sweeney Field—invitation of a friend!

The plagues have started for those with the mark. Makes me so glad I belong to Jesus. Jamie is a conscientious objector. When I shared with her that the plagues are God's judgments on those who take the mark, she said, "Another reason to avoid the mark like the plague!" She has no interest in Jesus; she's still hurting after losing both parents. But I have tried to prepare her for what to expect these last days.

Max was the sweetest, patting Jamie's knee, saying in his hoarse voice, "That's okay, Dad. Jesus will take care of us." And she said, "Thank you, Son. You've got your Jesus, and I've got you. We can do this."

Izzy stood up and yawned after journaling. Jamie and Max were already asleep. The garage only housed an old John Deer tractor. The rest of the floor was free for them to stretch out on. Izzy brushed her teeth with her toothbrush and a little paste, then followed up with a swig of water. She wrapped up in her poncho, used her hoodie as a pillow, and fell fast asleep.

At dawn the next morning, the sound of a dog scratching and whimpering at the door of the garage made Izzy wake up with a start. She sat up, and nodded to Jamie and Max who had, also, heard it. They quickly started rolling their beds and packing their bags. Within a minute they were all standing at the door wondering what to do.

Max rocked back and forth.

Jamie said, "Run to the bathroom. Quickly."

When he came out, Jamie went in, and finally, Izzy.

While Izzy was relieving herself, she heard a whistle, and a man's voice, "Rex! Rex! Come here, Boy!" Izzy sighed then smiled. Rex. *No coincidences in God's world.*

When Izzy opened the bathroom door, a tall lanky black man with curly hair wearing a straw hat opened the garage door. Max stood next to his mom, her arm over his shoulder.

The man jumped back. Jamie got poised to fight, and nudged Max back.

Izzy stepped forward to diffuse the tension, smiling her biggest smile. "Forgive us, Sir, for trespassing on your property. We just needed a place to escape from the rain as we were hiking." She stepped forward and offered her hand, "Hi, I'm Izzy. My friends and I were just getting ready to go."

"Well, I'll be. You nearly scared the heck out of me, if you know what I mean. And your friend here looked like a wild boar backed into a corner. I wasn't about to mess with her." He chuckled, then took Izzy's hand in a firm grip. "Alfred Jones, bus driver at your service."

Izzy, Jamie, and Max followed Mr. Jones up the creaky backsteps of the house. Rex nuzzled Izzy's hand, wagging his tail as she scratched his head.

The back door brought them into a kitchen with light speckled acrylic flooring, a steel sink and countertop, and cream colored wooden cabinets, all looking worn in the light of the two light bulbs still working in the fixture. A gang of water bugs went scurrying as the group of strangers walked in, disappearing beneath the sink and cabinet. A chronic drip of the water spigot had left a rust stain in the sink.

Oh, he's got water! Maybe we can clean up. Izzy looked with disgust at the dirt under her nails.

Everyone sat down around the table at Alfred's invitation. Izzy observed that their host did not have any telltale signs of branding. *Perhaps he is also on the run.* "So, Alfred, you're a bus driver?"

"Yes, ma'am. Montgomery County Schools, for twenty-five years already. Mostly serving east county schools. Yes indeed, kids these days are a handful." Alfred took his hat off and set it in his lap. His eyes had several rings of bags under them, and the skin of his droopy jowls appeared leathery.

"I know what you mean. I'm in education, too. I teach—taught—over at Overbrook Elementary. Second grade." Izzy smiled, thinking of her kids. *I wonder how they are?*

"I plum forgot my manners. It appears that maybe you all are in the same boat that I am in." Alfred placed his hands on the table, looking around at his guests. "Are you hungry? I've got toast…day-old bread discarded at the bakery. I got lucky."

He got up and took the bread down from the cupboard. He picked a plaid cloth off of the toaster and plugged it in.

Then he dropped four pieces in and turned around.

"So, you're awfully generous, sharing your hard-won bread with us when you don't have the mark to buy and sell." Izzy's stomach growled. She self-consciously leaned forward, wrapping her arm around her thinning waste.

"Oh, I've been on the receiving end. I had a gambling problem, real bad. There have been times I had nothing to give my wife to feed our little girl. So I'd go out and beg. Some folks don't give you the time of day. But others care. So yeah, I know what it's like to go hungry." Alfred brought a plate down from a shelf and ran it under the rusty water, drying it off with a tissue from his pocket. "It's clean," he said smiling with a smile that reminded Izzy of the Cheshire Cat.

The toast tasted good. *Thank you, Jesus. I used to be one of those who judged beggars. Please forgive my cold-heartedness. Bless Alfred.*

Alfred enjoyed the toast with the rest of them, nearly finishing off the whole loaf. Then he pushed back from the table with a chuckle, slapped the table and pointed at Jamie. "What do you do for a living? You nearly scared me half to death."

Jamie and Max looked at each other. Then they slowly stood up and moved away from the table. Suddenly Max jabbed at his adoptive father with his fist. Jamie got his arm in a grip and flipped him onto the floor.

Izzy and Alfred's mouths hung open in surprise.

Jamie helped Max up, and asked, "You okay, Son?" And they sat down.

"What?" Izzy was incredulous. "I didn't know you knew martial arts. Amazing, you two."

"He-he-he. I saw it coming!" Alfred clapped with glee.

"I used to be a Taekwondo coach. And before that, I studied to teach P.E." Jamie cracked her hands.

"Dad's the best!" Max's beaming face was framed by unruly blond curls.

"Oh? Dad, huh?" Alfred put his big hand across Max's matted curls. "You adopted?"

Max dropped his eyes to the floor and nodded his head.

"Hey, that's nothing to be ashamed of." Izzy nudged his arm with her fist. "Praise God for parents that love you."

Max sat up and grinned. "Yeah, it's been pretty cool." He put his arm on Jamie's back.

Alfred stood up and peeked out the kitchen window both ways. "Ah, we're alone here on this hill. Just hoping we don't get some company. The WOP Force is active in town. I tell you what. I imagine you might like to clean up a bit." He squished Max's matted locks in his hand.

"No, man!" Max squirmed.

"Wonderful idea." Jamie clapped her hands together. "Thank you so much."

"The water pressure isn't good, as we've got no pump now. But the good thing is that it is well water, so at least we have water. Let me show you to the bathroom and give you some towels."

"You are a lifesaver. Thank you, Mr. Jones." Izzy patted Max's back and leaned over to look into his face. "Won't a nice shampoo make you feel better?"'

Jamie and Max followed Alfred out. Izzy leaned down to get both sides of Rex's long face in her hands. She gave him a good scratch under his chin and behind his ears. He was a mix of collie and labrador, with long dark hair and deep brown eyes. "Rex, you look a little thin. I imagine it's hard to keep you fed now."

Alfred walked in, and hearing her comment responded. "When my wife and daughter disappeared, I'm afraid I lost my chance to buy poor Rex here more food. My world fell apart when I lost them. Especially when there's no way am

I going to take that monster Mr. B's ID. So, to tell you the truth, Miss Izzy, you all stopped me from putting me and Rex here out of our misery. At least for a little while." He leaned his chair back against the wall and closed his eyes.

Izzy saw tears moistening his eyes. "Alfred, I'm glad God sent us to stop your plan." She reached out and rubbed his arm.

"Well, it must have been God. Because I was all set to turn on the old John Deer and let me and my dog take a nap."

"Dear Mr. Alfred." Izzy got tears in her eyes. "You are precious to God. You and I missed the rapture, but God's love for you is real. And his promises will give you hope and keep you going during the tough days to come."

Izzy got out her pocket testament. "Look here. Romans 5:8—'but God shows his love for us in that while we were still sinners, Christ died for us.'"

"Yep. My wife told me the same thing. I've just always wanted to clean up my act a little bit before coming to God. That's the part that's tough—cleaning up my life. I still owe tremendous debt. That's why I left this place." He threw up his hands and indicated his house.

"I've struggled with addiction, too, Mr. Alfred. Everybody does to one degree or another. You are in good company."

"How's that?" Alfred sat up and clasped his hands before him on the table.

"You and I qualify for the love of Christ, because we're sinners. He proved his love for us by dying for us while we were sinners. And then he left us with this promise." Izzy turned back to Romans 8:38 and read—"For I am sure that neither death nor life, nor angels nor rulers..." Izzy looked up and whispered—"Not even Mr. B and The Prophet." Then looking down she read—"...nor things present nor things to come, nor powers, nor height nor depth, nor anything else in all creation, will be able to separate us from the love of God in Christ Jesus our Lord."

Tears were streaming down Mr. Jone's face as he held his big hand over both eyes. He searched for his tissue and used it. Smiling he said, "Well, that just about covers all my worries—death is the biggest, and the Beast and the WOP Force, and the unknown…even all of creation going crazy. Fears that just, well, have made me useless to myself, and others, including poor Rex here." Then the big man leaned over and gave Izzy a hug. "Thank you, Miss Izzy. You've given me hope. Now I can say, 'Thank you, Jesus!' I never really understood his acceptance and love before. Thank you."

Max came around the corner with a grin, with Jamie close behind him. "Thank you, Mr. Jones. That was fantastic. I feel so much better." Jamie stepped forward and offered her hand.

Mr. Jones started laughing and looked cautiously at her hand, waving his finger.

Jamie clasped his hand in a healthy shake, grinning.

"I guess I'd better quick get my shower." Izzy gathered her bag and waited for Alfred to show her the way. As they went Izzy encouraged him. "Jesus will never leave you or forsake you, Mr. Alfred. I'll be praying for you."

"Thank you, Miss Izzy. I do believe I hit the jackpot today!"

Refreshed and clean, Izzy, Max and Jamie bid farewell to Mr. Alfred Jones. *A most hospitable man with a big heart. I wonder when I'll see him again.*

They walked toward St. Joseph's University, thinking to explore the possibility of throwing their clothes into the washer and dryer under Vanessa's management.

Izzy thought it good to come up with some ideas for survival with her travel companions. "Do you know, with so many elderly people home alone, I'm sure some of them would appreciate some help around the house and yard, or with running errands. Perhaps God will provide for our physical needs as we serve others."

Jamie and Max nodded with agreement. "Excellent idea. Perhaps Max, also, could help babysit. He enjoys little children."

Izzy strained to get up the hills. Her eyes and her throat began to burn, and she coughed into her hand. "I wonder what's going on with the air. Maybe we'd better put on our masks."

No sooner had they put on their masks, than they saw the foreboding yellow form of a WOP Force jeep come around the corner in their direction. They exchanged knowing glances and picked up their pace as they moved forward. They all broke into a sprint, Izzy veering to the left, and Max and Jamie dashing down a street to the right.

God watch over us, Izzy prayed.

Izzy noticed a driveway going into someone's yard and dashed down the drive. Wheels screeched. *Oh, Lord, they've seen us!*

22. <u>CHLOE</u>

There was a gate accessing the alley. Izzy quickly opened it, then squeezed behind a shed next to the garage in the yard. Something crawled over her feet as she made her way in, and her breath caught in her throat.

Three WOP officers ran down the drive. They bolted to the gate and scanned both directions down the alley to find their prey.

Then Izzy heard voices. A woman's voice spoke from the back porch. "Is there a problem, officers?"

A man's voice answered. "Major House, His Highness Bandar's World Order and Peace Force of Philadelphia, Miss. We followed a suspect into your yard. It appears she escaped down the alley." The officer spoke again. "Miss, I can see that your home has four residents—you, your husband, a daughter and granddaughter, surnamed Anderson. Is that correct?'

"Yes, Sir. That is correct. Except that my dear husband just passed away a month ago; came down with a nasty case of the boils. There are three of us, now. We have all complied."

"So sorry for your loss. Do you mind if we look around,

Ms. Anderson?"

"No, not at all. Go ahead."

Izzy didn't dare breathe. She heard the men shifting things around in the garage. Sweat beaded on her forehead.

"Oh, hello, Kitty. How are you today?" Major House bent over to stroke the cat's back.

"Misty! There you are. I've been looking all over for you. You naughty kitten." Mrs. Anderson stepped off the porch to pick up her renegade pet, more like a bale of hay than a kitten. "Bad kitty. Mommy's got you now." Misty butted her head against her mistress's face.

"Rather affectionate, isn't she? We have a cat, too."

Izzy sweated. *Thank God for kitties.*

"That's all for today, Ms. Anderson. Have a good day. Peace and prosperity from His Highness Bandar's World Order for Peace."

"Thank you, Officers."

Izzy heard the men get into their vehicle and back down the driveway into the street. Her heart did flip-flops in her throat. She began to breathe a little easier, listening for the door to the house to close. When she thought it would be safe to exit her hiding place, Izzy pulled up her hood and squeezed back out to the opening.

Just then, a child came bounding out of the house and down the steps. She froze in her footsteps when she saw the hooded figure and screamed.

"Chloe! Don't be afraid. It's me, your second-grade teacher, Mrs. Goldstein." She put down her hood and stepped out into the yard.

"Oh, Ms. Frank! What are you doing here? I missed you when you did not come back to school. I thought you had disappeared."

Hearing her granddaughter's chatter, Mrs. Anderson ran out to the porch. "Mrs. Goldstein! Are you all right?"

Izzy raised her hands and nodded. "So far, so good. Would you mind if I came in so we could talk?"

They have received the mark. I'd better be careful.

When they walked into the living room, the TV screen caught Izzy's attention. Mrs. Anderson went to turn it off, but Izzy stopped her. "It's been a while since I have had access to the news. Would you mind?"

"You're one of those," said Chloe flatly. "I had to get the mark with Mommy and Grandma and Grandpa. Ms. Frank, shouldn't you get the mark to be legal?" She tugged on Izzy's sleeve and looked up into her face with a pleading look.

Izzy reached down and gently stroked her chin. *What can I say? It's too late to help her family. They already have the mark.*

"Yes, Chloe. Obedience is so important. You obey your Mommy and Grandmom, and your teachers at school."

Like an adorable puppy with big eyes and silky brown hair, Chloe nodded, not blinking once.

"That's a good girl. I have God to lean on. Don't you worry." Izzy gave Chloe a hug.

Mrs. Anderson shook her head and sat down. Just then, scenes of devastation from the week before flashed upon the screen. Flaming extraterrestrial rock like a mountain streaked across the sky.

> QUESPIE: His Highness deserves our respect and submission. It was absolutely amazing how quick the response was to the asteroid which exploded above the Danube River near Budapest. The world mourns the loss of about a million and a half people

in the greater Budapest area covering fifteen kilometers as the airburst flattened everything in its wake.

Oh, Father, have mercy! Looks so much like nuclear blasts! Izzy felt faint and sat down.

ROGERS: The magnitude of the impact of each of the two asteroids which struck last Sunday is like that of a thousand atomic bombs. The devastation from the asteroid which exploded over St. Louis Missouri covered a twenty-kilometer spread killing a million people. Subsequently, waters throughout the Mississippi River basin have been made undrinkable. This includes the Ohio River, which, as we know, feeds Pennsylvania's water system.

QUESPIE: Scientists do not recognize the elements dumped in the Danube, the Black Sea, and the Mississippi River basin, but whatever they are, they are poisonous to mankind. Plus, the fallout from such powerful impacts to our globe has rendered other water exposed to the atmosphere undrinkable.

ROGERS: But His Highness Bandar has wasted no time getting his teams and the water purification plants up and running to provide clean water for the masses. Already thousands of people have died from drinking the untreated water. So, we beg you, do not trust any water in your locality until you have been notified that the water has been treated

and is potable. Again, do not drink the tap water until you know it is safe.

QUESPIE: Now for the local news, today Independence Square filled with angry protesters shouting, "Nonconformists, Reform or Die!" You can see their placards of His Highness Bandar. They applaud his management of the world's response to the spate of natural disasters striking the earth these days. Mr. Bandar's ten percent tax on all monthly income to help with the recovery process should be shouldered by all. By non-compliance, people rob these humanitarian efforts of about twenty billion dollars!

ROGERS: Thank God I got the mark. (He held up his hand to show his mark.)

QUESPIE: Yes, otherwise we'd die of thirst! (She held up her hand to show off her mark as well.)

Mrs. Anderson picked up the remote and turned off the news channel. Stately, with a short white curly perm, she looked at Izzy and smiled. "I don't hold anything against you, Mrs. Goldstein. You must have been devastated when your husband disappeared."

Izzy looked down at her hands and nodded. "I learned to trust God enough to forgive others a little too late."

"So, you still trust God, after He left you behind?" Mrs. Anderson sat down, clasping her hands together. "I find that difficult. Especially after the rash of plagues which have debilitated us, broken us, and taken our loved ones."

She suddenly looks so tired. I wonder what happened to the rest of her family. Izzy extended her hand to the elderly woman's shoulder. "I'm sorry, you have suffered, too."

"Grandpa died of the boils," Chloe whispered, wiping a tear away with the back of her hand.

"Oh, that is so sad. How are you getting along?" Izzy grabbed Chloe's hand and rubbed Mrs. Anderson's shoulder.

"We miss him." The elderly widow stood up, wringing her hands. "You never know how much you depend on someone until they are gone. He used to be the handyman in the house. Now we are falling apart."

"And Grandpa's pancakes were the best." Chloe rubbed her belly and licked her lips.

"Well, I make good pancakes. Maybe I can make you all some, that is if it fits into your plans." Izzy's stomach gurgled. *Giving away how little I've eaten lately!*

"Why, you must be starving!" Chloe lay across her teacher's knees, putting her ear on Izzy's belly.

"Well, it is just about lunchtime. Breakfast is good any time of day. How long has it been since you last ate?" Mrs. Anderson grabbed a couple of aprons from the back of the basement door in the kitchen and handed one to Izzy.

Izzy thought for a moment. "Hmm, except for some toast this morning, it has been a couple of nights."

"It's unbelievable that it has come to this—no branding with the mark, then no freedom to use your own money! But I declare, no one has said you can't work for your dinner."

Izzy smiled at her senior hostess's kindness. *She waves her finger just like Aunt Anna used to. Thank you for a safe home to rest in, and a warm meal. Bless this family for their hospitality to me. And bless Jamie and Max wherever they are.*

The table set, everyone gathered around the table for the fluffy pancakes Izzy whipped together. Mrs. Anderson even put on a pot of coffee and cooked up some bacon. Izzy savored every bite. *Thank you, Lord, for friends and food!*

Suddenly one of the light bulbs over the kitchen table blinked and then went out.

"Oh dear, we have lost another bulb in that fixture. They never seem to last very long. Now with Grandpa gone, how are we going to fix it?" Mrs. Anderson folded her napkin and threw it on the table.

"If you have a ladder, I'm sure I can replace the bulb." Izzy stood up for action.

Mrs. Anderson showed Izzy where the ladder was, hanging longwise on hooks above the steps going down into the basement. Together they got it out and set it up beneath the light fixture. Izzy climbed up the ladder and straddled the top, waiting for Mrs. Anderson to find a new bulb. From her perch she saw the yellow form of a WOP jeep turn up their driveway!

Oh my Lord, I'm a sitting duck! Izzy scrambled down the ladder just as Chloe came bounding in from the front steps.

"Ms. Frank, you've got to HIDE!" Chloe waved at Izzy to follow her. By that time Mrs. Anderson heard the commotion and returned to the kitchen with a new bulb.

"Maybe I should just run," Izzy whispered, stooping down.

"No, Chloe has her favorite hiding place to show you." Chloe's grandmom, feeling a little faint, sat down at the table, waving the girls on.

Major House appeared at the back door and peered through the screen. "Mrs. Anderson, did we catch you at a bad time? Mr. Dodd from Utilities is here to give you a water-testing kit. May we come in?"

"Of course, Officer. I was just getting ready to try to replace the bulb. Now that my husband's gone, it's up to me to do repairs."

Mrs. Anderson shakily got up and unlocked the back screen. "Come in."

"Well, Ma'am, my men are pretty nimble. Let's ask them to do this job." Major House took off his cap and rubbed his scalp with a handkerchief before replacing it. "Mr. Dodd, please help Mrs. Anderson replace her bulb."

Mr. Dodd, whose uniform sported the water company's emblem, almost didn't need the ladder, he was so tall and nimble. He climbed a few steps and finished the job before Chloe reappeared from the basement. She had Misty in her arms.

"Oh, hello, Kitty, Kitty, Kitty! Hello, little girl." Officer House scratched Misty behind the ears, and patted Chloe on the head. "My cat loves to disappear into the basement, too, when company calls."

"Mm-hm. Exactly. Sometimes we don't see her for hours." Chloe scooted onto a chair. Misty looked like a big ragdoll draped over her arms.

"I'm sorry, I completely forgot my manners. Can I get you something to drink?" Mrs. Anderson stood at the back of her chair.

"No, thank you, Ma'am. You just take this vial and put some of your tap water into it." Mr. Dodd handed her the empty vial labeled with her name and address. "Our city water got contaminated slightly by the fallout from the asteroid that hit Minnesota. Terrible thing. But the portable water filtering machines, compliments of His Highness and all the faithful citizens of Philadelphia, have been installed, and we are hopeful the water is potable now."

"Thank you, Sir." Mrs. Anderson filled the vial. "We usually drink bottled water."

"That is going to be scarce now, I'm afraid." Mr. Dodd pocketed the water kit. "That asteroid poisoned all the waters of the Mississippi water basin. Plus, it obliterated a portion of the Ohio River, and we are in the process of rerouting the water. So water has become more scarce here in Pennsylvania. If you feel nervous about the tap water, try distilling it. You'll get the report next month, unless you want to pay extra. You will be billed one hundred for this service, but for another hundred, you can expedite this report."

"Let's expedite, then. Better safe than sorry."

Mr. Dodd made some notes on his phone. "All taken care of. You will be billed accordingly." He pocketed his phone, and looked to Officer House, who sat teasing the cat with his keychain. Coughing slightly, Mr. Dodd said loudly, "Well, Mrs. Anderson, you take care. Glad we could be of service."

Major House jumped up. "Yes. And we would be remiss not to let you know that His Highness B has declared it a crime to give aid to non-conformists. We know one made her escape through your property this morning. Please protect yourself. Anyone without His Highness's branding should be reported. People who lend them aid could be fined two-thousand dollars."

Chloe gasped, and everyone looked at her. She saw the attention and immediately began scolding Misty. "You bad kitty, you bit me!"

Mrs. Anderson cleared her throat, saying, "Misty gets a little excited when there's company around." Then she stood up slowly and offered her hand to Officer House and Mr. Dodd. "Thank you, Officers. We appreciate your help. That climb would have been much harder for me."

When the men were gone, Mrs. Anderson sank into a chair, letting out a shaky breath. Chloe stood at her knees, gently touching the face of her grandmother. "That's okay, Grandmom. We were only trying to help Ms. Frank. I had better go get her."

Chloe swiped her long brown curls behind her ears and thundered down the stairs into the basement. Less than a minute later she reappeared shaking her head and raising her hands. "She's gone!"

23. <u>LOST AND FOUND</u>

Blood flowed in the streets all over the globe as His Highness Bandar struck out in frustration and hatred for anyone committed to God. The WOP Force carried little images of the Beast wherever they patrolled, looking for offenders who refused to be branded for the Sovereign. Minors—seventeen years old and younger—were wrenched from their parents and sent off to reform school. They gave their adult captives one last chance to bow the knee before His Highness B. If they refused they were carted off to execution stations, where the law-abiding citizens with the mark liked to gather, shouting, "It serves them right! His Highness Bandar deserves our allegiance for all he has done for mankind."

People were divided into two camps—those who praised Mr. Bandar and his regime, and those who thought they were evil incarnate.

Vanessa was ambivalent. "I just go with the flow and try to do what I'm told. And I've been told that I am not allowed to let people from off campus use the facilities." She leaned forward and whispered to Izzy, who sat with her at her desk, "But you came at my invitation, so let's make it quick."

Izzy made her way to St. Joe's tennis courts at Sweeney Field the day after she left the Anderson home, hoping to find her friends. But Vanessa had not seen Jamie and Max.

Izzy followed Vanessa down the hall of the clubhouse to the laundry room. *It's so sad that Jamie and Max aren't here. Dear Jesus, send your angels to keep them safe.*

Vanessa gave Izzy a little hug and pat on the back. "I don't guess you have money for soap and such. My treat." She brought out her own stash of detergent and coins and handed them to Izzy. "It's a good thing you got here early; use a short wash so you can get out of here before the crowds come. I've got to get back out front."

Izzy worked at the elbows and soiled cuffs of her hoody with bar soap before throwing it in the wash with her clothes. *God, I'm getting grungy.* She scrubbed the dirt around and under her nails. Then she sank to the ground next to the machine, her eyes closed before she hit the floor. She thought of Marty and imagined his warm embrace. She prayed for Jamie and Max, Chloe and her grandmom, Alfred Jones and even Rex.

She put her laundry into a dryer. Then she sat back down with her pocket Bible. She opened it to Revelation, to skim. She read about the Beast being given authority to persecute the saints for a time. Her eyes fell upon Revelation 14:10— *"If anyone is to be taken captive, to captivity he goes: if anyone is to be slain, with the sword must he be slain."*

Izzy's head fell back to the wall. *That's not much of a choice, Lord.* She reread the passage—*"If anyone is to be taken captive, to captivity he goes; if anyone is to be slain, with the sword must he be slain. Here is a call for the endurance and faith of the saints."*

Izzy finished her laundry, and went out wearing a brighter, cleaner jacket. She waved and smiled at Vanessa who was hemmed in by a crowd of people at the reception desk.

As she walked down the hill from St. Joe's a cry rose in her throat. "O God, I'll endure with your help. Give me faith which won't waver!"

One day Izzy lay under some low-lying bushes overlooking the street below where there was an afternoon market. She enjoyed watching kids coming in and out of a candy store with their moms or nannies. She was delighted to see them skipping with joy. *Marty and I never got to have a family. It just wasn't meant to be.* She tried to brush the sorrow away by reciting a promise she had read.

Proverbs 10:22—*"The blessing of the Lord makes rich, and he adds no sorrow to it."*

Just then a commotion on the street below startled her. A WOP Force officer yelled, "Stop, in the name of Premier Bandar. Stop, or I'll shoot." Izzy noticed a string of three women being herded into a WOP Force jeep. But a fourth woman had broken away and fled up the street. Suddenly, the officer shot, and the bullet found its mark. The woman fell to the street as many observers screamed and rushed from the scene with crying children. The WOP officer checked the pulse of the fallen woman, and declared, "Death to Non-conformists. Let the people honor His Highness Bandar!"

To Izzy's horror, some people stood in their doorways or on the roadside clapping for the WOP Force. *I can't believe it. This cannot be happening.* Izzy wriggled out of her hiding place to run.

As she retreated, she heard some people shouting, "She deserved it. Follow King B!"

That night Izzy crept onto the grounds of Belmont Bible Church, looking for some solace. Of course, Pastor Michaels and the familiar faces of the Ladies' Fellowship were gone. Loneliness and fear gripped her heart. She found a row of bushes along the back wall to rest under in the shadows.

She munched on a half-eaten apple and bread crusts left in someone's lunch bag which she had found in the trash. She wrapped up in her poncho, sitting up and leaning her head against the brick wall, and dropped off to sleep.

In the middle of the night Izzy heard a muffled scream. Izzy's eyes opened. *Am I dreaming? Am I safe?* She waited and listened. Then she heard it, a low droning chant. She glanced over her shoulder and saw the soft light of candles coming from the Fellowship Hall. *Are they now using the church for their sacrifices?*

Izzy frantically wrapped up her poncho and stuffed it into her bag, hardly daring to breathe, fighting back tears. She crawled as quickly as she could behind the bushes away from view. Her left knee came down on something sharp, and she stopped and hung her head in pain, not daring to cry out. When she rounded the corner, rather than flee down the access road from the church, she hobbled off to the side, and found an alley which would take her to Fairmount Park.

She sobbed all the way to the glen. With no tissue, Izzy used one of her shirts for her nose and face. Her cheeks, already windburned, stung with her tears. A blood moon spied upon her path all the way to the park. Her knee left a trail of blood.

In the eerie moonlight Izzy made her way to the restrooms. In the half-light of a lamp outside the entrance she saw a jagged tear in her knee. She was grateful to discover warm water at the sink and tried to rinse her knee over the sink. It stung and bled as she used soap to scrub the wound. She pressed paper towels against the wound for a while to stop the bleeding.

Tired, she looked up into the mirror; the face of a waif stared back at her—scraggly hair framed her thinning red cheeks and tired eyes rested on dark rings. She gasped. *Horrors!* She went right to work splashing her face with water, cooling her chapped cheeks and scrubbing at the crevices along her nose. Gruesome memories and imagined fears flooded her mind. Her hands shook as she used a musty towel from her bag to dry her face.

Izzy decided to give herself a quick sponge bath without removing her clothes—using a thinning washcloth which she rinsed out under the warm water and wrung out, she swiped over her whole body thoroughly. *Thank you, Father, for the warm water and a refreshing bath. Now, please wash away the memories from today which haunt me. I don't know how long I can do this.*

She slipped into a stall and changed her clothes as the birds began to herald the dawn. Then she spent some time at the sink rinsing out her dirty clothes, scrubbing them with a shriveling bar of white soap. Her socks and pants still had the shadow of blood stains when she gave up on washing them. She rinsed and wrung them out and shook them out to dry. Then she gathered her things and climbed to the spot overlooking the glen where Marty had proposed to her. She sighed as she draped her damp clothes over bushes. Then she sat down under a familiar tree and began to work on her hair with a brush. From her perch she watched the sun rise over Philadelphia.

The sun warmed Izzy's body and she fell asleep. She dreamt of playing kickball with her students then awoke with a start, surprised that it had gotten so late. She looked down the hill and saw a cleaning woman eyeing her with a smile. Wearing a neon green vest with the words "Sanitation Department" the woman looked away and went back to sweeping and cleaning.

She seems friendly enough. What time is it? It feels late. Izzy stretched out her leg gingerly; the wound throbbed. She looked around and remembered her laundry hanging over the bushes. Slowly turning and rolling over to her good knee, Izzy managed to pull herself up. She limped as she collected her clothes, folded them, and stuffed them into her backpack.

Izzy scanned the park—it was practically empty, except for a mother and child tossing a ball in the field. She looked back to search for the cleaning lady at the bathroom, but she was gone. Izzy soaked up a few seconds of sunshine and peace before moving on.

I have to find Jamie and Max! I hope they're okay.

Izzy was determined to get to 30th Street Station, although she had a fever, and her sore knee slowed her down. She found that dragging her left foot with each step of her right foot helped her move faster. She kept her hood up to cover her forehead and wore her gloves. As she came into town, she noticed the News being broadcast in a store window. She lingered outside watching the screen.

She saw the two prophets of God who appeared in Jerusalem after the image of the Beast had been placed in the temple. They cursed the world with famine and no rain for three years. Some people attempted to capture them, but, to Izzy's surprise, the men called down fire from heaven which killed their attackers.

Next, Izzy nearly fainted when she saw three caskets being removed from Belmont Bible Church. The News revealed a replica of the Beast set up inside the Fellowship Hall and devotees burning incense and bowing down to it.

Apparently, non-conformists had become fair game for ritualistic sacrifices!

Izzy pushed back the fear by remembering a verse Marty had written in his journal—

"And they overcame him because of the blood of the Lamb and because of the word of their testimony. And they did not love their life even when faced with death."

By the time she got to 30th Street Station Izzy's legs felt like rubber, and the fever raged. She walked into the station with a determination to find her friends. She felt dwarfed inside, and also very vulnerable. But she wanted so much to find Max and Jamie. She thought she saw a head of hair like Max's, and she followed it into the food court. "Max! Max! Jamie?" Izzy's head spun. It wasn't Max. Izzy sank down into a chair at a table and put her head down. She slept, her head cradled in her arms.

Something woke her. The fever had gone. Izzy felt their presence and saw through her unkempt long blonde hair some men clad in gray. With a surge of energy, she stood to her feet.

"Stay where you are, I don't want to hurt you," she heard herself saying. "Why do you fight against the Lord our God, your Creator? Your life and breath are in his hands. Repent and come to him for forgiveness. He brought the boils, now he brings lingering death! Repent! Return to him. Perhaps he will spare you."

A swarm of strange scorpion locusts—their faces, demonic, their eyes, red—surrounded Izzy's would-be captors like a cloak, stinging them with their tails. The WOP force screamed and thrashed. Many fell to the ground in a fetal position, crying. People in the station ran for their lives. Others bent over in agonizing pain. Izzy stood up and walked through the crowd, everyone oblivious of her going.

How long, oh Lord? I am starving. My throat is so sore and dry.

"Take courage, my faithful servant. I will not give you more than you can bear. Be strong, be brave. Do you see that red car at the curb? Tap on the window."

This is crazy, Lord. But if you say so, what do I have to lose?

Izzy approached the red car and tapped on the window. A beautiful young woman rolled down the window, and, smiling, handed Izzy two bags of food and a tall bottled water. "Thank you so much. God bless you."

I sound like a frog, Lord. But I cannot believe your GOODNESS!

At that same moment, Max pulled Jamie's arm and pointed to the TV screen in the display window where Izzy had been standing not long before. When they saw Izzy at 30th Street Station on LIVE NEWS, they started running to find her.

The air grew dark with smoke, and they saw the strange creatures flying menacingly by. "Keep yourself zipped up," Jamie warned Max as she zipped up her jacket and put on her gloves.

People ran by them, crying. Then they saw Izzy, dragging her left foot as she walked.

"Izzy! Ms. Izzy! You're hurt!" Max ran right up to his teacher and yelled over the commotion.

"Max! Jamie! You're here! Oh, thank you, Jesus!" Izzy nodded toward a bench and deposited her packages there. Then she hugged Jamie, weeping. Max squeezed in to join their group hug.

The air became more difficult to breathe, and the three started coughing. "Let's find someplace safe, and indoors if possible. And we'd better put on our masks."

Max picked up Izzy's packages. Jamie supported Izzy on her left side. They moved along in silence because of the bad air. Before they knew it, they were already on the Schuylkill River Trail.

"Let's sit here and eat." Izzy motioned to some benches by the riverside. There was still a little bit of sunshine, and the air was easier to breathe.

"Food? You've got food?" Max hugged his waist.

"Yes, I think it's the gift of an angel."

"Really? Because I saw the bronze statue of an angel holding a man at the 30th Street Station, and I asked God if angels were real." Max cocked his head.

"Well, let's not just talk about it. Let's see how real this food is first!" Jamie sat with her hands on her hips.

Everybody laughed. Then they each shared a plate of pancakes piled high with pecans, whipped cream, and bacon pieces. The bottle of water seemed to be bottomless, as they were all able to fill their water bottles with it before it was empty. Izzy especially savored the moments with friends who were lost and then found. *God, you heard my prayer!*

After their meal, Jamie and Izzy walked together up the trail. "Look how dry the river is. There's just a trickle of water. The grass is turning yellow. It doesn't look good." Jamie shook her head.

Max peered at his parent through his matted bangs. "Dad, it's got to get worse before it gets better. But I'm not afraid. Jesus will take care of us."

"But he didn't take care of Grandmom and Grandpop." Jamie snapped at Max.

"But he did. I believe he took them to heaven that day. I heard Mom tell them to ask Jesus into their hearts that morning, because they were nervous about all the bad things going on—asteroids, wildfires, plagues."

Izzy put her hand on Jamie's shoulder. "Your mom and

dad didn't get Mr. B's branding either?"

Jamie shook her head. "Heck, no! They were more die-hard independent than I am. I've been tempted to get the mark recently. This starving to death is hard." Jamie's voice cracked.

Izzy noticed how baggy Jamie's pants were. *I'm not far behind.* But she was sure anytime there was food to eat, Jamie had made sure her son had some first. "I agree. We've not enough food. There's hardly any water. Our skin is itching and cracked. Our bellies hurt. And our greasy itchy heads are driving us crazy? Right?"

"So?" Jamie looked confused.

"So…" Izzy groped for the right words to say, words to give Jamie hope. "So, there's a day coming when Jesus will take us by the hand and lead us to streams of water; we won't hunger or thirst anymore, and he will wipe away our tears. Jamie, that's our only hope and comfort these days. As bad as it's got to this point, it's going to get worse."

"How do you know?" Jamie motioned to a bench they were approaching, and everyone sat down.

Izzy grabbed her worn bible from her bag and turned to Revelation. She showed Jamie the rundown of plagues which they had already encountered—hail mixed with blood and fire, the asteroid which had turned the sea to blood, and the meteorites which had poisoned the rivers. "We all have witnessed this latest plague of the locusts."

"What's keeping them from stinging us?" Jamie asked, looking around.

"Well, Max and I have God's stamp on our foreheads, sealed by the Holy Spirit. I believe he is protecting us." Izzy looked at Max. "Right, Max?"

Max nodded and grabbed Jamie's hand. "Please, Dad! Don't you want God's seal?"

Jamie looked down at Max's hand in hers. "So, you think

Grandmom and Grandpop went to be with Jesus? The car was gutted out by the fire. I just assumed their bodies were incinerated."

Max looked up at Ms. Izzy. "I hope so. Mom led them in prayer that morning before she disappeared, and the accident happened."

Jamie hung her head, and her shoulders slumped. "I don't know if Jesus will accept me. I've made some wrong choices, done some things I regret."

"Jesus will forgive you. Just ask." Izzy put her hand on her friend's shoulder.

Jamie nodded her head and started crying. "Oh, God. I've been stubborn and have clung to lies which I know weren't right. I hated you. And I wasn't satisfied with the way you made me, and I hope you'll forgive me. Wash me clean, please. Give me your seal. I want to belong to you."

A big smile spread across Jamie's face when she looked up, wiping her tears away on her dirty sleeve. "Do you see it?" she asked.

"See what?" Max cocked his head, a grin on his face.

"The branding! I've been branded by Jesus." Jamie reached out her arms and Izzy and Max, laughing, gave her a big hug.

"And the angels in heaven are rejoicing!" Izzy remembered Marty's story, his note in her lunch that day so many moons ago. *Father, another prodigal daughter has come home! Thank you for waiting with open arms.*

That night the three happy fugitives made their way to Alfred Jone's house. Darkness fell before they got there. But inside the kitchen window they saw the flicker of a candle.

Izzy's heart pounded. *Alfred? Dare we knock?*

Just then, Alfred opened the back door with a big toothy smile. "Well, bless my soul. We meet again. You know, it's not really safe around here. Rex and I were getting ready to go." He handed Izzy a notice from The WOP Force of Greater Philadelphia.

Izzy read it aloud. "This premise is absconded by The World Order for Peace of Greater Philadelphia, as the resident, Mr. Alfred Jones, has not yet entered the grid through receiving Premier Abdul Mutakabbir Asahd Bandar's branding."

Max and Jamie groaned.

Izzy bent over to rub behind Rex's ears. He had lost a lot of hair, and his skin clung to his ribcage. *Poor Rex. Hang in there, Buddy. It looks like we all need to run again.* Looking at her tired companions, Izzy asked, "Do we dare spend the night to rest?"

Mr. Alfred shook his head. "I'm feeling a little nervous, so Rex and I are ready to go. But Jesus has been a constant friend, Miss Izzy, ever since you introduced us. Thank you." He leaned over and gave Izzy a hug, Jamie and Max as well. He moved more slowly since the time Izzy first saw him. Putting on a warm, knit hat over his graying hair, gloves with holes in them, and a tattered scarf, Alfred put his hand on the doorknob, and bowed to all. "I'll see you all in heaven someday, if not before!" Then he pulled the door to and disappeared into the night.

Izzy and Jamie decided they should sleep for a few hours before heading out. They explored the house and found beds to sleep on. The tap produced only a slow drip of brown water, so they collected enough water in cups from the shelf to brush their teeth and to take light sponge baths. *I trust well water more than river water these days. Maybe I should collect some water overnight for drinking tomorrow.* Izzy found a larger container to collect the water and lay down to sleep.

Izzy swallowed. Her dry throat stuck to itself, and she coughed, waking herself up. She opened her eyes and sat up quickly. *What time is it?* The wall clock revealed it was four in the morning. *Thank you, Jesus. A good time to get out.*

She woke up her travel buddies and went to check on the water in the sink. The half-gallon container was two thirds full. The brown silt had sunk to the bottom, leaving a layer of cleaner water. *Thank you, Father, for water to drink.* She collected everybody's water bottles and spent about fifteen minutes ladling the cleaner water on top into each bottle. Hers was the last to be filled. *A little gritty, I think, but more to chew on.*

Jamie, Max and Izzy gathered together in the dark kitchen. They did not dare even light a candle. Shadows from the streetlamp shining through the trees danced on the walls. They held hands and prayed.

"Father, thank you for the rest, and for the new day."

"Thank you for water to drink."

"Thank you for our friendship. Watch over us and keep us in your peace. In Jesus' name."

And everybody said, "Amen." Then they exchanged hugs, wiping away a few tears, and ventured out.

24. <u>TURBULENT TIMES</u>

Dark clouds of swarming scorpion locusts—hellish and indestructible—engulfed whole cities, inflicting debilitating stings. The afflicted begged for death to escape the excruciating pain, but they were doomed to lingering torment for five months. Izzy heard the news that many people in Philadelphia tried to end their lives, the pain was so unbearable; she was saddened to hear that their friend at St. Joseph's University, Vanessa, was one of them—after a five floor jump from her dorm on campus, she lived on with multiple organ damage, splintered bones in her legs, spinal cord injuries, a concussion, and the overwhelming pain of the scorpion sting.

Then giant hail—some weighing one hundred pounds—plummeted the whole world, causing blood to flow as people were injured and died; fires spread from the damage to buildings and electric relay stations.

Electric fires spread into wildfires since the sun had baked the earth with no rain for months so that a third of the earth was scorched with fire. The asteroid strike caused a third of the sea life, as well, to pass away and the ocean waters were turning thick and dark red like old blood; a third of freshwater rivers were poisoned, also, by meteorite strikes. The air became putrid. Disease grew rampant. People by the millions began to die of toxins, thirst and disease.

"Cursed! Cursed be God! This sun is unbearable! It's like we're in an oven!" His Highness B yelled at his audience of one, The Prophet. "It's impossible to be out in the sun for even five minutes without getting burned. But I know The Prince of Darkness is stronger still. Let him not forget my sacrifice!"

Wherever His Highness B went, The Prophet kept the crowds committed to the regime through demonstrating supernatural power, performing miracles. One time the Premier and the ten partner nations organized a golf tournament to raise money for disaster relief. One of the kings lost his club in the lake. When The Prophet saw it, he threw a stick into the water where the club had fallen, and the club floated to the surface so that the player could retrieve it.

On another occasion, when dignitaries visited, and many fell ill with food poisoning, Khalil Yasin Hamza—the "powerful companion prophet"—put a common sweet potato in the water containers and ordered everyone who was ill to drink of that water, and they were healed.

Many times, pilgrims to Jerusalem who wanted to worship the Beast—the image of His Highness Bandar—were delighted when The Prophet made fire fall from heaven.

Still, he could not call down the rain to cool things off.

As foretold, God's two witnesses—the prophets dressed in sackcloth—took their stand in the square near the Wailing Wall. "Repent! Turn from your sins, and honor God!" they cried. They stood up against the violence, sin, and blasphemy of His Highness B, The Prophet, and their branded followers. They endlessly called down any kind of judgment they liked, including drying up the Euphrates River in Iraq, the homeland of The Sovereign B, as well as many other lakes and rivers.

The Schuylkill River began to dry up. Fish died. A stench lingered in the air. Fairmount Park turned brown for lack of rain. One day a wildfire roared across the park and continued devouring hundreds of acres of houses in its path—including the Belmont Temple, formerly the Belmont Bible Church.

Weeks crept slowly by for Izzy, who once more suffered separation from Jamie and Max as they fled from the WOP Force. She liked to look for work to do in exchange for food and the brief comfort of a home. But after about a year, people who realized she had not received the mark turned away from her without a word. One day, an old man whose face wrinkles easily crinkled into a smile told her, "There is now a bounty on the head of all non-conformists, Miss. Take care of yourself."

To make matters worse, as time wore on the nations woke up to the reality that Mr. Bandar and his World Order for Peace made empty promises they could not keep. World War III broke out as China and Russia joined forces to contest the sovereignty of Premier B and the WOP regime. Sophisticated tanks utilizing deadly chemical warfare overran the earth. Millions died of lung disease and nerve gas, destroying a third of the world's population.

One hot muggy day Izzy stretched as she awoke in the pagoda at Morris Park. *This is not life as you meant it to be,*

Father. Help me to endure. Give me wisdom to survive until it is time to go home. I long to rest in your arms, to quit running. I am surprised I am still alive. Looking around and seeing no one, she found a place in the bushes to relieve herself. The birds began singing, and she realized it would not be long before she should be moving on. Izzy opened her bag and pulled out her journal. She shook her head at the yellow tint of her broken skin when she picked up the pen to write.

October 7, 2035

"Dear Marty, I have been missing you so much lately. I wonder if it is time for me to go home. What will it be like? I can only imagine WONDERFUL! Life here has been tough. Many days I am only a step away from death. I hate the constant pressure of being hunted. But it is amazing how God has kept me fed and alive. Sometimes people just walk up to me and give me food. I even had a puppy drop a bag on the ground at my feet; inside was somebody's lunch—an apple and sandwich with some cookies. Then I'll never forget the day I meandered down to the 9th Street Italian Market, feeling terribly thirsty and more than a little bit of trepidation at the dark storm clouds and wind that had rolled in. Just as I ducked into the entrance, huge hail stones came crashing down. The tarps were no longer protection from the elements—the hail, some of them the size of basketballs, broke the tables and crushed and scattered the fruit and vegetables. The sound was deafening. I retreated to a corner within the pavilion, and crouched down to collect a piece of cantaloupe which had splintered off and flown to where I stood; I noticed an empty cup and used it to scoop up a couple of pieces of hail. It may have tasted like dirt, but that meal tasted so good and I felt loved through and through.

Then there have been sparse days…time to fast and pray

days. Lately, I am just feeling worn out, ready to go. Will I be one of the multitudes under the throne of God crying out, "How long, O Lord, before we are avenged of our blood?" What will it be like to see Jesus? I am so glad he gave me a second chance. I could have died in my bitterness, but he opened my eyes and heart to forgive, and he has forgiven me. He blessed me with a friend in Jamie—a gift which I could never have imagined. And it's an eternal friendship, because Jamie came to know Jesus, too!

Please, Sweetheart, pray for me. I miss you beyond words. Cannot wait to spend eternity with you. Oh, I know we won't be married in Heaven. But if the good Lord is willing, I would love to be on the same team. You will always, always be MY BEST FRIEND! Marty, I love you.

That day as Izzy walked down Woodbine Avenue to return to Fairmount Park, she heard a man calling her name. She broke into a run, crying. No more pretending she did not hear. Her well of energy seemed to have dried up with the Schuylkill, but she pushed herself to put one foot in front of the other. Blood rushed through her ears, her head thrown back, as she ran blindly.

"Hey, stop her!" she heard his voice behind her shouting. She looked to the right side and noticed a woman behind a tree. Immediately shifting to the left, Izzy dashed across the street and barely missed being hit by a silver SUV, but the woman chasing her did not. She heard the sickening thud and pop as the hound in pursuit went under the tires. Tears streamed down her face, but Izzy kept running. Her pursuers had stopped.

"Oh, God. I'm yours." Her sides ached, but she kept going at a slow trot.

The sun went down behind the tree line; a breeze across Izzy's chest caused her to shiver. She noticed a gate open onto a large parking lot, with a simple white building perched in the middle. Beyond that she saw an earth mover, its jaws curled up on the ground. Oblivious of any security cameras, she crawled inside and went right to sleep.

The predawn chill woke Izzy up. She was so cold, she almost dared not unwind from her fetal position. *How can I go on?* She struggled to crawl out of the shovel of the earth mover. She could hardly remember how she got there, but her burning legs reminded her of the run. Thankful she had the cover of night, Izzy stretched and twisted to loosen tight muscles. She tried hard to muster up some spit to swallow. Then she walked to the gate, found some weeds growing through the fence, cupped the leaves in her hands and drew off some dew to wet her lips; repeating this several times, her throat felt better, and she walked on.

Izzy trudged past miles of Victorian houses, row homes, and office buildings in the shade of night for a couple of hours. Dawn came, but not for long. She looked up into the sky as if through a gray blanket, although there were no clouds in the sky. *Strange. Something is blocking the sunlight.*

Ahead on the horizon lay what looked like an overpass. She veered off to a smaller road to avoid traffic, keeping her hoody up and her head down. Eventually, the highway hid behind a hill, and Izzy's momentum slacked with the strain of the steep grade. She then heard the hum of traffic and forged on, wishing she had a phone with a GPS still. Since she hadn't taken the mark, this was a luxury she could no longer access.

Izzy's stomach ached with hunger as she reached the top, but she had no time to think about it.

"Hey, girl! Stop in the name of His Highness Bandar!"

yelled a man to her left. She pulled her hood forward around her face with shaking hands. Her legs froze in place as she turned to see policemen standing in front of a slick modern police station, just three yards away.

Suddenly they were all inside the building, its interior as steel gray as its exterior. Two people dressed in uniform jumped from their seats and grabbed Izzy. Tears flowed down her cheeks as she let out an angry, "Rah!"

A strong arm pulled her hair to tilt her forehead up to the light. Shaking his head, he said, "Show me your hands."

Izzy shook uncontrollably and fell to her knees, her unruly matted blonde hair hiding her face as she bowed her head in despair.

"Shall we do it now?" Officer Annette Gregory asked when they found no chip in Izzy's hands.

"No, there's a few more being brought from across town." Officer in charge—Douglas Henderson—looked at Izzy, shaking his head. Then supporting Izzy's jaw trying to get her to make eye contact, he asked, "Wouldn't you like to take His Highness's branding? You look hungry. How long has it been since you last ate?"

A tear dripped from Izzy's nose and joined a puddle on the floor. "It's been a few days." She had a decent meal in exchange for cleaning house for an elderly woman two days before.

Officer Henderson got up and came back with a bagel. Officer Gregory looked aghast, her jaw dropped in disbelief, her double chin wagging her displeasure as she asked Henderson, "What are you doing?"

"What?" The man shrugged. "Last meal!" He sat down again across from Izzy, "Unless, of course, you want to take the mark. How about it?"

"No, I can't." Izzy looked down at her hands. *Make me strong, Lord.*

"What are you? A conscientious objector, clinging to your liberty? Life is better than death." The man put the bagel in front of Izzy. "Eat."

"Eternal life with Jesus is better than eternal death." Izzy raised her chin and looked into the man's eyes. "I have hope. Jesus is with me, no matter what happens."

"Yes, your Jesus is going to take you straight to heaven. Dang! Why don't you people take His Highness B's seal?" The officer got up and stomped off into another room.

Ignoring the bagel even though her stomach was audibly growling, Izzy became aware of a young woman waving at her to get her attention. Sitting at a desk filling out papers, she whispered, "How do you know Jesus is with you?"

Izzy mouthed back. "Because he loves me. He takes care of me. He died for me and you."

Officer Gregory slammed down her hand on the table. Izzy jumped and looked down at her hands as the irate officer barked, "No talking!"

Moments later Izzy looked longingly at the woman and gestured "Jesus loves you"—pointing up, then hugging herself, then pointing at the woman.

Walking over to the woman, Officer Gregory once more yelled, "Ramona Griffith, are you finished those papers? Because this is your only chance to take the mark and escape the penalty you deserve for disobeying His Highness B's edict. Quickly."

Izzy mouthed to her. "Don't do it."

Izzy didn't see it coming. The fleshy hand of Officer Annette Gregory plowed into her face, leaving it stinging. Izzy tasted blood.

"Don't you say another word. You'll be the first to die for

your obstinance!" Annette grabbed the bagel from the table in front of Izzy and gave it to Ramona.

"Here, you refuse the mark. Sign this." She slipped a clipboard with a pen onto the table in front of Izzy. Above a column of signatures, Izzy read the statement— "Being of sound mind and of my own volition, I refuse to receive the seal of Premier Abdul Mutakabbir Asahd Bandar. I am fully aware that the consequence is death by beheading." Izzy quickly signed—Izzy D. Goldstein.

Suddenly Izzy felt herself being yanked by the hair and led to a bench next to the open back door. The hefty female police officer thrust Izzy down with a heave and walked away.

Rubbing her sore scalp, Izzy noticed a growing crowd outside and saw TV cameramen. *Lord, you were despised and rejected. Help me to follow you. Blessed Lord, hold me close.*

Though outwardly, her body had shriveled to bones covered by itchy, broken skin, inwardly Izzy felt renewed strength and joy. *I'm finally going home!*

Izzy looked up as she heard a commotion at the front door. A WOP Force jeep had pulled up at the curb. She strained to see who it was.

Max's shaggy head poked in the police station door first.

Izzy shook her head in disbelief. *Poor thing. He has wasted away to skin and bones. What will they do to him?*

Next, the shaggy head with shoulder-length brown hair belonging to a bent-over woman appeared in the station.

Izzy sat up with anticipation. *Jamie?* When Jamie looked up—with the same sharp nose but darkened eyes—Izzy yelled, "Jamie!"

Jamie stood up straight. "Izzy?" She looked around for her friend.

"Quiet!" The woman officer glared at Jamie and turned to

threaten Izzy, raising up a long black baton in her direction.

Izzy locked eyes with Jamie. She raised her clasped hands up to her chin and bowed slightly as if in prayer. Jamie nodded back, a slight smile tugging at the corner of her mouth.

But the angry police officer lunged at Izzy and beat her shoulder with the baton. Then she handcuffed Izzy's two hands. "See if you feel like praying anymore!" The woman hissed.

"No!" Max and Jamie jumped to Izzy's defense, but two officers blocked their approach. "Don't hit her!" Max pleaded. Jamie wrapped her arm around Max as he wiped away tears with his sleeve.

Then another familiar figure came into the station from the WOP jeep—Mr. Alfred Jones.

Oh, Mr. Jones! We meet again. Still trusting in your friend, Jesus, I hope? Izzy sat up, wincing as her shoulder ached from the blow.

Jamie and Max were made to sit down at a long white table for questioning. Officer Henderson asked Jamie, "Are you willing to receive the seal of His Highness Bandar? This is your only chance to avoid capital punishment."

Jamie looked at Max and took his hand in hers. Then she and Max answered together, "No. We belong to Jesus."

"Very well. Miss, please sign here." The officer presented Jamie with the clipboard. Then he looked at Max. "How old are you, young man?"

"Ten, Sir. Ten years old." Max squirmed in his seat.

"Well, that makes you too young to be held responsible for not taking the mark. Rather, because of the kindness of His Highness Bandar and his regime, the World Order for Peace of Greater Philadelphia has prepared a Reform School for you. You will not be executed today."

Max and Jamie clung to each other in a long embrace.

"Go with God, Son. You'll be okay," Jamie whispered in his ear.

Tears streamed down Max's face as an officer pulled him away. "Mom, I love you!"

Jamie looked to the officer and said, "Please, he doesn't need to stay."

The crowd gathering outside the back door could be heard shouting—"Death to Non-Conformists! Honor His Highness B!"

"Oh, no, on the contrary. This is where he learns to reform his thinking. Allegiance to His Highness Bandar is the only right path." Two officers dragged Max to sit in front of a window overlooking the backyard where a stage stood—two muscular WOP executioners stood waiting, huge, sheathed machetes dangling from their belts. Max covered his eyes with his hands, sobbing.

Back at the front table sat Alfred. His hair had gone completely white. But he talked with vigor. "No way! I can't get that mark! Someone introduced me to Jesus," he shouted, glancing over to Izzy. Then, smiling, he looked back at the officer. "We've been friends ever since!" The disgusted Officer Henderson waved him on as he signed his death warrant.

Izzy smiled to herself. *Thank you that nothing can separate us from your love.* Then she remembered Ramona and lifted her head with effort to look in her direction.

When Ramona saw Izzy's gaze, she quickly got up with her papers and handed them to Commanding Officer Henderson. "I can't get the mark. I'm with them. Jesus loves me, too!"

"You Jesus freaks are all delusional!" Henderson kicked a chair, and Gregory eyed Izzy with the baton in her hand.

As Ramona approached, Izzy could not suppress a smile.

The crowd outside the door had grown to over thirty

people, some carrying heinous signs which read, "To hell with them!"

But Izzy knew where she and her friends were going. As they filed out—pitifully ragged, dirty, and skinny—she heard the angry mantra of the mob, "Death to Nonconformists! Let His Highness B be honored and vindicated!" A victory shout rose up in her throat as she mounted the steps to the platform where the executioners stood ready—"Our Father, who art in heaven, hallowed be your name, your kingdom come, your will be done on earth as it is in heaven…"

The crowd booed.

Strong hands covered her face with a black hood, then forced her down to her knees. "Father?" Izzy cried.

Then she felt a breath of fresh air fill her chest, and a breeze swirl around her like a cooling stream. The strong arms of two bright angels carried her through a dark valley. There she saw her doubts and fears, her sins and the lies that had bound her for years shrivel and melt away in the light of that palpable love emanating from the portal above. The closer she got, the more clearly she could see that the door was a man surrounded in brilliant white light, dressed as a king, with the kindest, most ruggedly handsome face she had ever seen. The man was standing with his nail-pierced hands outstretched and ready to receive her in a warm embrace.

25. NOBLER PEOPLE

"Izzy, I am The Door. There is no other way into my Father's house. I am your Shepherd. Just as a shepherd lays at the door to the fold, picking burrs out of wool, or doctoring the wounds of each precious sheep, in my embrace be perfected and healed."

Suddenly Izzy felt fire raging in her bones, brain, and heart, like a healing, cleansing furnace. She saw herself in Christ on the cross, and felt wave upon wave of his love wash over her. When she opened her eyes, she felt pure and clean inside and out, for her heart exploded with joy and her robe was dazzling white. *Oh Lord, your love is amazing. I feel such peace and joy.* Time stood still as Izzy basked in the Lord's presence. Then Jesus led Izzy by the hand to a bubbling stream of water. "Now drink deeply of this River of Life! Never again will you thirst, or faint from the scorching sun, or freeze in the cold, or go hungry."

Izzy cupped the sparkling clear water in her hands and drank until she was satisfied. She looked up into her Savior's face. *Oh, Lord, you are beautiful!*

"My Princess, you are beautiful." Then Jesus motioned for Izzy to look beyond him. "Come, your family awaits you."

Izzy stood with anticipation. The riverside, the lush green

lawn, fields of flowers, a glen of trees, and a gentle green slope up to a golden path all beckoned her from every side. She looked back to find Jesus, but he was gone. But she felt his nudge to go and explore. *Marty?*

First Izzy saw Ramona by the river—the newest of her family of friends. "I am so glad you trusted Jesus!"

"You and your friends were so sure of God's love! I had to believe!" Ramona laughed and twirled around in her new dazzling white robe.

Then Izzy laughed when she saw Jamie lying flat on her back in the middle of a bunch of daffodils. "Oh, Jamie, what a wonderful sight you are!" Jamie got up and she and Izzy hugged one another in a long embrace. *And to think that unforgiveness almost kept us apart. Thank you, Jesus, for your amazing grace. You led us from darkness into light and life and love!*

"My mom and dad are here!" Jamie beamed, her face young, radiant and pink as if all her miseries had slipped away. She grabbed Izzy's hand and nodded up the hill.

Oh, sweet Jesus! You really saved them! Izzy felt as if they flew over the ridge. There she saw Carol, Jamie's former partner, together with a couple. They were visiting together on a colorful blanket in the middle of the lush green lawn.

"Mom! Dad! Carol! Here's the reason I'm alive!" Jamie held up Izzy's arm as if she were the champion in a boxing match.

"Don't praise me! Praise Jesus! He's the one to thank. Without his love, I wouldn't be here, either." Izzy beamed as she greeted Carol and met Jamie's parents, Sylvia and Fred. "For a long time we thought you had gone up in flames. I am so happy to meet you here!" Izzy felt love radiate through her entire being as she took a deep breath and exhaled. "You two are a real answer to prayer!"

"You're right about that." Jamie put her hand on Izzy's shoulder and motioned for her to sit with them on the blanket. "Carol prayed for them and us all the time. But I didn't have it in me to believe. I resented her prattle about God and his love. Then after the rapture, Max came to trust in Jesus. I had no idea, Mom and Dad, that you had trusted him, too."

Izzy sat down to listen with interest to Sylvia and Fred's story. *Amazing how young they look! And so much joy and peace in their faces! And what is that on Carol's brow? I believe she's wearing a crown!*

"Well, you know how nerve-racking the events happening in the earth were! Who would have ever thought that the good old Earth would have been shaken by so many earthquakes, volcanoes, and meteorite strikes!" Sylvia spread her hands as she began her tale.

Fred nodded his head. "When the volcano blast flattened Rome, it got hard for us to sleep! What was the world coming to? It felt like the end of all things."

Yes, I remember how shaken we all were with that news. That was before the asteroids took out millions of people in Europe and the U.S.! God warned us through the Bible, but no one could anticipate how bad it would get. Izzy reached out and sympathetically squeezed Sylvia and Fred's hands. "I'm so grateful God got your attention!"

"We are, too!" Sylvia squeezed Izzy's hand. "Thank God! That fateful morning Carol heard our fretting, and she told us that things were happening just as the Bible warned that they would. She told us to give our lives to Jesus, and that he would take care of us."

"And am I ever so glad that we did!" Fred said with a big smile. "I just can't get over the love of God for us." He grabbed Sylvia and Carol's hands. "We almost missed it."

"I'm so grateful, Mom and Dad, that you missed the

Tribulation." Jamie spoke quietly.

"Yes," Izzy reached out with sympathy.

Jamie closed her eyes, then opened them and looked around with a grin. "Well, look who's here! Eee-Yah!"

Izzy's face broke into a huge smile, and she giggled at the sight of a very youthful dark-skinned man robed in dazzling white, his robes flying as he leapt into the air and landed by their happy family. "Mr. Alfred Jones! You're here!"

Everybody watched as Izzy and Jamie gave Alfred a welcome hug.

"How was it, friend?" Izzy asked, rubbing his shoulder, Jamie nodding knowingly by his side.

Alfred wiped away tears from his cheeks, and shook his head, looking down, a long grin brightening his face, eyes closed for a moment. When he looked up, he spread his hands, shaking his head. "Just too good for words. Too good for words. I'm flabbergasted by the love of God."

Jamie introduced Alfred to her family. "Here's the man who gave of the little that he had to us perfect strangers the day we met. His home was a welcoming rest stop for us."

Alfred held his hands high. "I'm the one who was blessed. Believe me."

Izzy beamed as she received his nod in her direction. *Thank you, Jesus, for giving me the privilege of pointing Alfred to you.*

Finally, Izzy joined Alfred, Sylvia, Fred, Carol, and Jamie for a group hug and a prayer.

"Hallelujah, Jesus, for your deep love and sacrifice for us."

"Thank you for giving us all faith to believe you."

"Thank you for welcoming us into your Heaven, our home."

"Lord you are amazing!" Izzy declared. "Thank you for being The Door, our entrance into Heaven."

Jamie added a prayer for Max. "Oh, Father. You must have work for Max to do, or lessons for him to learn. Make him brave. Give him your peace to walk with you through each day until his work on Earth is done. In Jesus's name."

Everybody chimed in, "Amen!"

"Surely, Max will be okay." Jamie said to Izzy as they hugged, her green eyes sparkling.

"You're right, Jamie. God just has more work for him to do on earth. He is God's child. Jesus will take care of him. Someday we will see him again."

Izzy hugged the rest of the family. "It's been wonderful spending this time together."

"You go ahead, Izzy. We've got forever together. We'll see you around." Jamie's beautiful face portrayed deep peace within.

Izzy turned to go. She heard some laughter. Two women were bantering back and forth. That sounds so familiar. She slowly turned around. Listening. Looking. She walked up the slope to the golden path. At the crest, sitting on a big white rock, were her mother and Aunt Anna waiting for her. They jumped down and ran to her, their robes flying, their joyful countenance making them appear as if they were both as young as when Izzy knew them as a small child.

"Mom! Aunt Anna! You're here!" The three held each other in a long embrace.

A variety of flowers in a rainbow of colors surrounded the many benches along the path. Izzy sat down between her mom and aunt on one of those inviting pine benches. "Mom, when you died, I missed you so much. I hated seeing you go. And I hated God for not answering my prayers. But here we are together again."

"Yes, I prayed for you, Sweetheart." Izzy's mom stroked her daughter's hair. "Your Aunt Anna did a good job filling in for me, didn't she?"

Izzy leaned over and laid her head on Aunt Anna's chest and gave her a hug. "Yes. She was amazing, like a mother hen. I loved you, Aunt Anna. Don't know what I would have done without you. And thank you for warning me about not taking the mark of the Beast. And thank you for welcoming Marty and me to make our home with you."

Marty? Where is my Love? Izzy stood up, not so much worried as excited to see her new husband. She looked longingly around, then turned back to her mom and aunt. They both waved her on with their signature laughter. *So good to hear them at it again. And to think it will never end.*

Izzy walked further up the golden path, breathing deeply of the crystal-clear air, quietly conscious of the undercurrent which swirled around her—the love of God.

Finally, she saw Marty standing at the pearl gate of the heavenly gold city. *Oh, Marty, I have missed you so much!* Izzy started running.

Marty leapt down the hill, his face beaming. Laughing, he lifted her up to the blue sky and swung her around. Then they stood at arm's length, gazing at one another.

"How I adored you, Marty. You were always so thoughtful and kind. You loved me and tried to point me to God's way of forgiveness. I'll be forever grateful. And, Marty, your face looks as handsome as ever, but nobler. Does that come with living here for a while?"

"Oh, Izzy. As glorious as the rapture was, I missed you dearly. But the Lord assured me you would make it here later. As for the nobler look…it comes with prayer. Come, I want to show you our prayer room."

"Prayer room?" Izzy turned around. She looked up. On every side she saw homes of different shapes and sizes, all beautifully emanating light. Then looking up at Marty—who gazed at her with amusement—she asked, "Which one is the prayer room?"

"Ha, ha!" Marty laughed. "Izzy, Heaven is huge. If you want to go anywhere, just name the place." Then he took her hand and said, "Prayer room."

Suddenly Izzy found herself with Marty in a huge round room about two football fields long and wide, with windows all around the rim. Amazing! There at the window looking out was her librarian friend Laura.

Grinning at Marty, Izzy reached out to tap Laura on the shoulder. A current of warm power coursed up her arm. "What was that?" Izzy jumped.

Laura turned around laughing. "Izzy, you made it!" She went to give her a hug, but Izzy backed away cautiously.

Marty chuckled. "Izzy you just tapped into the power of prayer."

"Wow!" Izzy shook her head. "I have a lot to learn."

"Yes," Marty and Laura agreed. "Now Jesus is ready to take the throne." He looked soberly at Izzy. "He wants us all to pray through the last sufferings of the day of His wrath. Look out this window and he will show you what you need to see and pray over. May his Kingdom come, and his will be done on Earth, as it is in Heaven. Are you ready?"

Izzy nodded. "Father, I'm yours. Teach me to pray."

As Izzy gazed out the window looking out over the earth, she watched a tragic scene unfold.

Izzy and Marty saw three spirits like slimy green frogs come out of the gross mouths of the unholy trinity—Mr. B, his image The Beast, and The Prophet. They went to every nation whispering lies to leaders and those with influence.

To some they gave power to duplicate the plagues of Moses saying, "This is what awaits us if we let Jesus and the Jews get by with the plot to rule the world! Nations of the world arise! Let us stop them once and for all time."

Izzy could see the entire world laid out on the screen. She viewed Egypt and saw frog-infested homes just like in the days of Moses. In China, she watched as gnats infested homes and businesses alike. In South Africa, locusts destroyed the little bit of greenery that was left right before her eyes.

She saw millions of people starving, their flesh covered in boils, locusts and gnats, enraged that the Jews appeared shielded from attack, untouched by the boils, the scorpion locusts and the suffering which had become the lot for the rest of the world. People in the square in Jerusalem—where the two mysterious men were still calling down disasters on the belligerent world as they had been doing for over three years—waved placards decrying the destruction they had brought on the world.

"These Jews have to go—the whole lot of them!" His Highness B snarled as he paced back and forth at the World Order for Peace Administration Building in Ramle—the very room where he and The Prophet had called down the flood onto the escaping Jews. The last seven years his nerves had been worn to a frazzle like the oriental rug he had worn bare there. "Why is it that this Jesus moves about with impunity, together with no small crowd of followers? He is a fake! An imposter! What are you going to do to deal with this treason?" He reeled around and placed his strong hands on The Prophet's shoulders, glaring into his eyes with his own fiery red ones.

The Prophet arose from his perch where he had been meditating. "We have summoned the armies of the world to face off with the rabble. They gather as we speak at

Armageddon. The Prince of Darkness will plunge the forces of the enemy into confusion and make them easy prey. You have nothing to dread."

"Oh God," Izzy prayed, "Send the Beast and his regime confusion and darkness instead!"

Marty prayed alongside her. "Yes, thick darkness to immobilize them and derail their evil plans, in Jesus's name!"

Suddenly a thick darkness descended from the ceiling like the black ink of a squid in water. His Highness B saw it coming and grabbed his partner's arm just before being engulfed in the dark shroud. It covered the entire compound in Ramle.

Screams erupted on every side.

"I can't see! Oh, God! What's happening?" Mr. B screeched.

"My hand, I can't even see it right in front of my face!" Even The Prophet was screaming.

"The pain. Ahh, it hurts. Help me! Will somebody help me?" Darkness and pain immobilized Mr. B. "Do something!" he implored.

But The Prophet's efforts brought no relief.

After the darkness lifted, His Highness Premier Bandar and Vice Premier Hamaz were seething with rage. They ordered a siege on Jerusalem to destroy the remnant of the Jews there. International forces ransacked the city, raped the women, and took half of the inhabitants captive.

Izzy groaned. "Oh, God, comfort them, and give them grace to endure. Finally, bring your people safely home." Marty put a comforting arm around her. "God will hear you Sweetheart. Remember who wins in the end."

The two holy men robed in sackcloth cried out together, "It is enough!"

The scene on the big screen changed. Izzy saw Chloe and her grandmother, Mrs. Anderson, watching the news. She pointed out to Marty that Chloe had been one of her favorite second graders in her class and how she and her grandmother had rescued her.

"I know darling, I watched it unfold, praying for all of you," Marty said gently.

"But Chloe and Mrs. Anderson got the mark of the Beast!" *Oh, Chloe, dear sweet child! Father in Heaven, is there hope for her?*

Marty nodded, watching silently with her.

> ROGERS: From their enclave in Ramle, His Highness Bandar released a statement today—
>
> BANDAR: "Let our Lord Liege, Lucifer, vindicate himself upon the two troublemakers!"
>
> PROPHET: "At His Highness's word, they must die!"

"Grammy, why is Mr. Bandar talking about Lucifer? Wasn't that the devil's name? He's the bad guy. I don't like him. He makes me scared." Chloe snuggled closer to her grandmother.

Mrs. Anderson stroked Chloe's face. "I had no idea. This is the first time I have heard him call on the devil. It makes me regret getting branded with his ID. Shh. Let's keep listening now to see what happens."

> QUESPIE: Julie Quespie here with FOX29 News. I am in the center of Old Jerusalem, not too far from the Wailing Wall. This is where the two holy

men, supposedly from God, have often stood calling down judgment. These two monk-like men have certainly worn out their welcome. His Highness B is determined to get rid of them. One is speaking; let's listen in.

"The kingdom of the world has become the kingdom of our Lord and of his Christ. And he shall reign forever and ever!"

"Amen!" Izzy and all in the heavenly prayer room cried out.

She and Marty kept watching the screen. Suddenly the shadowy black form of a dragon swooped down upon the two men, causing them to bend over as if in pain. They fell to the ground, dead.

The cameraman must have lost his footing, for they lost video coverage. But Izzy could still hear Ms. Quespie as Chloe and her grandmother listened in.

QUESPIE: Oh my God! What was that?

ROGERS: Julie, it looked like smoke in the shape of a dragon! Are you okay? We have lost your video.

QUESPIE: That was hair-raising, but we are alright. Different news, though, for the two troublemakers. They have died, not too far from where I stand, thanks to His Highness Bandar. He truly is all-powerful!

ROGERS: Folks, Rodney Rogers here broadcasting from the city of love, Philadelphia.

We were just speaking with our reporter on the ground in Jerusalem with some earthshaking news—the two fire-breathing men who have troubled the world these three-and-a-half years are dead. That's right, friends. After His Highness B declared that his Lord Lucifer himself would have to make things right, what looked like dark smoke in the form of a dragon overpowered and killed them. Now we return to our correspondent, Julie, in Old Town Jerusalem.

QUESPIE: Rod, the scene here in Jerusalem is electrifying. People have gathered around the two fallen troublemakers and are laughing and joking. The police have come in twice to try to remove the corpses, but nobody will let them. It feels like people just want to savor the victory.

"Ahh, no, no, no!" Chloe whimpered from Mrs. Anderson's lap. "Grammy, that monster killed the good guys! Ah, ah!"

Chloe and Grammy continued to watch the news about the two prophets of God. People from all over the globe refused to bury them, but rather came to defecate on them, and to taunt their corpses like a cat playing with a dead mouse. Everyone exchanged gifts to celebrate like it was a holiday.

"Disgraceful, how low the human race has fallen! Chloe, we do not treat each other like that. We need to be kind to one another and treat each other with respect. Come, let's see what is happening in Jerusalem now." She and Chloe once more settled themselves before the screen and Live News.

"Grammy, look! The two good guys! They are standing!"

"Unbelievable," murmured Grammy.

A deep voice shouted from the sky, "Come up here!"

"Wait. Was that God speaking?" Grammy held Chloe close and almost stopped breathing.

> QUESPIE: "The men are rising into the air. They have been transformed into angelic beings and are dazzling white! Now…they are gone. This is unbelievable. This cannot be happening. You can see people here in the square falling to their knees. Let's see what they are saying.
>
> I am approaching a group of young men huddled around one of their peers kneeling on the ground. He is crying out."

Ms. Quespie held out the microphone to listen in. The grieving man screamed a heart-wrenching cry.

> "He's real! God is real! We've been all wrong! What are we going to do? We're doomed! We're doomed with this mark! Oh, God, I'm so sorry!"

"Oh! Grammy! I don't want this mark anymore! I…don't…want…it! Please, let's take it off. Let's take it off, Grammy!" Chloe retreated to the corner of the couch and rubbed at her wrist, desperately trying to erase the mark.

Grammy inched over to scoop her grieving child into her embrace. "Don't, Baby, don't! You'll hurt yourself! You don't have that monster's ID."

"I don't? But I got the mark with you and Mommy and Grandpa." Chloe wiped her face with her hands.

"No, Sweetie. You are the lucky one. Your mark only has our family name. You were too young to receive our banking chip with Mr. B's ID. Oh, how I wish I had refused it, too!"

Julie Quespie's screaming grabbed their attention back to

the screen. Chloe's mouth quivered as she saw stucco structures sway and crumble, crashing down upon Julie and all in the square.

A huge CRACK split the air, and Chloe and Grammy felt the floor lurch as they toppled onto the floor. Grammy managed to pull herself over Chloe to shield her from falling objects. The whole house rumbled for several minutes, throwing books and breakables off shelves, sending them crashing to the ground. Walls creaked, then the house first swayed side to side and bumped up and down, shattering windows. Suddenly, all grew quiet, except for the sound of water spraying in the kitchen and the buzz of the TV.

The senior Anderson tried to push herself off of her granddaughter. "Chloe?"

"Grammy, oh Grammy! You're bleeding!"

"That was an earthquake. We never get earthquakes here in Philly." Mrs. Anderson struggled to sit up and leaned against the couch. She glanced over at the TV screen and gasped. "Oh my stars, some highways in town collapsed."

Izzy looked on in horror as Chloe sat up to watch the TV screen. It showed a row of a half a dozen thin, bedraggled, shabbily dressed men and women kneeling on a platform outside a steel gray police station. They were all faceless, their heads covered with heavy black coverings. Two WOP officers stood behind them brandishing huge, raised machetes. One officer raised his dramatically over the first one kneeling and a female voice was heard crying "Father!" before the blade came down on her neck, and her covered head rolled off to one side as shrieks filled the air.

"That was me," Izzy whispered. She looked up into Marty's eyes and saw they were filled with tears. She didn't think she'd see people in heaven crying, and she reached up her hand to wipe away his tears.

"I am so sorry you went through that, Sweetheart," Marty

whispered back, pulling her into his arms and kissing her hair.

"Thank you, my love," she said, smiling. "It was pretty awful. But I see now that we were not alone."

Rogers was reporting once again.

> ROGERS: There you saw it, folks—several citizens in our own city were decapitated when they swore their allegiance to Jesus and refused to get the brand of His Highness Bandar. Among them was Mrs. Izzy Goldstein, a second grade teacher at Overbrook Elementary School in Wynnefield.
>
> And in breaking news, correspondent Julie Quespie was among two dozen Americans and about three hundred Jews and Arabs killed in the town square in Jerusalem when buildings fell on them in an enormous earthquake. We were down for a few minutes as the earthquake shook our building and some wiring came loose, but we're back up again using generators. Rest in peace Julie and all of the victims of this horrible…

Izzy saw Chloe crying into her grandmother's arms. "Oh, Grammy."

Izzy cried out in prayer, "Oh, Lord, save Chloe! Comfort her, sweet Jesus." Then she witnessed another great shaking of Chloe's house. The house imploded, the walls caving backward. Izzy saw Chloe roll out the front door and down the steps as the house collapsed. Then she witnessed angels in the air above proclaiming, "Honor God and fear him, for the hour of his judgment has come! Worship him who made the heavens and the earth! Come to him."

Oh Father, little Chloe is your little lamb. Help her find you, gentle Shepherd. Then Izzy saw Chloe sit up, crying, holding her right arm to herself. She wiped the wound, and out of her skin came the chip which she had received when her family received the mark. She cried even louder as she saw her hand, sticky with blood, holding the chip. "I want God, please! I don't want that monster. He killed Miss Izzy! Oh, Grammy, Grammy!"

Then two young men dressed in jeans wearing yarmulkes ran to her aid. One, tall and thin, knelt down beside her. He supported her back and gave her a cup of water, saying, "Chloe, Jesus sent us to take care of you. My name is Reuben." Then the other youth, who was stocky and strong, said, "And I'm Joseph. Jesus loves you, Chloe." First Joseph cleaned her wound, then Reuben picked her up, cradling her in his arms. "Let's go find, Jesus."

"Jesus. I want Jesus." Chloe murmured, as she fell asleep. Then Izzy lost sight of Chloe as the scene changed once more in the window where she prayed. She looked up to Marty with concern on her face.

"Don't worry, Sweetheart. Just pray. Jesus will take care of each situation as we pray."

Izzy and Marty then saw Uncle Amos stand to address his people as they gathered in the huge meeting hall cut into the mountain. "Hear me, my friends. Yeshua appeared to me in a dream last night. He is coming as our victorious king. We need to prepare for his arrival. Pray for yourselves. Pray for each other. If you have offended anyone, or have been offended, make it right. We need to be of one heart. Stand firm in the love of God. The day has come to emerge from hiding and take a stand for the last great battle."

A murmur rippled through the crowd as people gripped

the arms of their loved ones.

"No need to fear," added Amos, his face radiant. "Jesus has told me we will not be fighting this battle. We need only to pray and see him conquer our enemies."

"Hooray for Jesus!" Benjie—taller and thinner than Izzy remembered him—waved his fist in the air and did a little jig.

Benjie, may you be God's man as you grow up. Izzy looked proudly on from her portal in heaven.

Then Izzy and Marty saw everyone fall to their knees and burst into singing the familiar song of deliverance, the song of Moses—

"I will sing to the Lord, for he has triumphed gloriously;
the horse and his rider he has thrown into the sea.
The Lord is my strength and my song,
and he has become my salvation;
this is my God, and I will praise him,
my father's God, and I will exalt him.
The Lord is a man of war;
the Lord is his name."

Father, give them the victory! Jesus, do the fighting for them!

A deep voice resonated throughout heaven. "Saints, to your steeds. The Kingdom of the Lamb has come! I want you to see the victory at Armageddon. To your steeds!"

Izzy and Marty looked at one another. But before they could say a word, they found themselves mounted upon beautiful white horses—with wings!

The stately stallions brought them through the portals of heaven to emerge in the stratosphere surrounding Armageddon–a huge plain of panoramic proportions where many battles were fought through the ages. "This is where King Saul and his sons met their doom, and surely where Mr. B and his Prophet will meet theirs!" Marty encouraged

Izzy.

She and Marty, on horseback, fell into line with their company. What Izzy saw—horses and their riders fanning out in their ranks, all dazzling white—took her breath away. Quickly all the mounted troops in the sky lined the horizon around the nations gathered at Armageddon.

Strange. Not a cloud in the sky, but the day is dark and gray. Izzy recalled what Pastor Michaels had shared about that last great battle foretold in Revelation—it would happen on a strange day when the sunlight would lose its luster like the dusk; it would happen in the plain to the east of Jerusalem near a town called Megiddo, where all the nations of the earth would gather for God's ordained final battle.

I can't believe I am witnessing this with my own eyes! Izzy watched below her, seeing the Jews in Qumran come out of hiding and march in groups of one hundred down the road toward Masada, singing songs of praise to their King Yeshua. Likewise, those gathered at Masada marched up the road to meet their comrades in procession, leaving thousands on the top of the fortress waving banners and singing songs of triumph. *This does not look like the front line of a war zone. Lord, let them see your deliverance!*

To her horror, Izzy saw missiles launched by the enemy speeding toward the Judean Desert where the Jews sang songs of praise to their coming King Jesus!

Then her sorrow turned to excitement as she witnessed the missiles make a U-turn and strike the enemy troops. *God has caused his enemies to fall into their own trap!*

As if she was watching a gruesome horror movie, Izzy saw the flesh melting off the bones, and eyes rotting in the sockets, of His Highness B's key commanders.

She closed her eyes tight against the sight, then turned her eyes to King Jesus, whose eyes shone like flames of fire, and his face like the sun. Majestic on his steed, Jesus wore many crowns and a white robe dipped in blood with a banner which read "King of kings, and Lord of lords!" He raised his head high, his jaw set firm.

The Saints prayed. Their steeds stood still.

Izzy whispered, "Lord, how we long to see evil ended and all your enemies under your feet!"

Marty proclaimed, "Stand still and see the salvation of our God."

Izzy saw the Jews in Masada kneel and lay prostrate on the ground. Amos Asher and his family huddled together on their knees. "Come victorious King Jesus!" Izzy prayed.

What happened next made Izzy rub her eyes and look again. Suddenly a sign appeared in the sky—Hell like a fiery sulfur pit—opened above Armageddon so that those on the ground and in the air saw its pulsating hungry flames. Four strong angels appeared clutching The Beast—Mr. B—and The Prophet! They were screaming hysterically. The angels tossed them—screaming—into the fiery pit of Hell. Flames leapt up to engulf them. Then—with an explosion of heat which Izzy felt on her lofty mount--the apparition disappeared as quickly as it had appeared.

Izzy watched as the soldiers on the ground panicked. They desperately fought one another in their efforts to escape. The army's periphery melted away as many left their gear and started running for the hills, the crevices, valleys and caves—anywhere to hide.

King Jesus opened his mouth and His voice rumbled like thunder. "By receiving the mark, you have despised my sacrifice and denied the power in my blood! So die, now, in your own blood—everyone of you with the mark of the beast!"

Men cried out.

Marty and Izzy looked at each other in amazement at what happened next. Men were bleeding from their eyes, nose, ears, and mouth—holding their heads and dropping to the ground, dead. Armageddon became a field of blood. Birds swarmed in, one black cloud after another from north, south, east and west. They alighted and started feasting upon the dead—both man and horse.

Around the world, men as well as women, the young and the old, all who had received His Highness Bandar's branding hemorrhaged to death, and the birds ate up their flesh.

The clean-up of the world had begun.

Izzy sat on her steed, which was still airborne in the clouds, and saw a magnificent angel—his robes like burnished bronze, his face, stern—coming down from heaven, and with a key unlocking the door to the Abyss; black flames licked around the opening.

Izzy saw Marty was spellbound as the scene unfurled.

The angel seized the dragon—Lucifer—now in the form of a huge black serpent, bound him in chains and hurled him into the gaping inferno. Billowing darkness like the smoke and flames from a gigantic oil spill engulfed him.

Then the angel slammed the door shut over Satan—the serpent and usurper of peace upon the Earth. He took the key and locked and sealed the shaft of the Abyss for a thousand years!

Izzy found herself with Marty in the ecstatic crowd around the throne of God in heaven. King Jesus had taken his place on his throne in Jerusalem, where he would reign for a thousand years. Now, in the Throne Room of Heaven, he presented his saints to the Father—Izzy and Marty, her mom and Aunt Anna, Laura, Jamie and her parents, Carol, Mr. Alfred Jones, Ramona—all the saints, saying—

"Look at the reward of my sacrifice—all the children which you have given me! Let them be with me in my glory and serve with me as I reign and restore peace upon the Earth."

EPILOGUE

"Izzy, I am The Door. There is no other way into my Father's house. I am your Shepherd. Just as a shepherd lays at the door to the fold, picking burrs out of wool, or doctoring the wounds of each precious sheep, in my embrace be perfected and healed."

"Hallelujah, for the Lord God omnipotent reigns!" Izzy raised her voice in praise with the throng, and it seemed like the thundering of a mighty waterfall in her ears. "Let us be glad, and rejoice, and give honor to him: for the marriage of the Lamb of God—Jesus—has come, and his wife has made herself ready."

Izzy felt radiant and pure in her white linen gown trimmed with lace. She sat at a long table spread with a white tablecloth and set with crystal, fine china, and golden flatware. Flowers dazzled her eyes with their vibrant colors against all the white. An angel brought Jamie to sit next to her and Izzy reached out to give her a hug. Her mom and Aunt Anna sat across from her with smiles as wide as the sky.

But Izzy's eyes were on the Lamb—the King in his glory—whose pierced hands reached out and radiated love for each one. O Lord, you are BEAUTIFUL!

"You, my Bride, are beautiful.," she heard him say.

Izzy detected a twinkle in the King's eye as he raised his goblet and said, "Let the feast begin!" Everyone returned the gesture, raising their goblets high. When Izzy looked down at her plate again, she saw a stack of fluffy pancakes smothered in butter and syrup, and she laughed.

Benjie came running into the house, shouting, "Dad! Mom! You won't believe it! I can understand the Arabian kids, and they can understand me. Come and see!"

Amos and Abigail ran out to the street with Hannah and Daniel close behind. There Benjie stood in the middle of a group of Palestinian children. They were all jabbering away, scratching their heads. Then they all threw their hands up in the air, their faces breaking into big smiles, and impulsively formed a group hug. "God is love! No more war! Now we can work for peace, hand in hand!" Benjie shouted.

"Out of the mouth of babes!" The Ashers began shaking hands and sharing greetings in their new language to the many adults gathered on the street.

Suddenly someone came around the corner of the street walking toward the Asher home. The last time they had been there the Great Disappearance, known as the Rapture, had not yet happened. So much had changed since then. Benjie saw them—they wore white robes, belted with multi-colored sashes, and wore simple crowns of gold. When he recognized them, Benjie ran to them but stopped short of embracing them.

"Cousin Marty! Izzy! You're here! I can't believe it. You look so…different."

Marty and Izzy looked at each other and laughed. There was no denying it! Their bodies were quite different in some ways—no more maleness or femaleness, and they no longer had to use the bathroom. "The Lord has given us new bodies that can still enjoy our five senses, but on a magnified scale." Izzy stooped down and gave Benjie a big hug.

Marty added, "Everything tastes so much better, colors look so much more alive, and we can hear people whispering across the room! It's true, Benjie. We are not the same people we were the last time we were here. Now we are glorified priests of the King of kings, and Lord of lords."

"King Jesus! Woo-hoo! He's the BEST!" Benjie, Hannah, and Daniel gathered around their company, gingerly stroking the deliciously soft fabric of their priestly robes. "Ahh, I love the colors of your belt. You even have crowns on your heads!" The children looked up to Izzy and Marty with admiration.

"Ok, children, let's give our guests a chance to come in and rest." Amos greeted Marty and Izzy with a hug and motioned for them to come into the house.

Benjie's mom Abigail, smiling shyly, bowed to them as they came in, her long brown hair falling gently off her shoulders. She welcomed them with tall drinks of fruit juice and some cookies she had made. "What adventures we have all had since we last spent time together."

Everyone had their own stories to tell, and they talked, it seemed, nonstop for hours. The Ashers shared of their lives at Masada, and of God's abundant provision.

"That place was huge!" Benjie could not contain his excitement. "There were so many floors of apartments, grocery stores, meeting halls, fitness rooms with all the equipment, and even a swimming pool! I wish you could have seen it!"

Then Izzy listened with interest to Marty's experience when the Lord called him to join Him in the sky at the Rapture.

"It was amazing! I heard my name called, and the blast of

a trumpet, and suddenly I found myself robed in white with the Lord and thousands of saints in the sky! Glorious!" Marty's face seemed to glow as he talked.

"I, on the other hand, still had to come face to face with my Savior!" Izzy bowed her head, then looked up to begin her tale, her fingertips pressed together.

Benjie, who was lying on the rug looking up at Izzy, burst out, "You look so much like an angel!"

Everyone laughed.

"Hush, now, Benjie. We want to hear Izzy's story." Big sister, Hannah, put her hand on Benjie's head.

Everyone sat in silence after the flurry of stories ceased. They broke into a song of praise to their Savior and King, Jesus. Love seemed to be the very air they breathed.

Marty produced a small book from the folds of his robe and handed it to Amos. The cover read, "To Prime Minister Amos Asher—Gameplan for the Restoration of Israel," embossed with an ornate golden seal.

"Prime Minister Asher." Amos rubbed the seal with his thumb and looked up to Marty with tears in his eyes. "It will be my pleasure to serve my king!"

"There is much to do, and not all people will immediately submit. But God has given us authority to help." Izzy and Marty talked and prayed with Prime Minister Asher, answered his questions and reassured him of their support.

"Next time we will introduce you to the rest of the team assigned to help reinforce your rule here in Israel. But for now, the hour is late. We need to let you get some rest." Marty and Izzy stood to go.

"And you, too." Amos stood, and Abigail and the children came to see off their special guests.

Marty raised his hand in blessing, saying, "May the blessing of Father, Son, and Holy Spirit abide upon each one. And may the love of our matchless King keep you by

His grace."

When the Ashers opened their eyes, Marty and Izzy were gone.

AUTHOR'S NOTE

"The Spirit and the Bride say, 'Come!' And let him who hears say, 'Come!' And let the one who is thirsty come; let the one who desires take the water of life without price." (Rev. 22:17)

These are welcome words to sin-sick souls and weary travelers along this road called life. Humanity has spiraled into unrestraint and violence. It is a scary time to be alive. This book is an invitation to come to the Spirit who created all things. It is an invitation to choose life when the day comes that you must decide whether to choose the mark of the Beast to live.

Perhaps at this point you are tempted to put the book down because you cannot believe there is a God in heaven who cares when the world has unraveled so. Someday—and most likely someday soon—someone will arise who will seem to restore order and give hope; the world will be in such a mess that many people will gladly follow him. Whatever he asks, they will do, even though the consequence will be forfeiting that gift of eternal life which flows on forever and ever.

The story within these pages is fiction. There will be elements from world news, and from scientific and sociological studies. But it is still fiction written with this goal in mind—to inform readers of the signs of the end times as recorded in the Bible, so they will not be caught off-guard. The Bible is a manual for life whose Creator spells out very clearly what is to happen at the end of the world so people can make informed decisions.

It is this author's hope you choose LIFE over the temporal convenience of doing business as usual by receiving the mark of the Beast.

<u>ABOUT THE AUTHOR</u>

Ruth's passion is spreading the message of this, her first, novel—that is, the love of God and His full redemption. She has spent over forty years in Taiwan as a missionary. Now, in her retirement, God has put an urgency in her heart to help people be ready for the soon return of the Lord Jesus Christ, because he promised—*"And if I go and prepare a place for you, I will come again, and I will take you to myself, that where I am you may be also."* (Jn. 14:3)

Ruth, with her husband, Mark, is a member of Global Outreach, International and has retired to Taiwan to continue the work of reaching the resistant west coast for Christ through a non-profit called Taiwan Harvest 119 Caring Association. She also aspires to better love and encourage her five children and fifteen grandchildren. Ruth received her Master of Arts in Worship from the

Conservative Baptist Seminary in Shiluo Taiwan in 2022 where she majored in violin and discovered the joy of composing music. So Ruth aspires to write for many audiences, from children to adults, music lovers to aspiring missionaries.

For more information about Ruth and her book,
visit her website:
www.RuthHarbour.com

www.ingramcontent.com/pod-product-compliance
Lightning Source LLC
Chambersburg PA
CBHW061056100726
47911CB00012B/252